Stephanie Theobald

Stephanie Theobald was society editor of *Harper's Bazaar* for three years. She has written extensively about the art world for *Harper's Bazaar* as well as for *The Sunday Times*, *The Observer* and *Arena* magazine. *A Partial Indulgence* is her fourth novel.

ALSO BY STEPHANIE THEOBALD

Biche

Sucking Shrimp

Trix

STEPHANIE THEOBALD

A PARTIAL INDULGENCE

SCEPTRE

First published in Great Britain in 2009 by Sceptre
An imprint of Hodder & Stoughton
An Hachette Livre UK company

I

A CIP catalogue record for this title is
available from the British Library

ISBN 978 0 340 82392 7

Typeset in Monotype Sabon by
Palimpsest Book Production Limited
Grangemouth, Stirlingshire

Printed and bound in the UK by CPI Mackays, Chatham ME5 8TD

Hodder & Stoughton policy is to use papers that are natural, renewable and
recyclable products and made from wood grown in sustainable forests. The
logging and manufacturing processes are expected to conform to the
environmental regulations of the country of origin.

Hodder & Stoughton Ltd
338 Euston Road
London NW1 3BH

www.hodder.co.uk

For Jake

Trompe L'œil

Claridges, London, 12 August, 1981

What a sun!
Like a scoop of marmalade.

In the mornings, I have a full breakfast. Chilled grapefruit juice made the night before and put in the fridge so it's just the right temperature. Scrambled eggs and two types of sausage with bacon and English mustard. A couple of slices of toast thickly spread with butter and a smidgeon of marmalade on the very last corner . . .

What a way to start the day. Sometimes it's bananas and cream. The thick, yellow top of the cream, naturally. Then I am ready for the plunge. Perhaps a trip to Sotheby's for the sale of one of my Picassos – the snatch of a whisper, the sparkle of a cufflink and then the mystical hush as bids soar far above the reserve price: one million, two million, three million, four – on and on, a thrilling flash in time and space, as if the patient might live after all, as if skies might be bright after all, and then the gasp as the hammer goes down and the Great Houdini emerges from his tank . . . alive!

I will shake a number of hands, nod to a number of my 'pupils', as I like to call them, and then take a cab to have lunch with the Duke of Beaufort. The 12th of August, also known as "The Glorious Twelfth", is the opening of the shooting season and should always be celebrated with a memorable repast. We will have caviar followed by roast grouse with bread sauce and game chips, a cheese course and then summer pudding and cream. The grouse will be cooked for twenty-two minutes, served on a piece of toast spread with duck pâté, while the bread sauce will be very white; not too many cloves and naturally no crusts.

And the wine. Ah, the first glass of the day, rushing from the bottle like a wave crashing on a beach on a sunny morning in June. Many say to drink burgundy with grouse, but a friend of mine insists that the night before he goes to heaven, he will drink a bottle of the best vintage bordeaux of the twentieth century: Mouton Rothschild 1945: *L'Année de la Victoire*. I agree that such a vintage deserves an extraordinary occasion, but personally prefer to marry game to a more simple claret. Fragrant and light. Bracing! The herald of a new lily-pad moment: leaping from one pad to the next, when all the lights are green, when nothing can hold you back, when the wave is only building and you must ride it all the way. Breathe deep and claim your prize: the odour is not merely of oil and varnish – you are smelling immortality!

Look around you and you will see my immortality: The de Vere van Dongen, the de Vere Cézanne, the de Vere Picasso. I could go on. I sell to billionaires – British, American, Greek, Japanese – but the paintings themselves must shine for ever with my aura. My pupils come to me after they've bought their jets and their horses and their fourth home. Picasso, Gauguin, Van Gogh – the name is of small importance. Artists are mere entertainers selling their frivolity or their insanity to me, Charles Frederick de Vere, so that I may spray a sheen on a fortune made from rendered pig fat or used aeroplane parts. My pupils know that a de Vere picture will cover up a *parvenu* glare with a respectable coat of tradition. They know that acquaintance with me will gain them entrance to the great country homes of the nobility and if the owners are looking for a little lose change for the sale of some ancestral portraits then I flatter myself that I may be of some assistance to both parties. I provide my pupils with jewels, wines, brides, mistresses. I tell them what clothes to wear and how to wear them, I instruct them how to be idle with panache. To the Japanese, I say that a picture is the only thing they can spend a fortune on without incurring a great deal more for its upkeep. To Australians I say, 'If you can float it, fly it or fuck it – rent it, don't buy it!' I wait for the dirty laughter to subside and then I look them in the eye and tell them gravely, 'You can always make more money but this picture is unique. If you let it slip through your hands you will never forgive yourself.'

Then there are my ladies. Ah, my ladies. The wives of the titled and the rich come to see me in my permanent suite on the fourth floor at Claridges where I am surrounded by my paintings, my sculptures, my *objets d'art*. I am never without my favourite picture – the most recent one I have bought, naturally – on an easel in the outer chamber where we eat scones and drink tea. Like Disraeli and Queen Victoria, we become engaged in flights of artistic fancy. Like a Troubadour with the flair of a Provençal poet, I offer my ladies hopes, dreams. I beguile with visions of a banquet at which only the most cultured may feast, I conjure an Elysium where only the wealthy may walk victorious with acclaimed artists (of the past, naturally. Few of my pupils are interested in the grubby realities of living artists).

My method of instruction is entirely non-Socratic. I have everything to tell my pupils. They have nothing to tell me. 'Consider this!' I say, with a theatrical flourish of the hand. 'Picasso was just nineteen when he sketched these *corrida* scenes. The bull represents the duality of Man.'

I pause before concluding with flirtatious eye contact, 'Man being at once both savage and tender.'

I breathe life into my paintings. I express no surprise when a ray of sun breaks through the window and swathes the picture in a glow of golden light. My clients are amazed, but I expect nothing less from the universe. My pupil will often express a desire to purchase the work in question, although pictures have a tendency to fade when I am not present. How often have I heard the regret, 'But Freddie, the paintings always look better when you are in the room.'

It has been said that no one is more moody, emotional or untrustworthy than an art dealer and while this is true, other important factors must not be overlooked. Namely the luck of the devil and the knack of turning insecurity and greed into desperate concupiscence. I offer my pupils the exquisite torments of unrequited love: *You like this picture? Alas, I have it reserved for a favourite client. You like this one as well? You are right to find it beautiful but I doubt you can afford it.* If my art does not conquer you immediately, I may allow you to keep it in your house as a non-paying guest. Your fondness will turn to lust and your desire will soon demand satisfaction. You will tell me that you long for my art and I will ask you what your longing amounts to in pounds.

I am unstoppable. Each painting is greater than the last one. Until the next one. To each collector I offer a better, more alluring vision of immortality. Depressions prove lucky for me as does rising income and inheritance tax. I show my clients how to avoid both oblivion and the tax inspector in one triumphant swoop. Philanthropy. Bequeathment. A gift bequeathed to the Nation. Ah, the Nation. A smell of oak and leather and cigars lifted from boxes with lids that close with a sigh.

Naturally, I am not merely concerned with the rich and the titled. Far from it. It is scrupulous attention to detail that has distinguished the career of Charles Frederick de Vere as much as it has of any notable army general. Valets, concierges, waiters and the household staff of my pupils have all been of vital service to me since the path to immortality is not paved with gold. On the contrary, its flagstones come remarkably cheap. One of my most significant stones was purchased here in Claridges not two years ago when it transpired that one Earl P. Johnson VI, a Texan Croesus had taken up residence on floor three of the hotel. I had been following this man's artistic flowering ever since he came to my notice in a piece in a newspaper article where he had announced that, 'Works of art are my friends. Beautiful things inspire me.'

So when the chambermaid knocked on my door at 11.28 to ask if I required the turn-down service, I twinkled into her eyes and asked her to ascertain the afternoon plans of Mr Johnson in room 304. When she responded with an almost imperceptible wink, I eased a crisp note into the top pocket of her white blouse. I have always adhered to the precept that when directing servants, one should never say, 'Please' but always, 'Thank you'.

Maids have let me down before now, but Carmen is one of my better spies. At 13.46 she knocked again to explain that Mr Johnson was just finishing his lunch and that afterwards he had plans to leave for the National Gallery. She offered to keep him talking in his room and then to bring him to the lift on the third floor by 14.30.

'My dear girl,' I told her. You are my favourite thing in the world!'

I confess, I will lie on occasion, although only the sharpest will notice the black sediment behind the periwinkle blue. Luckily, I am not a man to dwell on morality. Not mortality, either. Mainly, I am punctual. Pathologically so. It was raining that day and I needed time to chose my attire carefully. I knew that Earl P. Johnson VI would soon leave his room to begin his after-noon of cultural betterment and I wanted to arrive at the lift early in order to hold it on the fourth floor until I heard signs of life from below. The plan went like clockwork. At 14.29 I heard Carmen's voice. I smiled as I stepped into the shiny brass contraption, slamming the cage shut and beginning my descent as I prayed she would not betray me now.

At floor three the lift stops, the doors open and in steps Earl P. Johnson VI. He looks younger than his newspaper photograph and much taller. Six foot four and sporting a fringed suede jacket that emphasises his strapping shoulders.

When I flash him one of my smiles, his big face lights up and he tips his Stetson.

'And they say that only Englishmen carry umbrellas!' I announce in a voice heavy with geniality.

'Pardon me?' He speaks quietly for a Texan.

'I am on my way to the National Gallery to look at some

pictures,' I reveal, glancing at his large golfing umbrella. 'But given the inclement weather, I seem to be shamefully under-prepared.'

I get ready to look surprised.

'That's the darnedest thing,' my man replies. 'I was just going to the National Gallery myself!'

'Incredible!' I exclaim. 'A lily-pad moment!'

I hold out my hand. 'Charles Frederick de Vere. Delighted to meet you.'

'Lily pads?' he says, his warm hand, the size of a baseball glove, embracing mine.

I have him. The lift reaches the ground floor and the doors open. The grill is ripped apart by the bell hop.

'Special moments of synchronicity,' I explain, gesturing with my hand that he may leave the lift before me.

'Maybe . . .' He falters for the first time.

'Express your thought,' I implore.

He steps into the marble-floored lobby. 'Maybe you'd like to share my taxi,' he suggests. 'The rain and all?' He hesitates. 'Maybe you could show me some of your favourite pictures at the National Gallery . . .'

My expression suggests that the idea has only just landed in my head.

'The pleasure would be mine,' I exclaim. 'Are you interested in art?'

'Well . . . I buy art.'

'Really?'

'Put it this way: if I just bought real estate I would be one boring person.'

At the entrance to the hotel, I nod at Flip as he prepares to spin the revolving doors so that Earl P. Johnson VI and I may make our exit into the world. By the tone of Flip's, 'Good morning, Mr de Vere, sir,' I can tell it will not be long before I bump into another rich stranger with an interest in immortality.

Part One

CHAPTER ONE

Everything is frozen, nothing moves. A dead fly dangles in an ancient spider's web. Three sheep outside, half hidden by a crumbling tower, they've been shot with stun guns too.

The fly starts to tremble in its dust-laden safety net and the door smashes open. The girl looks up.

'Oh!' She sounds disappointed. 'It's only you.'

The boy's eyes bulge out with sadness and blankness. There are specks of blood all over his pale face as if he's been on a shooting spree. There is blood and fat all over his fingers and red wine and blood all down the napkin stuffed into his neck. With a hysterical whinny he jolts back into life.

'Cosima, darling! You are funny!'

His teeth plunge into the bird's carcass. He has stripped it pretty much bare but he still manages to rip off threads of meat, chunks of cartilage, licking at purple clots. He takes it from his mouth and looks at it with a panicked squint before ramming it back to begin another bloody battle.

'Pigeon,' he pants from one side of his face. 'Wonderful. Should always have pigeon. 'Licious, absolutely 'licious. Pigeon . . .'

The girl sits at a desk covered with sketching pads and pencils. She might be somewhere in her twenties as might the boy who wears jodhpurs, a holey cashmere jersey, odd socks and shoes with no laces. She watches him inspect a long table which is covered with an off-white cloth and is formally laid for a meal. Looming above the table is a tarnished coat of arms – a golden owl embossed on a shield with a scrolled motto underneath: *Dum Spiro Spero*.

'Four of us for dinner tonight?' the boy inquires, nervously.

The girl abandons her drawing. She goes to sit on the window ledge by the piece of dead coral (sugary with age), the twisted ram's horn that turns into a cheese toasting fork (rusty), the Red Indian head dress (moth-eaten) and a scattering of dead flies. She is followed by two whippets whose gleaming grey coats suggest they might be fed on caviar.

'Sykes thinks that someone rather special is coming,' the girl says with a trace of a smile.

The boy makes a desperate inhalation and the bird carcass drops to the floor. The girl twists strands of long black hair around her delicate fingers as she watches him dive on to the faded blue carpet.

'You only ever turn up at mealtimes,' she says.

'Conversation,' he mumbles on hands and knees. 'I like good conversation. Very elegant . . .'

'I can't wait to hear what this one's story is,' the girl muses, looking over at the dining table.

The boy retrieves his booty and stands up, panting. 'Let's hope there was blood involved,' he says, slyly. 'You'd like that!'

The girl frowns and the falsetto whinny erupting from the boy's mouth only stops when a fly drops down dead on the carpet.

The flies are a constant at Summer Crest Hall. There is always the distant sound of flies spinning in their death throes, like champion skaters on ice. There are flies dropping from the ceiling on to the floor, from lamp shades on to out-of-date magazines. Or you find one buzzing like a broken Messerschmitt in the Spode china cup you were about to pour your tea into. Sometimes they just crawl – the crippled ones, the half-dead ones that can't fly any more. You see them on windowsills, on the mantlepiece, on the oil paintings – settling into the chipped white of a dandy's limp hand.

Franck pretends he doesn't see them. Franck pretends he never sees anything sad or shocking. He says, 'I'm very content. Very happy,' at least three times a day so you know that he's not content at all. Sometimes he sits in the Long Room, flicking through illustrated books of German Wehrmacht fighting uniforms. 'Oh darling,' he croons sadly to no one in particular as he sips at something in a tankard.

Franck comes and goes like the vapour of breath on a glass or a shadow on the ground on a cloudy day. He is a dandelion clock, a directionless piece of fluff, the pale stranger emerging from the mists of a frosty morning who turns out to be the Tarot card Fool with eyes in the sky, a smile on his face and a cliff edge he's about to step over.

He hobbles out of the Long Room, avoiding Cosima's gaze.

'Sykes,' he whines when he reaches the kitchen. He waves the remains of the pigeon in the air without meeting the house-keeper's eye.

'Any more, Sykes dear?'

A girl barely out of her teens is wearing a floral rayon pinafore. She sits at the table applying mascara from a long pink box with a wand the size of a tooth brush.

'Bloody stuff,' she mumbles, spitting on to something resembling boot polish. 'Is it smudged? It's a bugger without a mirror.'

Franck lets out a high-pitched giggle.

'Lovely,' he says, laying the spindly rib cage quietly in the bin. He takes a spoon from a dresser filled with antique dinner plates and stirs a bubbling pot on the Aga.

'You seen my Evening in Paris scent?' Sykes barks.

Franck jumps.

'No Sykes, dear. But your Max Factor Crème Puff is on the table.'

'I can see that. You keep your paws off it. You and that Kenneth Sketch.'

Franck purses his lips.

'Got to keep up standards,' Sykes mumbles. 'We've got a right one coming to dinner, by all accounts.'

There is a thud from the scullery room and as Sykes turns her head, Franck pulls his sleeve over one hand and fishes a hot grey body from the pan. He shuffles quickly out of the kitchen, noting the orange light shining on to a blue and white landscape filled with crumbling towers and sheep. A man in breeches points a stick at a woman in a voluminous skirt which is covered in blood the colour of ketchup.

CHAPTER TWO

The beds are like opium beds, they make you sleep and sleep. It is only a whirlpool of fruit and cream and chocolate sauce that finally propels Carmen Costello into the land of the living. She wakes with the sound of a man yelling, 'I want to talk dirty . . . get another woman up . . . hire a hooker . . . let's get crazy!' still ringing in her ears.

She groans. Her eyes focus on a cherub with a squashed head and then on a man's arm. The muscles are deformed, as if there are bagfuls of stoats wriggling under the skin. Then Carmen becomes aware of sheets. She feels along the bed with her hands. *Nice quality. Linen. Darned.*

She is conscious of a stream of orange-coloured light flowing into her eyes and when she sits up, she notices that the strange human biology is part of a tapestry and that the light is shining through a latticed pane of glass in a granite casement window. Then she remembers. *England.* She groans and flings herself back into the four-poster bed. She looks up at the carved oak canopy.

Another hotel, another promise.

She wonders what it'll be this time. Nothing surprises her any more about the so-called high life. Topiary on the table in the Henry James dining room, toilets done out in Louis Vuitton leather (*what the hell, rich people still piss on the seats*), marble staircases, oatmeal walls, rooms so overheated they make your lips chap, mini croissants for breakfast, gigantic shrimp for lunch.

It was ironic that Larry was so undiscerning when it came to his private pleasures. His addiction to a holy trinity of Champagne, Cocaine and Lesbian Sex Acts was an endless source of grief to Carmen. *Private dances with fruit and cream and chocolate sauce, for Christ's sake.*

It is not the girls in the strip clubs that Carmen has anything against. She comes from the same place as they do: the wrong side of the tracks. Southie. It hadn't been easy growing up in a blue-collar ghetto of Boston famous for mobsters, car-theft rings and a huge Irish population when you had straight black hair, dusky skin and a name like 'Carmen'. Even her Irish relatives used to give Carmen a hard time, referring to her affectionately as 'The Spik'. Her mother, who was Mexican, told her not to take any notice while her Irish father just laughed and said the experience would toughen her up. *And I guess it did. I got the hell out of Southie, didn't I? But where did I end up?*

Every time Carmen wakes up like this in another strange hotel, she swears it'll be the last. No more tacky clubs, no more private dances, no more letting Larry invite hookers back to the room. She can't even remember where last night took place. Or how it finished. She has a terrible hangover and when she closes her eyes, the white glare behind her lids makes it worse. The lighting isn't much better with her eyes open. It reminds her of a photo taken in daylight with a flashbulb. She sits up again but everything looks a little bloated, slightly unreal. She glances again at the grotesque tapestry cherub and flops back down on the bed.

When she met Larry, he'd never denied that he liked strip joints. He'd reasoned that they were an antidote to his glamorous professional life and less harmful than gambling. He stopped going the first few months after they got together, but then he started again. He was smart enough not to go to Spearmint Rhino in Santa Barbara where Carmen now lived, but that didn't stop him from driving twenty minutes along the coast to sleazy places in Ventura. The Glitter Gulch, Mary's, Ginger Tiger. Naturally, he always forgot to get rid of the credit-card slips.

Carmen decided to accompany him in the end. She only needed

a couple of Bend Your Ass Overs to get into the mood. She'd even laugh when Larry would hire a private room and have her and one of the girls dance together.

'Hey babes! Don't write cheques your bodies can't cash!' he'd yell as he sat with his legs spread, one hand gripping the neck of a champagne bottle, the other stuffed down the front of his pants. He thought he was being exotic, trying out different establishments around the world but they were all the same. Guys with no shirts pumping their fists into the air, sticking small denomination bills in girls' underwear.

Carmen sighs and pulls the sheets up around her neck. She notices a fly drop down from the bedside lamp and buzz around in a sleepy twirl on the bedside table. A sensation of déjà vu hits her. She feels around her body for familiar signs: silk La Perla teddy, *check*; hair crunchy from too much alcohol the night before, *check*; VIP party manacle, *check*. Her hand lingers momentarily on the plastic identification bracelet on her wrist. She closes her eyes but the white glare returns so she rips back the sheets and gets out of the warm feather bed, suddenly realising how freezing cold it is. *Fucking England.*

She looks round the room for the temperature dial, cursing the fact that she's not back home in California. But she sees nothing apart from a mirror on the wall, so corroded that her face looks dim and far away. *Just as well*, she thinks. *I probably gained twenty pounds since I last looked.*

She pads over the creaking floorboards towards the sticky orange light coming in through the window. When she peers out, all she can see is a valley shrouded in a moat of cloud. She walks back past the bed, noticing three mythology-themed tiles on the headboard: two entwined lovers, a guy spearing a bull and a man in winged sandals brandishing a shield. She carries on to what she assumes is the bathroom and when she pulls on a frayed tassel, she finds herself in an even colder room. Icy, this one with moist walls, a gurgling wooden commode and a smell of damp carpet. She runs her fingers along the edge of a bath with rust at the bottom of the taps. *Fucking minuscule European tubs.*

She goes shivering back to the bedroom and decides to pour herself a stiff drink. But when she gets to the middle of the room she stops dead.

Wait a minute.

She looks around.

What kind of hotel . . . Where's the mini bar?

She realises she has no memory of checking in and yet when she goes to open the wardrobe door, she is reassured to see her clothes hanging in their usual impeccable order. All the stuff she normally brings on her travels: her cashmere, her Dolce & Gabbana *puta* dresses, her Versace daywear – the most low-key pieces she could find although they're not exactly subtle and each one glints with gold buttons embossed with the head of Medusa. She sees that her black corset is on the seat of the dressing table and that her favourite kitten heels are by the side of the bed. There's her rhinestone clutch too. She grabs it and when she opens it, she sees that all the contents are intact: her lipstick, her sugar-free cinnamon gum, Melatonin capsules, Senna, the keys to the house in Santa Barbara.

She sits back on the bed. She really is feeling strange. Not the customary pain of tobacco craving mixed with food poisoning – the tell-tale signs of love addiction according to her Santa Barbara friend Charlene. No. This is more like jet lag, although it can't be jet lag, she reflects, since she's been in London for . . .

She can't remember how long. She pauses, as if the tantalising plot of a dream is about to come back. But it doesn't. She fights the growing feeling of lethargy by deciding to get dressed. She takes off the pink teddy and puts on one of the Versace numbers, a sleek black cocktail dress. *Tighter every time I squeeze into it*, she curses as she tussles with the line of buttons that runs down one side.

Stepping into the kitten heels and tossing a pink cashmere throw around her shoulders, she walks back to the window. She'd

18

ask Larry what the hell was going on but she suspects he's off on one of his early morning guilt walks. She's used to the guilt walks.

And then it strikes her that London didn't have any misty fields the last time she was there. Just as a tingle of panic starts to settle in her belly, she hears footsteps outside the door. Carmen has been in English country hotels before. Any minute now, a student waitress in a grubby white pinny and cheap shoes will enter the room apologetically, bearing a tray of tea. *Forget the tea*, she thinks. *But I could use a cup of coffee.*

When nobody knocks, she grabs her clutch and goes to open the door herself. She is immediately hit by a rush of cold air and the sight of a vicar on a cricket pitch trying to hit a ball with his umbrella. A framed black and white cartoon hangs on an oak-panelled wall next to a tarnished sword and a knight's helmet stuck with a droopy red feather.

Carmen sees a chambermaid at one end of the corridor. A glimpse of a bun of hair, a short black skirt and a pair of athletic legs.

'Hello?' she shouts, but the woman rushes off. Carmen decides to follow her. She needs to find the manager. Noting that her room is number 1981, she closes the door and steps into the corridor, which groans with the sound of ancient pipes. The place smells familiar somehow, like a dining room in a Victorian hotel before the guests have arrived and warmed it up.

Carmen follows the direction she thinks the chambermaid might have taken and finds herself at the top of an enormous staircase. The gnarled wooden steps are shiny with age and the walls are hung with fading oil paintings. There are bursts of flushed *décolletage* and tiny feet in pearl-embroidered slippers but few distinct faces or bodies. And yet they feel familiar to Carmen. She dismisses this notion as ridiculous. *Damn cold's freezing my brain.*

As she continues down the staircase, she passes marble busts placed in dusty granite alcoves, she overtakes more corroding mirrors and a large crystallised spider that hangs by a mummified thread from another decayed painting.

At the bottom of the staircase she sees something that looks like a dungeon door. It is studded with rusty iron bolts covered in lichen spores. She manoeuvres her way past a collapsed sedan chair, an array of axes, some fencing swords and a set of something that resembles medieval dental equipment.

She has nearly reached the enormous door when the sedan opens and a pale young man emerges. Carmen thinks he could be anything between twenty and forty, although mainly she notices the clot of blood on his chin and the gnawed bird carcass he is holding in one hand. He looks startled when he sees Carmen but soon composes himself and starts talking in a way that reminds Carmen of a child saying lines from a school play that they haven't learned properly.

'Ve'y pleased to meet you,' he says, extending a greasy hand. 'I'm Franck. Welcome to Summer Crest Hall.'

'Nice to meet you, Franck,' Carmen says, making a brief wave. Franck breaks into a high pitched giggle. 'Seeing you's like the first day back at boarding school!' he says, before his face suddenly stretches into a sneer. He slides a plump thumb on to a worn latch and pulls the gigantic dungeon door open with such confidence that Carmen is aware of a pulse in her body for the first time since she woke up.

CHAPTER THREE

When Carmen follows Franck through the dungeon door, she finds herself in a long room with a faded blue carpet. Her eyes are drawn to a golden owl staring down at her from above the fireplace and then to a young woman with snakes of black hair.

It is 20.00 precisely, according to an eighties-style digital clock on the mantelpiece. Carmen can no longer see Franck but she does spot the maid with the athletic legs (who she now sees is rather older than she thought – maybe in her late sixties). She is putting coal into the unlit fire as if it breaks her heart to part with each lump. Carmen notices a long table formally laid for dinner and more faded oil paintings: a maiden on a swing; two fleshy sea nymphs sprawling on a rock. Mainly though, she keeps coming back to the girl with the long, dark hair.

She is sitting at a desk and appears to be drawing, while a man with a shaved head sitting next to her is cutting pictures from a magazine. As Carmen gets closer, she sees that there are two dogs lying at the girl's feet.

When she looks up, Carmen freezes to the spot. It is a response that both confuses and irritates her, given the girl's relative youth. She can't be thirty yet. When she stands up and pulls the sleeves of a paint-splattered shirt over her hands like an awkward school-girl, Carmen sees that there is blood on the ends of her fingers.

'Oh,' the girl says. 'You must be the new arrival.'

This isn't quite the manager Carmen had in mind. She is trembling like a thoroughbred horse and her eyes make Carmen think of mist on a lake in the early morning when the sun hasn't broken through yet.

'Pleased to meet you,' the man with the shaved head says in a soft, American monotone. 'I'm Kenneth Sketch.'

His voice sounds like a Persian cat padding over a velvet carpet. In spite of his preppy appearance – a navy blue jersey draped over the shoulders of a stripy blue shirt – something about him reminds Carmen of Jack Nicholson. Possibly the slightly deranged smile or maybe the startled-looking eyebrows.

'Hi,' Carmen says. She glances over at his collage. 'You look like you're having fun.'

'I count myself lucky to be here,' he drawls, picking up the glue stick. 'I'd start the night at a fancy dinner and end up hanging out with people with no teeth. People with no teeth for goodness' sake!'

Save it for Oprah, honey, Carmen thinks. 'No kidding,' she says. 'I bet it was warmer than this place.'

The girl comes over to greet Carmen properly.

'I'm Cosima,' she says.

'Hi, Cosima,' Carmen replies, shaking the girl's pale hand and noticing that the marks on her slender fingers are not blood but red paint. 'Great house you have here. Although you're going a little overboard with the shabby chic, if you don't mind me saying.'

'I don't mind at all,' Cosima says in clear, upper-class tones.

'Thing is,' Carmen ventures, 'I'm not actually sure where I am right now?'

'We're in the Long Room,' Cosima tells her. 'The really freezing cold room.'

Carmen nods slowly. It crosses her mind that the girl might be a little simple.

'I noticed you had some heating problems,' she says.

'Yes. Franck always wants to eat in here but it's silly. Laying linen and cutlery on dusty tables when you think, "Why can't we go in the kitchen with the dogs, where it's warm and you don't have to use the candelabra?"'

'OK,' Carmen nods. 'We're getting somewhere. So, this guy Franck – he runs this hotel?'

22

Cosima smiles. 'Oh, no!'

Carmen changes tack. 'Would you have a mirror?'

The girl bites her lip.

'It's a small thing,' Carmen goes on, 'but I couldn't find one in my room.'

'They don't have mirrors here,' Cosima says.

Carmen narrows her eyes. 'No, you don't understand. I really need a mirror.'

'Why?' Cosima says with a sudden giggle. 'Do you want to kill yourself?'

Carmen feels a stab of paranoia. People say her face shows experience, but she knows that forty per cent of that experience is sun damage. Charlene told her to wait until she was fifty for surgery because the later you start the better, but she's not sure she can hang on for another two years.

'Now listen . . .'

She stops when she feels Cosima's hand on her shoulder.

'You poor thing,' Cosima says in a new voice tinged with authority. 'You must be starving. Do join us for dinner.'

Carmen realises that she doesn't want to go back to her bedroom on her own, and now that Cosima seems to have turned into the grand hostess, she decides to take her up on the offer. She is soon joined at the table by Kenneth Sketch, and when Cosima pulls up a chair beside her, Carmen is aware of a flutter in her belly.

'OK, babe,' she says. 'I'll be straight with you. I woke up just now in your . . . establishment, and I can't find my partner. Larry Pfister? You might have seen him on TV . . .'

She is distracted by the almost indecent way Cosima seems to be staring at her.

'KSBY? It's Californian. The NBC affiliate in San Luis Obispo and Santa Barbara counties. Larry does this show . . .'

'I know Larry Pfister!' Kenneth Sketch breaks in. 'He does that gossip show, right?'

Carmen feels a glimmer of hope.

'Well, it's pretty dumb but . . .'

23

'Oh no, I love that show. I was in Santa Barbara one time at a personal growth retreat. Las Colinas. You know that place?' He smoothes his napkin on to his lap. 'I watched a lot of TV . . .'

There is the sound of a distant door opening and closing very loudly. All three turn to the end of the Long Room to see a man in a woollen hat walking briskly towards them. *Thank God*, Carmen thinks. *Maybe he'll know what the hell's going on.* As he walks closer, she hears him saying something. One word she can determine is, 'Doctor.' Her hopes rise once more but the man carries on marching, his eyes fixed on the kitchen door, his lips mouthing a furious rant, '*And guess what he told me? Guess what he told me!*'

Carmen hears a tinny beat coming from his woollen hat just before she sees the bulge of earphones. Another door slams and he's gone.

'I love Sinead O'Connor, don't you?' Kenneth Sketch asks Carmen.

The blood drains from her face. She thinks about Kenneth Sketch's childish collage. She looks at the deranged expression on his face. She glances at the clock that says 20.20 and then she remembers the plastic party bracelet. When she inspects her wrist properly, she sees that it says, 'Carmen Costello. Card No. 3385. 17/07/1956.' Her date of birth. Her eyes bulge as if she's just had a brainwave.

'That asshole,' she mutters. 'He put me in that place.'

'What?' Cosima says.

'That hospital. The place the rich Brits get sent when they go loopy loo . . .'

She gets up and starts pacing the carpet. 'Asshole! I remember now. Before we came over on this English trip he was promising me a spa weekend. But I know his presents. One time he checked me into this place in Zurich. Fucking kooky! Bath tubs with hoses under the water. Electronic massage chairs. Little chats every day with a guy in a white coat.'

She shakes her head, looking round the room.

'Still, nothing compared with this. Fucking C-Wing, as well!'

'C-Wing?' Cosima says.

24

'Don't give me that!' She glares at Cosima. 'A-Wing for the recovering drug addicts. C-Wing for the real crazies!'

She returns to the dining table and sits noisily back in her seat. 'He can't do this to me,' she tells Cosima. 'This is 2004. You can't check your girlfriend into the nut house while you spend the week with some sleazy hooker you picked up one night and tried to turn into a goddamn banana split!'

She tries to calm her breathing as she watches a bluebottle limp its way across the tablecloth.

'I'm sorry,' she says. 'I sound like I need to be in C-Wing, right?'

She tries to laugh but another fly falls from the ceiling and lands on her hand.

'For fuck's sake!' she shouts. 'Damn flies in this place! What kind of rehab is this?'

'It's OK, Carmen,' Kenneth Sketch soothes. 'You can share with us.'

'No, Kenneth!' she explodes. 'It is not OK! I wake up in the freaking Munster Mansion and nobody will tell me what's going on!'

There is silence. Carmen starts to feel foolish. She prods the dead fly with a long, red fingernail. 'Would you look at that,' she mumbles. 'Leg muscle definition like Naomi Campbell. Now that's just unnatural.'

'Not as unnatural as those fake tits you get!' A girl in her late teens marches into the room carrying a tray of steaming tankards. 'Barmy!' she says, slamming one of the mugs down in front of Carmen. 'Like erect penises on ladies' chests!'

The girl's eyes are thick with mascara and she is wearing too much face powder. Over a hand-knitted twinset she sports a floral rayon pinafore that rustles as she moves and leaves a smell of toilet spray in her wake.

'Depends which doctor you went to, honey,' Carmen snaps back, realising that this creature is one of those British girls into really ugly clothes. *Thrift-store shit. 'Vintage' they call it.*

'Meet Sykes, our wonderful housekeeper,' Cosima says quickly, giving the girl a meaningful glance.

'People should grow old gracefully,' the girl insists, tossing her blonde ponytail back. 'I've seen the people in those magazines.' She nods towards the pile by Kenneth Sketch's collage. 'Cheek implants I saw the other day. Disgusting. Like golf balls sewn into your chops.'

The way Sykes is looking her up and down is making Carmen feel uneasy. And then, in a flash, she understands. *Of course! The lipo! That's what Larry booked me in for!*

She looks at Kenneth Sketch and it suddenly registers why he looks so permanently startled. *They do shit botox in this place too*, she thinks, with a sigh of relief.

'That's it! Larry promised I could have liposuction before the end of the year,' she tells Kenneth Sketch, patting her right buttock. 'The fat-sucking machine's going to have its work cut out, right?'

Kenneth Sketch looks as surprised as his frozen forehead will allow and the mists lift momentarily in Cosima's eyes. But Carmen is not fooled. She always wished she'd been better at being a drug addict. Cocaine might have kept her thin. As it is, her favourite drugs are sugar and the sun. No paranoia. No dealers. Not that she doesn't have to go to elaborate lengths to sneak all those gourmet candy apples into the house. At Sparky's in Santa Barbara she'd have fifteen of them in her shopping cart and pretend they were for the children that she doesn't have. At the check-out she'd be saying in a loud voice, 'This one's for Jerry, this one's for Maria . . .'

'Butter pecan popcorn,' she explains to Kenneth Sketch. 'Key lime pie, dulce de leche . . . no wonder I'm so big.'

'Dulce de leche,' Kenneth Sketch croons.

'When I'm desperate,' Carmen tells him, 'I won't even put the condensed milk in the microwave to cook it.'

'Oh, I'm the same,' Kenneth Sketch says. 'I'm only faking it when I order protein in a restaurant. All I ever really want is sugar.'

'You should try condensed milk with sardines,' Cosima says, suddenly.

Kenneth Sketch and Carmen both glance at the tall, thin girl as she strokes the whippets at her feet. When they turn back to each other, Kenneth Sketch gives Carmen a smile that reminds her of the bland beam of a flight attendant. As she observes the motionless muscles at the corners of his eyes, she feels herself warming to him. It strikes her that Kenneth Sketch must have been attractive when he was younger.

'Why don't you phone a friend?' he suggests.

Carmen feels her heart beat faster.

'You spoke with someone?'

'Sure. I spoke with my lover yesterday.'

'You did?'

'They don't like you to talk to people when you first get here.'

Carmen has to concede that this is regular practice in some of the better rehab places.

'But some days you can call. Oh, I couldn't do without John Paul. He's been really good to me. Especially since I fell off the wagon. Take it from me, magic mushrooms and lobster when you're on a six-hour internal flight from New York to San Francisco – they don't mix.'

Carmen's jaw starts to tremble. 'That's why Larry sent me here, right? Oh God, I love that asshole. Surprise lipo for Christ's sake . . .'

It is 21.01 and Franck suddenly appears out of nowhere.

'The Bullshots!' he exclaims, rushing to the table. He stuffs a new napkin into the top of his jersey and clasps his hands around the sides of his steaming tankard.

Carmen has almost forgotten the mug in front of her. She eyes it suspiciously.

'Excuse me, ma'am,' she snaps at Sykes. 'What is this, please?'

Sykes shrugs. 'You boil up twenty birds and then you throw them all away. You just keep the stock.'

'The consommé, Sykes,' Franck corrects her.

Carmen sniffs the steam. 'But . . . isn't there alcohol in this?'

'Vodka and consommé,' Franck tells her. 'A hunter's Bloody Mary. 'Licious. Very civilised.'

He puts his face into his mug, grunting like a child in the throes of a delicious night's sleep.

Carmen pushes the Bullshot away from her.

'Could I please see the spa menu?'

Sykes looks puzzled. 'You mean slimming stuff?'

The red nails begin to tap the table. 'If that's not too much to ask, yes, I would like to eat something that's not going to turn me into even more of a friggin' whale than I am already!'

Sykes stomps back to the kitchen, hollering, 'Mary! Shift your bloody arse!'

As Franck sniggers, Kenneth Sketch confides to Carmen, 'I think magazines put too much emphasis on diets. I know a girl who can hardly fit in the back of a taxi. But she thinks she's hot and so I think she's hot.'

'Try telling that to a heterosexual TV anchor,' Carmen growls as Sykes returns to the room with the grey-haired kitchen maid. Both are carrying plates of charred meat.

'Pigeon,' Sykes announces, banging a heavy grey plate down in front of Carmen.

The plumes of steam rising from the birds, coupled with Sykes's faint whiff of toilet spray, mesmerise Carmen for a few seconds. She watches Cosima pass strips of meat under the table to the whippets.

'Marvellous, eating off my great-grandfather's pewter plates,' Franck enthuses. 'When you've got roast beef and Yorkshire pudding on pewter it's like being in the middle of a battlefield!'

'Roast beef,' Sykes mutters. 'Chance'd be a fine thing. All I'm ever given to cook is pigeons.'

'Pigeons!' Mary shrieks. 'How much longer must I be punished!'

Carmen tries to place Mary's accent as she watches Sykes chase the sobbing old lady back to the kitchen.

'We have birds to eat every day,' Kenneth Sketch tells her.

'I don't mind, actually. Don't you like it when things are exactly the same? Over and over again?'

Carmen looks at her plate with growing concern. She pulls the meat off the bones with her knife and fork and then, taking her fork in her right hand, begins picking at the crispy flesh. When Sykes returns to the room holding a blue-and-white Spode china bowl, Carmen hopes it might contain a salad.

'Forgot this,' Sykes says, clanging the bowl down on the table.

'Heaven!' Cosima exclaims.

The bowl is filled with fried potatoes carved with smiling faces.

'Potato smiles,' Cosima tells Carmen. 'I love the smiles. It's sort of sick. Cutting up faces on your plate.'

She asks Sykes to bring in some tomato ketchup, explaining to Carmen that 'It's for the blood.'

When Carmen says, 'I thought you guys had blue blood,' Cosima suddenly stops feeding the dogs and Franck breaks into one of his nervous whinnies. Carmen observes the storm brewing under the translucent surface of Cosima's cheeks and her absorption is only interrupted when she suddenly bites into a piece of lead shot. Her eyes bulge and she cradles her jaw with her hand. There is silence in the room as everyone waits for the outburst and yet she controls herself. Carmen's discoloured teeth are one of her less attractive features and she is not keen to draw attention to them.

'Vodka and food with bullets in,' she says, quietly. 'Who needs Reiki and psychotherapy?'

Franck starts mumbling under his breath. 'Darling. Darling . . .'

'I mean, why should I care if I'm at the fat farm or the nut house anyway? And who needs botox? ECT makes you look much more relaxed.'

Franck starts to guzzle faster.

'I'm going to love it here!' Carmen's voice is becoming more shrill. 'I'll starve! The weight'll drop off of me!'

Sykes rustles back into the room with a blue-and-white gravy boat filled with tomato ketchup. When she sees Carmen's face she looks concerned. She glances at Cosima and then turns back to Carmen.

'Shall I fetch you some lettuce, love?' she asks in such a kind-sounding voice that Carmen bursts into tears. Carmen's mother graduated from cleaning bars in Southie to becoming a house-keeper in Boston's ritzy Fisher Hill neighbourhood. It would really upset her when the owners of the house were mean to her mother.

'I'm sorry, Sykes!' she weeps into her napkin. 'I'm being a bitch!'

She wipes her eyes and asks Sykes for directions to the nearest bathroom, explaining that she needs to go and 'freshen up'. She excuses herself from the table and follows the young housekeeper through the kitchen, noticing a sparkling, cat-shaped brooch on her pinafore.

'That's lovely,' she tells her as they climb a narrow stone stair-case. 'Mother of pearl and . . .'

'Marcarsite,' Sykes shrugs. 'Poor girl's diamonds.'

'Oh no,' Carmen says, softly. 'Stars are the diamonds of the poor.'

Sykes's face lights up.

'That's a lovely thing to say,' she says.

She gives Carmen another unsettling once-over which leaves Carmen wondering if all the women in this house have the hots for her. But then the scowl returns.

'Too romantic for my own good,' Sykes grunts, rubbing her caked lashes and smudging mascara over her powdery cheeks. As she reaches over to open a door with the sound of hissing water behind it, Carmen is struck by the delicacy of her wrists.

Carmen is in much better spirits when she returns to the Long Room.

'You know, babe,' she tells Sykes. 'Romance has been my down-fall, too.'

Sykes shrugs as she tops up Franck's Bullshot mug.

'And the liposuction's not going to solve anything,' Carmen

goes on, turning to Kenneth Sketch. 'See, my therapist thinks I'm suffering from love addiction.'

Kenneth Sketch nods gravely. 'You're one of those strong women looking for a flakey man to dominate her, right?' he says.

Carmen nods. 'It's terrible. But hey, maybe *that's* why Larry sent me here to be cured.'

'Oh honey, I've been there,' Kenneth Sketch says, holding her hand across the table. 'I was looking for Mr Right, too. I went to a bunch of shrinks. But you know what?' He pushes his pigeon away. 'I'm so over that psychological stuff. I go to psychics now. Or Catholic mass. So beautiful. That's where I met John Paul.'

Carmen starts to well up again and when Franck has finished manoeuvering Kenneth Sketch's half-eaten bird onto his own plate, he pours her a glass of red wine.

'Here you are, dear,' he says. 'This will make you feel better.'

Carmen frowns. In spite of her other indulgences, she prides herself on the fact that she has never cared for wine.

'It's not wine,' Sykes tells her. 'Pre-meds, they call it.'

'Oh, yeah,' Kenneth Sketch drawls. 'The pre-meds are great.'

'Pre-meds?' Carmen hesitates. 'I guess I have to get ready for the operation, right?'

'They grow the grapes here at the house,' Franck tells her.

'Organic, huh?' Carmen says, picking the glass up. She takes a sniff and wrenches it from her face.

'Gross!'

'You don't need much,' Cosima says.

'Don't give up,' Kenneth Sketch adds in his soothing voice.

So she tries again. The taste is bitter. And then suddenly a glow lights up in her head. A sublime heat seeps into her body and she feels warm for the first time since entering the house. She beams at everyone round the table, realising that the sun she has been worshipping all these years was only a pale imitation of the incredible solar system contained in her wine glass. She knows that everything is all right. She knows she is sitting in a freezing cold room but she doesn't care. She doesn't care about the cold or the heat, if she's happy or sad, if Larry dumped her or if she put on more weight. It suddenly strikes her that she doesn't feel scared any more and it's a wonderful sensation.

'Mmmm. This is a tasty glass of wine.'

'We have an endless supply of the stuff,' Franck tells her.

'Well, you're pretty self-sufficient here aren't you?' Carmen says, cradling the glass in her hand. 'Who shoots the birds?'

When Franck giggles, Carmen just smiles and breathes in the colours of the Long Room which are much brighter than when she first came in. She sees now that the paintings on the walls are in ice-cream pinks and baby blues. She notes how the ribbons and the bows and the folds of rich taffeta all seem to shimmer in a breeze. She closes her eyes and sees fruit and foam and cherries and when she opens them, she sees a blue-and-white shepherdess in a voluminous skirt and then Cosima's hand on top of hers.

Sykes has returned to the kitchen. Franck is polishing off Kenneth Sketch's pigeon, informing him about Waffen SS officer trousers. Carmen feels as if she and Cosima are the only people left in the room.

'You must find it strange here,' Cosima says quietly. 'I paint in the attic during the day. Come and keep me company. I'm looking for a new sitter.'

Carmen is struck again by the girl's beautiful skin. A luminous white, as if a choir of angels is giving it a permanent back lighting. She takes another drink of the pre-meds, still looking at the hand resting on hers. Such a sensitive hand. She can't remember the last time someone touched her with such tenderness.

It is 22.22 and Carmen feels a pure, unearthly peace.

'I'm going to propose a toast to blue blood,' she announces suddenly to the table. But as she reaches for her glass, she knocks it over, staining the cloth with a dark red puddle. When Franck cries, 'Oh dear, the Mistress of the Beasts won't like that!' Cosima excuses herself and walks quickly out of the room.

CHAPTER FOUR

Carmen wakes up feeling a lot calmer, which is surprising considering that she still finds herself marooned in some kind of deranged rehab centre. What has changed is that she managed to speak to Larry on the cell last night.

> *Larry! it's you! Baby, I miss you so much!*
> *Hey hon, how you doin'?*
> *Some crazy spa you got me booked into, baby . . .*
> *Lost any weight yet?*

She pulls the phone away from her face as if it just threw a bucket of cold water down her ear. Funny. When Carmen first met Larry in Santa Barbara she thought he was a food fetishist. He used to kiss her face like he was eating a chicken dinner. And he said such beautiful things. On their fourth date – twilight on Butterfly Beach – he'd suddenly taken her hand, pointed to the first star of evening and whispered, 'That one's for you,' adding, 'The stars are the diamonds of the poor.'

She thought that was the sign. To do the thing. To pull the 'I love you' party popper. So she pulled the string and there was the big bang and the pink and the purple and the green tissue paper spilled out all over the floor. Only Larry didn't pull his, and Carmen's 'I love you' just lay there in a little heap of coloured paper. And like a party popper, she couldn't push it all back in and pretend it never happened because it was there, her guts, splayed out all over the floor, embarrassingly present.

Carmen decides not to tell Larry about the pre-meds and the strange food. He asks her what she's been up to but what does

Carmen tell him? That she's been moping over him for the past twenty-four hours? That she sees his face in every conversation she has? That he's hiding behind every door, every chair, every crumbling oil painting in the house? And maybe he's not even looking at her anyway. She's convinced he's peeking at other chicks, younger chicks, chicks with thinner waists, smaller asses. So much for her tough Southie upbringing.

So babe, any of the girls in that place trip your trigger?

Carmen makes a long sigh and Larry starts enthusing about how he's just had a great meeting with a 'very intelligent British woman' about his new TV show. He tells her he's going to be busy for a few days but that he'll call her soon.

Bye hon, take it easy.

Larry, I . . .

After the cellphone conversation, Carmen almost relishes the icy conditions of her bedroom. She feels strangely affectionate towards the man with the ferret biceps in the tapestry, she feels kinship with the squashed cherub's head. She still has a problem with the sporadically dying flies though. As the umpteenth blue-bottle drops down from the bedside lamp, she decides to take Cosima up on her offer to be painted. To tell the truth, she is excited by the idea of taking her clothes off in front of this girl and who knows, Larry might get a kick from it when she next speaks to him.

She leaves her room, follows the draughty corridor, goes up some chunky granite steps until she reaches what seems to be an attic room. She hesitates in front of the door, wondering if Cosima still wants her to pose. She seemed upset at the end of dinner last night. But mainly Carmen is having second thoughts about taking her clothes off. She has been naked in some strange circumstances but nothing like this.

When Cosima opens the door, Carmen almost fails to recognise her. She is still wearing the large, paint-splattered shirt, but last night's trembling thoroughbred has vanished. Today, Cosima

34

looks radiant. She is holding a roll-up cigarette between fingers that show fresh signs of dark red paint. Carmen feels her heart thump as Cosima smiles and beckons her into a high-ceilinged studio that smells of turps and foie gras and is even colder than Carmen's bedroom.

'Welcome to my parlour,' she says. 'I come here to hide. Recovering drug addicts aren't nearly mad enough.'

Carmen feels a shiver pass through her body and it isn't the cold. That cut-glass accent; it gets her every time. She distracts herself by looking round what seems to have once been a children's play room. There is a rocking horse and a fort with soldiers spilling out on to the floor. The walls are pasted with hunting-themed toile de Jouy wallpaper, although the peeling motifs of dogs and deers and classical females in diaphanous robes are obscured in places by piles of art books balanced precariously one on top of the other. By the window, there is a trestle table covered with sketch pads, turps bottles, a pot of brushes, some Montecristo cigar boxes filled with tubes of paint, an oyster shell ashtray and a plate of biscuits topped with pâté.

Carmen turns to a stack of paintings leaning against a wall. She hesitates in front of it but when Cosima says, 'Be my guest,' she starts to flick through the different canvases. An array of strange rabbits and girls in Edwardian dresses and huge flying horses with tiny children on their backs passes before her eyes.

'Old work,' Cosima tells her, lighting the cigarette. 'This is the newer stuff,' and she lifts a sheet covering some easels to reveal three pictures awash with dramatic reds, bobbing with disparate fragments and drenched shapes. The paintings move Carmen.

'Great . . . colours,' she says, at a loss for words.

She makes herself turn away and notices that the only picture actually hanging on the studio wall is a large tapestry, less lumpy than the one in Carmen's bedroom. For some reason, she feels as if she's seen it before. It shows a dark forest and three robed girls dancing together next to a dreamy young man who is reaching up to pluck fruit from a tree. It's the young man that catches Carmen's eye: a beautiful boy with pale skin and plump lips. He reminds her a little of Franck. But also of someone else.

'Are you all right?' Cosima asks.

'Sure,' Carmen says. She points to the tapestry. 'Interesting picture.'

'Burne-Jones,' Cosima tells her. 'Typical Victorian, don't you think?' She turns to look at it. 'An anodyne copy of—'

'Botticelli's *Primavera*.' Carmen finishes her sentence.

'Very good,' Cosima says, looking impressed.

'Put it down to my terrible taste in men,' Carmen quips, still gazing at the tapestry. 'I saw Botticelli's *Primavera* in the Uffizi one time. I was honeymooning with my first husband. He didn't really get it. He was too busy worrying where in Florence he'd be able to get an over-cooked steak and a glass of milk for his dinner.'

She turns and notices a bottle of wine on the trestle table. She wonders if she'll be offered any more of the pre-meds.

'My first husband, Six, he'd have appreciated that piece of Burne-Jones . . . cheesecake.'

She gets another flash of déjà vu but decides to ignore it. She wanders over to a threadbare, bottle-green chair where the two whippets are curled up like sea horses. As she crouches down to stroke them, she asks Cosima if she's the Summer Crest Hall art-therapy teacher.

'Sometimes,' Cosima replies with a sigh. 'Dreadful unimaginative stuff. Most of them paint flowers and landscapes and ideas of unconditional love.'

She walks over to the trestle table. 'The worst bit is talking to them. It's exhausting, don't you find? Being sociable?'

The pale fingers start to roll another cigarette.

'When I was a child I tended to hide under the furniture when the guests arrived.' She smiles. 'I'd draw doodles of decrepit horses. And then cover them with all sorts of reins and bits and spurs. My imagination could be quite cruel. Sometimes I'd draw people and dress them in theatrical costumes. And then I'd hang them.'

She shrugs.

'I'd biro them all out, of course. You're not supposed to draw hanged people.'

Cosima lights the cigarette and sprawls into a battered chair with unselfconscious elegance.

'My childhood was intensely social. My mother was a very eccentric woman. It was daunting.' An enormous puff of smoke floats up to the rafters. 'Not that the parties were all bad. My favourite guests were the chic homosexuals and the drunks. They were extremely louche and very nice to children.'

She sits up to flick ash into the oyster shell.

'That kind of naughtiness doesn't seem to exist any more. Don't you think? Everyone's getting on with their life, getting themselves sorted out.'

'I guess that's why we're all here,' Carmen says.

'In the seventies there were some really good losers,' Cosima goes on. 'Vomiting in the plant pots. Things like that.'

She takes a biscuit from the plate on the table before turning to look Carmen in the eye.

'Of course, I'm very good at doing the drawing-room thing when I have to.' She takes a bite. 'I was highly trained for it.'

When Cosima sees Carmen looking at her biscuit, she says, apologetically, 'Oh, it's not pâté. It's dog food.'

'Excuse me?'

'I longed to be a dog when I was a child,' she explains. 'They got more physical affection than we did.'

She considers the biscuit in her hand. 'Funny, I never used to like the wet stuff . . .'

She puts it back on the plate. 'Franck was always such a goody-good. He never wanted to eat dog food.'

'You knew Franck as a kid?'

'He's my cousin,' she says, sounding suddenly bored. 'We used to play together.'

Carmen notices a drawing propped up against Cosima's chair. Two baboons in the woods prowling around a tree. A naked female sits with her back to the tree, although at the moment, the woman is only a pencil outline. Her arms and legs resemble nerve endings.

'That's cool,' Carmen says, pointing to the sketch.

'Good,' Cosima says, brightening up. 'That's the one I was hoping to put you into.'

'Yeah?' Carmen tries to sound casual.

'My aim now is to draw as clearly as I did as a child.'

Carmen nods, wondering when she's supposed to strip off.

'Do you mind if we plug that thing in?' she asks, spying a hair dryer on the windowsill. 'It might warm the room up.'

'Good idea,' Cosima says. 'I haven't used that for years.'

Carmen wonders how long she's been inside this place. But then the ancient contraption starts to whir and Carmen relaxes a little. She moves away from the dogs and begins to undo her gold Medusa buttons. It is a clumsy undressing. One of her worst ever. Cosima mentions that she might like to go behind the screen and Carmen feels foolish. She tiptoes behind it, thinking how ironic it is that the older you get, the less confident you become. She wishes Cosima were painting her after her operation when her body would be in better shape, her stomach and her hips so much smaller. But at least her hair is still good. Still thick and still mainly black. She can thank the Beaner genes for that. Leaving her clothes folded neatly on a chair, she remembers what Kenneth Sketch said last night about projecting a confident image and she steps out from behind the screen. Hand on hip, looking Cosima saucily in the eye, she says, 'So, where would you like me?'

She is put off her guard when she sees the way Cosima is staring at her. She can't tell if there is awe or horror in her eyes. Then Cosima composes herself. 'Perfect!' she says. 'You've got the perfect body.' She adds, 'It might not work, of course. Some people are like foreign countries to paint.'

'I guess.'

'I'm hopeful though,' she says. 'The last pictures are often the best.'

'The last ones?'

But Cosima doesn't answer. She goes over to the bottle-green chair and strokes the two dogs before gently inviting them up.

'Come, Fido! Come, Phèdre!'

They move away and Cosima puts a piece of sheepskin on the chair. She invites Carmen to sit down, telling her, 'I'll have to make some sketches of you first.'

Carmen sits down gingerly, cupping her hand over her crotch in what she hopes is a nonchalant manner. Cosima takes her place on the battered chair. She takes a pad and a pencil from the trestle table and starts to make marks on it. Carmen marvels again at Cosima's long, delicate hands. So fine. Never a day's work at the kitchen sink.

'I'm so sorry,' Cosima says, looking up suddenly. 'I didn't offer you anything to drink. Pre-meds might be a good idea. Do you think?'

'Sure,' Carmen shrugs, watching Cosima pour the dark liquid from the wine bottle into a glass. She recognises the smell of fox as she raises the glass to her lips. She tastes the bitterness just before the explosion of calm. Soon, she doesn't mind being left on her own, naked on a sheepskin rug in front of a girl whose face and body twitch with concentration as she looks from her sketch pad to Carmen and from Carmen to her sketch pad. Convulsing and writhing around in her seat, she makes Carmen think of some of the crazies she met in Zurich. *Strange,* she reflects, *how inspiration makes you look like an unhinged rabbit.*

She sips some more at the liquid in her glass. Incredible how it tastes like bliss in a bottle and yet leaves no hangover. She puts the glass on the arm of her chair, thinking how she must remember to tell Charlene about this when she gets back to Santa Barbara.

She relaxes into the sheepskin rug as it strikes her that Cosima is only interested in the way the light falls on her skin. She remembers that this is how painters paint flesh. She feels excitement at the thought that Cosima might be able to put the sheen back on her body, just like the old days. She wonders if being an artist's model will feel anything like sex. And to start with, it does. The intensity comes and goes in waves. At some moments she is exquisitely aware of her body, as if her body is breaking up into thousands of tiny bits, minute pixels flying up, spreading round the room and dissolving into the toile de Jouy wallpaper. The whole room is encased in her naked flesh, her warm, soft skin and she thinks of dogs spraying against trees, of amazons pulling back arrows. She feels something she hasn't felt in years: sexual defiance.

Exotic sounds rush through her ears: the flowing of pencil over paper sounds like a distant river; the rumbling hair dryer could be a tropical wind. The longer the sitting goes on, the more the room seems a way of escaping the room, of escaping the house – escaping herself. She falls into a trance where there is just the rushing of the river and the blowing of the wind, the sight of the fauns and the nymphs and the goddesses. She smiles at the tapestry boy with the pale skin and plump lips and a pink robe slung over his shoulder. When she smiles at the whippets, curled up on guard outside the toy fort, Cosima seems to read her mind.

'Sometimes I like Fido and Phèdre better than humans,' she says, without looking up from the sketch pad. 'If rich people were animals then the men would be hippos and the women would be the little pecking birds on their backs.'

Carmen grins and takes another sip of the pre-meds, relishing the sensation of all being right with the world and deciding that the flies now sound as if they're purring. Her eyes hover around the room until they are drawn back into the inferno of reds on the easels. She fixes on one painting where streaks of black seem to pulsate on a sheen of bright ruby Madder Lake, making her think of a mascara overdose.

'Is that Sykes?' she murmurs.

'Possibly,' Cosima says, still drawing.

The river rushes on.

'What about that one?'

Carmen is looking at a canvas whose red is slightly duller than the others, the hue of meat left out too long in the sun.

'I'm speaking a foreign language into one of his ears,' Cosima tells her. 'And blood is pouring out of the other.'

'And who is "he"?' Carmen teases.

'Oh, that would be telling,' Cosima replies in a voice that is both shy and flirtatious. Then the river stops. 'The trouble with love is that it doesn't last very long,' she says. 'You taste mortality in the first kiss.'

Carmen nods. 'Picasso used to say that a love affair is like an hourglass. Once the sand starts falling, it's not long before it's all used up.'

Cosima frowns.

'Who told you that?'

And that's when Freddie pops into Carmen's head. Just like that. Charles Frederick de Vere. Black velvet jacket and red foulard. 'I knew an art dealer once,' she tells Cosima. 'He lived in a luxury suite in a London hotel. It was all gold and fancy. One day, he told me he was going to install a cage of monkeys and when I asked about the smell he said he'd spray them every day with Guérlain's Jicky!'

She waits for the laugh but it doesn't come. The river starts up again, a mad torrent this time, gouging and slicing into the paper.

Carmen suddenly feels horny. She likes the angry river. She realises that the power in the room has changed, that she, Carmen Costello, has said something to disturb the inscrutable whippet girl.

'But then,' Carmen drawls, looking again at the baboons in the drawing. 'I guess you dig monkeys too.'

The giggle comes at last.

CHAPTER FIVE

I was working in the tea room at Claridges when I first saw him. The first thing I noticed were his eyes. That his eyes were actually alive. So alive it took me a while to come round to the other things: the forelock of salt and pepper hair, the jungle red foulard in the breast pocket of the black velvet jacket, the gold chain around the neck, the out-of-season tan.

There was the voice too. It was deep and spiffy, like the British guy in the smoking jacket from *The Rocky Horror Picture Show*. Although mainly he made me think of James Bond, Roger Moore era. There was something theatrical about him. He made you think of trick pens and fast cars and buttons that you push and a bed springs out of the wall.

It was the spring of 1979 and I was twenty-three years old. I'd just finished a masters in tourism and hospitality management at a small college in Boston. The joint was run-down but the fees were cheap and my tutor had a crush on me, which is how I ended up with the Claridges gig in the first place.

De Vere was having tea with some broad, one of the dried-up society ladies with a crisp blonde bob and too much foundation on her face. When I came to take his order he looked surprised. He leaped to his feet, exclaiming, 'Ah, a newcomer!' before making an elegant bow, checking out my tits and heels as he went.

I knew his type. Guy who always wants extra jelly on his scone, extra cream on his cake. Dirty little fucker. Not that I mind the buttery boys. They notice stuff. You should have seen the shoes the other waitresses used to wear. Typical English. Not just flats but cruddy flats – soles peeling off, all scuffed and curled. A Latina would never have left the house looking like that. A lot of men don't notice those things. They notice if a girl isn't wearing heels – they know that something's wrong, but they don't put two and two together.

De Vere was different. He was always kissing hands, clicking his heels, telling stories. I'd come up to the table with a fresh pot of hot water and he'd be in the middle of some elaborate tale: *'The salons of Paris were aghast, Mrs Thorougood!'*

He could tell a story, there was no doubt about that. He could do fairy-tale ending stories, bleeding-heart stories, victory-snatched-from-the-jaws-of-defeat stories. *'The year is 1790 and Fragonard is a broken man. Can you imagine his despair, Mrs Thorougood! His final masterpiece, commissioned by Louis XV's mistress, Madame du Barry, rejected at the eleventh hour . . .'*

He could do flashing eyes, dreamy eyes, flirtatious eyes (he never failed to mention how an artist called François Boucher used to sleep with all his models). I soon figured out that he was an art dealer. Eighteenth-century paintings were his speciality. Boucher and Fragonard the main boys on his books. I learned how their delicately coloured work was all about frivolity, sensuality – *volupté*, de Vere called it. I topped up his teapot more than was absolutely necessary. I wanted to see how he'd pull his 'ladies', as he termed them, into his web this time.

He was good. It was as if he was promising to paint *them* into the oil paintings. He would insist that one of his pictures hanging on the wall of their house would make their husbands see them in an erotic new light. *'But an eroticism, Mrs Thorougood, that is never vulgar.'*

Most of them didn't give a shit about their husbands. They didn't really give a shit about art. The shit they cared about was Charles Frederick de Vere.

By the early summer I'd been promoted to the post of chamber-maid. It was easier work than the tea room and you could make more tips. You just had to appear to give clients special treatment: enquiries about their health, chocolates on their pillow, personalised notes left on their desk.

De Vere's suite was my favourite. It was spotless. Kind of anal, if you want to know. I didn't even have to clean the bedroom because I'd been told by the housekeeper not to enter there under any circumstances and whenever I tried the door, it was always locked.

Given the lack of work there was to do, I spent a lot of time sprawling on a crimson damask couch in the huge reception room, my head propped up on a dragon's wing. De Vere's suite was in the high Victorian section of the hotel and there were animals all over the furniture: lion paws for legs, dragon wings for arms, a rosewood card table with griffon claws. And there was a tangle of gold vegetation swirling and twirling all over the walls and ceiling – fronds and ferns and petals and vines.

There was never any beer in his fridge, so for want of anything better I'd siphon white wine from opened bottles and kick back and enjoy the view: the stuffed owl with a coloured mohawk bigger than the ones the postcard punks were working on the King's Road; the screen painted with a girl whose breast was falling out of her dress as she shot an arrow at a guy with a deer's head. But my favourite thing was the paintings on the easels. It was a lot of high-class cheesecake, if you ask me. A lot of light pinks and baby blues, a lot of faggy white boys and a bunch of chubby chicks flying through the air in flapping chiffon or lounging around in the woods on pieces of crumpled velvet. There was a lot of cellulite going on also: cellulite on butts, cellulite on backs of knees and the nipples were weird, all the same kind – the neat, pink, cherry kind.

Even so, I couldn't stop thinking about those pictures. I liked to go up real close and skim my fingers over some of the lumps and bumps of the paint, wondering if there were flakes of 300-year-old skin under the cracked caramel of the varnish or if some eighteenth-century mistress of the house had stood just where I was standing and beat herself up about not being as chunky as the big girls in the painting.

I was running my finger over a porky thigh one afternoon when suddenly the bedroom door burst open. I jumped and my glass of wine fell on to the carpet. When I turned round, I saw a flicker of gold and then Charles Frederick de Vere, framed in the doorway. His legs were spread and his hands were thrust deep in his pockets, like Monty just returned from the battle of the Alamein.

The gold vanished as he slammed the bedroom door shut and I dropped to my knees, pulling a cloth from the front of my apron. I could feel him there, looking down at me, doing that English public schoolboy groin thing as I sponged frantically at the carpet. Before I knew it, I was sponging in a way that I knew would make my big Mexican bohonkus look indecent in my tight black chambermaid skirt. De Vere didn't say anything but I could smell him: buttered broccoli and cigars in gentlemen's clubs. It turned me on, if you want to know the truth.

'I'm glad to have found you again,' he said, locking the bedroom door behind him. 'My teas were starting to become a little dull.'

His voice sounded like warm cream poured over a naked body from a porcelain jug. I started rubbing faster and then suddenly I smelled shoe polish and there was a tan hand above my head. I took it. It was warm and dry. It clasped mine and helped me to my feet.

'I'm sorry, Mr de Vere,' I said, pushing my rack forward slightly. 'It won't happen again.'

'Oh, but I hope it will,' he said, glancing at the top of my white blouse which I always left unbuttoned a little too low. 'Now that I know you like the *vin de table* I've been leaving out for you, I think we might progress the education of your palate.'

He turned sharply on his heel and walked over to the fridge.

'Does art interest you?' he asked, opening a bottle of white wine.

45

I wondered if I should tell him that where I come from, art means 'dirty'. Or it means graffiti expressing support for the Irish Republican Army sprayed all over the walls of the Southie projects. And anything with John Wayne. In Red River, the Irish pub where my dad works, they have a huge poster of John Wayne over the bar.

'Sure, I like art,' I said. 'I mean, my mom definitely likes art. One time she bought my little brother this Blue Boy outfit. You know, like the kid in the painting by . . .'

'Gainsborough.'

'Yeah, him. There was an offer in the *National Enquirer*. You got a blue cape, blue breeches, a blue sash. The hat with the feather in. You got everything. All in for a hundred and ninety-nine dollars.'

'A bargain,' he said, handing me a glass of wine the colour of urine.

'My dad wasn't so pleased. Said she was trying to turn Billy into a fag. Said she should have gotten him a cowboy outfit.'

'Then you have a good grounding,' he said.

'Excuse me?'

'The eighteenth century.' He cast his arm toward the easels. 'The century of lightness, frivolity. An embodiment of the spirit of the *ancien régime* on the eve of the revolution . . .'

De Vere predicted that the nineteen-eighties would turn out to be another such era of whimsy and fancy. He told me he'd just returned from an auction in Monaco where the star lot – an eighteenth-century closet – had been bought by the Getty museum for nearly a million pounds.

'A phenomenal sum!' de Vere exclaimed. 'An extraordinary piece of furniture!'

He showed me the catalogue, explaining that the closet was actually, 'A nine-foot-high Louis XV corner cabinet made by Jacques Dubois in polished oak and rosewood with gilt bronze mounts.'

When I looked at the whacked-out photograph, I wasn't

surprised that the cabinet had come from the cheesecake times. I mean, I love a little glitter, but this was beyond over-the-top. It had four dainty rabbit paws for legs and it was crusted all over with gold like a lot of ornamental eczema. There were a bunch of the naked fat people stuck on to it also, only they'd been painted gold instead of light pink and baby blue.

The wine was thick and heavy. It nearly made me choke.

'So, that guy,' I said, turning to one of the pictures on the easels.

'Boucher?'

'Yeah, Boucher. If he slept with so many of his models, how come the chicks all have the same kind of nipple?'

His eyebrows arched provocatively. 'What other kind of nipples are there?' he enquired.

I was enjoying the attention. I sipped some more at the urine and walked over to the window.

'And what's this?' I asked, running my hand over the bow and arrow girl on the painted screen.

'School of Titian. *The Death of Actaeon.*'

'The artist must have slept with the same models as Boucher.'

'I'm sorry?'

'Check out the nipples.'

It was obvious to me. The hunter chick had the same type of nipple as the Boucher girls'.

'Everything that deceives may be said to enchant,' he said with another expansive hand flourish.

'Is that why the guy's got a deer's head?' I asked.

'A stag's head,' he corrected.

'How come?'

'Diana was very vicious. Actaeon was a mortal whom she caught spying on her as she bathed.'

'What'd she do?'

'She turned him into a stag,' he said with a smile. 'Had him ripped apart by his own hounds.'

He patted the crimson couch and I went to sit next to him.

47

I didn't get too close though. I took another swig of the gross wine.

'You're like an indulgence salesman, right, Mr de Vere?'

'Indulgence?' The eyes were twinkling.

'You know, like the Catholic church used to do – sell people bits of paper so they could get to heaven quicker. Except you're selling bits of canvas. You're telling people that if they buy one of your paintings, they're going to be on a higher plane than the people who invested their money in, like, pig iron. You're promising them . . .'

'Salvation?'

'Yeah, but only a piece of it. Most indulgences were partial. They only got you a few days off your stretch in purgatory.'

De Vere smiled. 'So I must carry on selling my pictures?'

'Absolutely. And you're pretty slick. I've seen you in action. You make your clients feel like they just scored themselves a piece of the burning bush, five drops of Mary's milk . . .'

'My holy relics,' he said softly, gazing at the gilt frames in front of us.

'High art, holy relics, get-out-of-jail-free cards. It's all the same.'

He turned and looked at me in a strange way. I figured I'd better lighten up.

'You know what, Mr de Vere?' I said. 'I bet you could sell potatoes to Idaho.'

'Call me Freddie,' he insisted, topping up my glass. Then he fixed me in the blue of his eyes and said, 'Would you care to see my "secret potatoes"?'

I was pretty tipsy by now. I just said, 'Sure, Freddie, you show me what you want.'

He disappeared into a small room off one end of the reception area and when he returned, he was carrying two small canvases.

'Meet Jean-Honoré Fragonard,' he said, turning the pictures to face me.

One showed a young girl lying on a bed with her nightdress pulled up. She was holding a miniature dog in her arms and its tail was tickling her pussy. The other one was of a girl in another hoisted-up nightdress but this time she had a swan in her bedroom. The swan had a very long neck which was located a few inches from a very finely detailed vulva that had a better Hollywood wax than I did.

'Get out of here!'

'Very naughty, the eighteenth century,' he chuckled, sitting back down. 'Pornography was the preserve of the well-to-do.'

'Pornography?' The word shocked me.

'I use the word *entre nous*, Carmen. To my clients I talk of "erotica".'

I nodded, thinking they were right, what they said about art back in Southie.

'A little spice is a good thing, don't you find?' He gestured back to the more modest paintings on the easels. 'To paraphrase Shakespeare: sweetness is a commodity of which more than a little is by much too much.'

I tried to sound foxy. 'To paraphrase Jacqueline Susann: too much is never enough.'

When I felt him move closer, I got up from the couch and sashayed over to the window. See, I wasn't too keen. He didn't like people who were too keen. It was like his theory for selling a picture: make out they can't have it, that they're not ready for it, that they don't have enough money to buy it. Then they can't resist.

CHAPTER SIX

That was when the room service calls began. Five, six, seven calls a day. He was smart about it. He found out my shift times so that when he rang down it'd always be me on duty. I knew he didn't really want another pillow, a new clean towel, an extra bucket of ice. Actually, he did want the ice. He loved to drink champagne and he was true to his word about 'educating' my palate. The next day when I knocked at his door, he was brandishing a bottle like a magician who's just pulled a rabbit out of a hat. 'I've chosen a Pol Roger for our first lesson,' he announced. 'Churchill's choice of breakfast beverage.'

I shrugged.

'Whatever,' I said.

His eyes lit up.

Every day, when I took my place on the crimson damask couch for my forty-minute lesson, he'd tell me something new about the *méthode champenoise* or how champagne is made. About the two years it has to stay in an underground cellar, 'sleeping' and thereby increasing its alcohol content; about how the bottles are put on a rack three weeks before they're ready and get turned daily so the sediment collects in the neck; about how the bottles end up in a 'dressing room', where the necks get covered in gold paper, the purpose of which is, 'to save one from the vulgarity of knowing when the champagne ends'.

I learned that you can say pretty much anything about wine if you say it convincingly enough. 'Lively on the palate', 'a long delivery down the throat', 'the length is slowly descending, it's a very attractive descent'. I learned that you talk about the 'dress' to describe the colour of the wine and the 'legs' and 'shoulders' to describe the kind of kick it gives you. I was convinced that de Vere was only giving me these lessons because he wanted to get his hands on my big rack. That was why I was taking the precaution of chucking most of the contents of my glass into the plant pots when he wasn't looking. But it wasn't only a chastity-saving device; I didn't have the heart to tell him that I didn't like wine, that I was more of a Tab or a Fresca kind of girl, that I'd have been more psyched by a crash course in Golden Syrup or Bakewell Tart (my best discoveries about Great Britain up to that point).

Still, I can't say it was boring, and at the end of each grandiose lecture I'd always be rewarded with a ten-pound note folded into a long, crisp torpedo and inserted into the pocket of my tight-fit shirt. Occasionally, de Vere would ask me about myself, so I'd tell him a little about the South End of Boston, about my dad, the Irish deputy barman at Red River and my mom, the Mexican cleaner.

In the beginning, I wondered if I should point out that in spite of my champagne ignorance, I'd always been very aware of 'high society' and the importance of social nuance. See, as far as I can make out, colonial Mexico was as stratified as it gets. My great-grandmother Carmen was born illegitimately in Monterrey, Mexico in 1870 to a middle-class Criolla woman (a Mexican born of Spanish parents) and a native Indian father. Naturally, having an illegitimate baby was bad enough back then, let alone making one with mixed-blood. I figure that my great-great-Criolla grandmother called her daughter 'Carmen' because she wanted to give the kid a kind of nest egg. The Spanish were the ones who ran the show back then in Mexico, and by calling her kid 'Carmen' (you can't get more Spanish than that, right?) she thought it might inspire the little girl to grow up and kick a little ass. As it turned out, baby Carmen set the ball rolling. By the thirties, her own daughter – my grandmother Bertha – had moved to Texas and in the fifties, Bertha's daughter – my mom – broke out of cattle farming once and for all by running off to the East coast with a blue-eyed Irish Catholic boy with hopes as high as hers.

But I soon realised that de Vere wasn't so much interested in me as in increasing his own pleasure. And like a lot of guys, he found the 'Latina' thing kinky so I decided to work on that instead. Sometimes I'd treat him to a few Spanish phrases. Something like, 'Cállate la boca', or 'Vámonos de rumba'. It was a pity I didn't know what a lot of them meant. See, Spanish is still the servant-class language in the United States of America, the language of cleaners and babysitters. My mom only ever spoke to us in English because she had this thing about 'bettering' me and my brother. Still, I picked up her vibe. My dad's too. 'There's a lot more to life than they let on,' he used to tell me. He advised me to get an education and figured there'd be money in hotel management.

'Business school was a cinch after my weekend job at Red River,' I told de Vere, sneaking another glass of Dom Perignon into the rubber plant. 'Inter-personal communication, listening skills, public presentations, that kind of bullshit.'

His face clouded. He was silent for a while and then he said, 'I was sacked from my school.'

My ears pricked up. De Vere was pretty good at not saying anything about his own life story. He explained that 'sacked' meant 'expelled', but when I asked what he'd done wrong, he just shook his head. He stood up, walked to the far end of the room and stood tapping his fingers on the glass doors of a tall, mahogany bookcase.

'What is the name of the greatest vintage claret of the twentieth century?' he said, suddenly.

I'd never seen Freddie cranky before and worst of all, I always got my Moutons and my Margots and my Millessimes mixed up.

'Give me a moment . . .'

'Mouton Rothschild 1945,' he said, tightly. *L'Année de la Victoire.*'

'Oh Freddie,' I said, trying to sound playful. 'There you go again with your details.'

His face froze. 'I have made my career from taking an interest in details,' he said. 'This cabinet, for instance, contains information about the birthdays, the anniversaries, the secret tastes of some of the richest people in the world.'

He unlocked the door and perused a row of alphabeticised, leather-bound ledgers with an index finger. He stopped at G.

'Mrs Goldfarb.'

He pulled the ledger out and turned to the correct page.

'Forty-two DD bust,' he read. 'Waist 34 inches.' He read it all out as if he was declaiming some great speech: 'Laces to be made from reinforced calico. Extra elastic panel measuring 4 inches by 7 to be added to central panel.'

He closed the ledger and returned it to the cabinet.

'Precise instructions for the alterations to be carried out to Mrs Goldfarb's corsets,' he explained, walking slowly back to the reception room. 'I had them shipped to Paris at my own expense.'

'Neat.'

He wouldn't meet me in the eye.

'Mrs Goldfarb's husband is a very good customer,' he said briskly, delving into his pocket. 'And now, my dear Carmen, I'm afraid I have work to do.'

This time, he put the ten-pound note straight into my hand.

I was furious by the time I got back to the laundry room. De Vere was wrong about my lack of attention to detail. Only that morning, I'd found out something extremely beneficial to him. I would have told him, only it appeared that I'd been 'sacked' from his suite.

See, I was more interested in art than in champagne. I already knew that the head doorman, Flip, was giving de Vere tip-offs about collectors who were staying at the hotel. But I didn't think that Flip was so smart. The guy was a classic hotel-industry sleaze, if you want to know. He tried it on with all the new girls and when it came to his spying activities, he only went for obvious targets: not just rich people but rich people who were known to spend money on old paintings.

Flip would never have bothered with someone like Earl P. Johnson VI. Nor would de Vere, for that matter. As far as they were concerned, Earl was just another rich Yank philistine. Not only did he have no record of collecting art, but he wasn't twitchy enough or paranoid enough. Basically, he wasn't like most art tycoons: pallid grey men who get lost in crowds.

Earl had been on my radar for a while. You couldn't miss the guy with his Johnny Appleseed smile and the huge Stetson he used to tip whenever he was addressing a female member of staff. The first time I cleaned his room, I noticed a small Precious Moments porcelain figurine on his bedside table. It was a boy with a huge head and teardrop-shaped eyes who was looking at his watch. Underneath his feet, an inscription read: 'Wait Patiently on the Lord'.

It was like an itch, a hunch. See, John Wayne isn't the only art they have at Red River. In the ladies' rest rooms, they have a Precious Moments poster of a little kid with a huge head and teardrop-shaped eyes wearing a sailor suit and looking up at the sky through a telescope. Through the graffiti, you can just about read the message underneath: 'Turn your eyes upon Jesus'.

I decided to follow my hunch.

Normally, the personalised notes I left for guests were sayings copied out from packets of fortune cookies I'd bought in China Town. *Dig the well before you are thirsty. A rat who gnaws at a cat's tail invites destruction.* But with Earl, I adapted. Precious Moments pictures always come with an inspirational Christian message and thanks to Red River, I knew a bunch of them. I left a trail of those cheesy breadcrumbs so that when I finally met Earl face to face (I'd observed that he always came back to his room right after lunch) he'd want to strike up a conversation with me.

One day, at ten after two I knocked on his door and asked if he'd like the turn-down service.

'Did you leave me those messages?' he asked, timidly. With his puppy dog eyes and his eager-to-please eyebrows, Earl P. Johnson VI looked a little like a Precious Moments statue himself. He invited me in, offered me a glass of water and explained how his fiancée had given him the figurine just before he left Texas for his trip to Europe.

'My fiancée, Sandy and I,' Earl said with a blush. 'We have the same taste in art. We sometimes pray over my collection.'

'You collect art?'

'Oh, I love art. Sandy believes that God can speak through beauty.'

I soon had him eating out of my hand. I was cute with him. I called him 'Six' because he was the eldest son of a generation of Earls that went back to the original Earl Johnson who set up a tiny farm just outside of San Antonio. Over the years, his family had amassed a fortune from hamburger meat and now he was using the proceeds to travel around Europe speculating on property.

We talked about back-home stuff, about how we missed the open spaces, the bacon, Super Bowl Sunday. I was still wondering how to broach the subject of him buying a bunch of fat chicks from the eighteenth century, so I suggested that he should start checking out some of London's art galleries on his afternoon walks.

One day, I asked him about his art collection and he handed me a copy of the previous week's *USA Today* folded open at the property section. There was an article about the latest piece of real estate Six had just bought in the South of France. 'Works of art are my friends,' he was quoted as saying. 'Beautiful things inspire me.'

When I'd finished reading, he told me that he had some photographs of his collection with him and would I like to see them? My heart started pounding. Until I saw the photos. What the journalist had omitted to say in the article was that aside from a bunch of original Precious Moments posters, Earl P. Johnson VI's art collection consisted of a few Navajo Indian rugs and a lot of crap painted by burned-out businessmen who'd run away to live in Santa Fe.

The Picasso was a piece of luck.

See, even though I didn't have high hopes for Six on the art front, I still liked the guy. One November afternoon when I went to turn down his room, he told me he'd decided to move on to somewhere with a better climate. To the villa he'd just bought in the South of France, outside of Cannes. The place had been very run down and Sandy was there now, supervising the renovation. It seemed that the former owner, an eighty-year-old lady, had left a lot of stuff behind. Some of it was art work that had freaked Sandy out.

'A bunch of old plates and pots painted with . . . crazy stuff.' Something verging on excitement appeared in Six's eyes. 'Goats with men's bodies and . . . genitals and things.'

'No kidding.'

'Sandy thinks the signature says, "Picasso", and it would make sense. He had a house nearby.'

When I asked why the old lady would have left them behind, he said he figured that the place had bad memories for her.

'She wanted a quick sale. She didn't seem to care too much about the money.'

He added that Sandy had also found some paintings in the house. Mainly watercolours by local artists but one of them was an oil painting with Picasso's signature on it. Sandy wanted to get rid of that also.

'I know what she means,' Six said.

'You do?'

'The trouble with high art . . . well, it scares me.' He shrugged awkwardly. 'When you go into a store to buy a picture of a little girl with big eyes and a basket of puppies, the floors don't echo like they do in an art gallery. You can drink a Slurpy as you walk round. There's a person sitting there who's not an art expert.'

I had to admit that I understood his concerns. I put my hand on his strapping shoulder. 'Six, man,' I said. 'You need to sell that Picasso and I know just the person to help you.'

I hadn't seen de Vere for a while. The champagne lessons had come to a mysterious end the day I forgot the name of the greatest claret of the twentieth century. But that afternoon I was summoned.

When de Vere opened the door, his tie was loosened and I noticed a grease stain on his shirt. He was already halfway down a bottle of champagne but he didn't look too bubbly. He looked old.

'Want to buy a picture?' he said, flopping on to the couch.

There was a painting on an easel that I hadn't seen before. It was amazingly realistic. It showed a peacock with a jewel-blue body and blood-soaked feathers and a hare with a gashed side and tethered hind legs. The butchered animals were draped elegantly on a bloodstained tablecloth and nestled artistically between a gold flagon of wine, a spray of honeysuckle and a fancy platter of fruit.

I sort of liked it. It was kind of sick. It was good to know that the 18th century wasn't all about whimsical women falling out of their clothes. Still, whichever way you looked at it, it was a painting full of dead stuff.

'The ladies didn't go for it, huh?' I said.

'My ladies aren't keen on blood in their soft porn.'

He told me that still lifes of dead game were very popular with the *ancien régime*. That this artist, Alexandre-François Desportes, had been employed by both Louis XIV and Louis XV to follow the royal hunt with a notebook and make on-site sketches of the animals the kings considered trophies. De Vere had decided that this dead game was 'rather too extravagant' for modern tastes and muttered something about having to 'take the picture back'.

'Take it back where?' I asked.

He looked irritated. 'Darling,' he said. 'You just concentrate on the buckets of ice and the little notes on my desk and we'll get along very merrily.'

Something exploded inside me. 'You can be really fucking patronising, Freddie!' I turned and marched towards the door, yelling, 'You never tell me anything about art. It's like some secret you want to keep to yourself . . .'

I looked back just in time to see de Vere looking vaguely amused.

'My dear Carmen,' he said, lighting a cigar. 'I detest talking seriously about painting. In fact, I detest talking seriously about anything.' A smoke ring bobbed from his mouth. 'It's the best way for people not to understand each other. Don't you think?'

'Quit being clever!' I said. 'You think that only Flip can do your tip-off stuff but you're wrong! Did Flip get you any good Picasso deals lately?'

I thought I saw something change in his eyes but I couldn't be sure. I mean, maybe de Vere didn't buy pictures. Maybe he only sold them. And maybe he didn't want a Picasso, anyway. Picasso was modern stuff and he sold old stuff.

'Earl P. Johnson the sixth,' I carried on. 'Third floor, room 304. Ring any bells? Any of your spies tipped you off about him?'

I played it too fast. I should have held on to my trump card. But I was naïve. I gave him everything: the name of the guest, the villa in the South of France, the painting in the cellar. I even showed him the clipping from *USA Today*.

Finally, I ran out of steam. I waited for him to say something but he just carried on smoking. He got up and went to look out of the window.

'So?' I wanted to know. I moved away from the door and came back into the room. 'What do you think?'

'I hear many such stories every day,' he said, staring down into Brook Street.

He was a goddamn liar. I later found out he always got more of a rush about buying a picture than he did about selling one.

'I must ask you to leave,' he said, turning and walking quickly to his office at the end of the reception room. 'I'm sure you have things to do.'

It was so abrupt. I felt stupid. I was used to de Vere being nothing but totally attentive to me. I rushed out of the suite, ran back to the laundry room. Fucking country, fucking job. Fucking slimy art dealer.

When I got a request for a new pillow at nine the next morning, I was still angry with him. He could tell. I threw the pillow down on the couch.

'A nice morning,' he said, awkwardly.

'Is there anything else you'd like, Mr de Vere?' I said.

He came closer. 'I upset you yesterday, didn't I?'

I sighed. I knew I couldn't win. I'd already given him the important information. He could do it without me. Then again, it would
be easier if he had me on his side.

'I have go to Germany tomorrow,' he said, sitting on the couch
and idly picking up a newspaper. 'The wife of the director of the
Cologne art museum has invited me to dinner.'

'Whoopee doo,' I deadpanned.

'My!' The periwinkle blue eyes appeared over the top of the
Financial Times. 'I *did* upset you.'

I couldn't help smiling.

'She is an amateur artist,' he went on, throwing the paper down
and patting the seat next to him. 'I will buy one of her monstrosi-
ties for £30,000 and in return she will instruct her husband to buy
one of my Fragonards for his museum.'

'So?' I sat down.

'Lesson number one, Carmen. Gentlemen have the money but
it is often the ladies who tell them how to spend it.'

That was when I twigged. He wanted my help. And I still wanted
to play. I thought quickly. I thought about how Six was always back
in his room by two in the afternoon. How he usually took the lift
to go for his walk shortly after that.

'You need to speak to Six today, right?' I said. 'I'll keep him
talking, I'll tell him to take a trip to the National Gallery. I can
guarantee to have him by the elevator on the third floor by two
thirty.'

I folded my arms, looked de Vere square in the face.

'Fourteen thirty hours, Freddie. Think you can be there?'

De Vere stood up, thrust his hands deep into his pockets.

'Carmen Costello,' he said, narrowing his eyes. 'I do believe you
are ready for your art education.'

CHAPTER SEVEN

It was an unconventional education.

It begins with a phone call the day he arrives back from Cologne. He wants me to come round to his suite that evening for dinner and do I want lobster, caviar or Chinese? Chinese? I'm thinking. Alongside two-dollar stores, welfare centres and dozens of nail salons, there is more Chinese food in Southie than anywhere else on the East Coast. Really I want lobster but I figure maybe that's too expensive, so I say caviar.

When I walk into his suite, I'm pleased to hear him exclaim, 'Knock-out!' because I've spent a lot of time planning my look. I've worn a *décolleté* top that puckers my tits up good and I spent the day at the hairdressers having my hair done in the style of my childhood heroine, Lupe Vélez, the 1930s Hollywood actress, also known as the 'Mexican Spitfire'.

But when I close the door, I realise he's not even looking at me. He's got his back turned and he's staring at a picture on an easel in the middle of the room.

'Knock-out, don't you think?'

When I see what he's looking at, I almost forgive him. The room is dark, but a spotlight illuminates a ferocious blaze of colour. It's the most arresting painting I've ever seen in de Vere's suite. Maybe in my whole life.

A genuine Picasso.

See, back home in Southie, nobody knows what a Boucher or a Fragonard is. Picasso, on the other hand, is one of the big names up there with John Wayne or Bruce Springsteen. Even my dad has heard of Picasso ever since the summer my mom bought him an 'I Heart Picasso' BBQ apron from the Shopping Channel with a harlequin boy on the front.

Actually, I've already heard about de Vere's Picasso coup from Flip. Even Nick the head chef and Mrs Patel the housekeeper got interested in the story. Like I say, Picasso trumps eighteenth-century French painting any day of the week and it doesn't put de Vere in a bad light either. De Vere on his own, I might have passed on. But de Vere in a room with a real Picasso painting? I can't deny it, it adds a certain dimension. Pretty much within two minutes of walking into his suite, I've decided: tonight's the night I'm putting my picture on the market, putting the butter back on Freddie's broccoli.

'Marie-Thérèse Walter,' de Vere says in his dramatic voice. 'The greatest sexual passion of Picasso's life!'

'Wasn't she the doormat?' I say.

A smile bleeds on to his lips. 'The more innocent and virginal he made his images of her, the more satisfying her degradation became.'

You can't see a virginal woman as such in the picture because Marie-Thérèse is part jug, part guitar, part watermelon. Picasso had to disguise his affaire with her, de Vere tells me, because he was married at the time. He was forty-seven and Marie-Thérèse barely eighteen when he invited her up to the Brittany fishing village of Dinard where he used to spend the summer with his Russian wife, Olga, in the late 1920s. He hired a beach hut where the biddable new mistress would be summoned in the afternoons.

The guy could obviously paint. The strength of the arm, the bend of the waist, the spring of the wrist – you could see it all in that painting, you could see he believed that the flow would never end. My favourite thing is the signature that shot across the bottom of the canvas like an arrow:

Picasso

'Note the virility in the stroke,' the fruity voice whispers in my ear. In spite of the low lighting in the room, I can see a pair of twinkling eyes and for a moment I think he is going to kiss me. He doesn't. He turns sharply on his heel and walks over to the ice bucket.

'Time to celebrate!' he announces, grabbing the golden throat of the champagne bottle. When the cork pops, I whoop 'Hallelujah!' I don't intend to throw a single drop into the plant pots tonight.

'Here's to Carmen Costello and her hidden talents,' he says, handing me a frothing glass. 'Like the cigar smoke blown by his uncle into the lungs of the apparently stillborn Picasso, you, my dear Carmen, have brought me back from the dead!'

See, the Picasso was a big deal. According to the famous Zervos *Catalogue Raisonné* – the place where all Picasso's legitimate works are recorded – the painting (*Bathing Cabin with Jug*, 1928) had been lost after the war. Over the next few weeks, a ton of articles would appear in the international press and de Vere's address book would quadruple. Suddenly, he was being offered other paintings to sell, not just by Picasso but by other post-Impressionists – Gauguin, Van Gogh, Cézanne. And that night, he could feel all this in his bones. He knew he was about to step up into the big time.

He strides over to a table with a platter of caviar on ice as the centrepiece.

'I do *believe* in caviar,' he says with feeling, sliding a spoon between his lips.

He loads another spoon up with the black spawn and hands it to me. Even before I've put it in my mouth, the smell of the stuff is grossing me out. See, I thought I liked caviar but it turns out that the kind I've been eating is the cheap stuff they serve at some of the receptions at the hotel. The stuff where the eggs are black and springy on your teeth and when you crunch them they pop in your mouth and a sweet juice comes out. De Vere tells me that this isn't caviar at all, it's called lump fish. I personally get a kick out of it, but apparently the best kind of caviar is what we're eating tonight – the sludgy black stuff that de Vere got at a special black market price from a street hustler outside the Hermitage museum in St Petersburg. I manage to swallow some of it but it tastes like I just fell into the ocean and swallowed a ton of salt water.

When I spit some of it back into my hand, a flash of irritation crosses de Vere's face. He snaps into business mode. He walks over to the window and starts talking about how he's getting out of the eighteenth century. That's when I notice that all the Bouchers have vanished. De Vere says that times are changing, that people don't have the big houses any more or the wall space to put this, 'Guff, all this . . . half-arsed hedonism' on.

His lips are twisting up and I feel a little nervous when he picks up a knife and goes over to the screen of Diana and Actaeon. He pulls it back to reveal a big eighteenth-century art dump. I can't believe it when he starts cutting one of the flying fatties' nipples off.

'But, Freddie, you can't . . .'

'Oh yes I can,' he cries. 'No more Boucher! No more Fragonard! I'm taking them all back to where they came from. This one, that one . . .'

He gestures to the canvas of the tethered hare and the bloodied peacock. '"*The Dead Stuff*", as you so rightly called it.'

He walks back toward me, brandishing the paint-smeared knife. 'Too much poetry for a century that has no time for poetry!'

As he rants on, I'm sitting on the crimson couch, gradually working my way through the bottle of champagne. I've been too nervous to eat all day and I downed a few Dutch courage Campari sodas before I arrived, not to mention the couple of shots of Mexico's national drink. But I've pushed all thoughts of Campari and tequila from my mind. I wink at de Vere. He hasn't seen my wink yet. It never fails.

'You just calm down now, Freddie and come over here,' I tell him in my *puta* voice. He looks surprised but does what I say. He finally even notices my plunging neckline.

'My dear Carmen,' he says, 'You're looking very . . .'

I cut him off. I put my hand on the itchy fabric of his pants and start my ego-boosting routine. 'Now Freddie,' I tell him. 'You are a very talented man . . .'

He drinks it up.

'Why, thank—'

'. . . Very talented, Freddie. You can do whatever you put your mind to . . .'

My hand starts rising up his leg.

'Yes,' he says, looking back at the Picasso. 'You and I are about to embark upon an exciting adventure.'

I take this as the sign. I look at his hand holding the champagne glass and I see suntanned hands made of fresh baked bread. I see a striped sailor's jersey, a pair of espadrilles, a bronzed god at the easel, a monster in the bathing cabin.

I've been reading books on Picasso since this whole thing started. Turns out that the giant of twentieth-century art was a dirty fucker too. He first hooked up with Marie-Thérèse Walter when she was modelling stockings in a Parisian department store. All you could see was a pair of legs coming out of two wooden holes, but Picasso found out who the legs belonged to and the rest is history. Blue Period? The guy's whole life was a blue period.

I don't care any more about the gross caviar because the more I drink, the lighter I get. I look at the Picasso painting and then back at de Vere and then over at the Picasso painting until they blur into one and the same. The blue eyes turn to black, the black eyes turn to blue and the stroke of the brush under the signature is as long and hard as the swelling I know is getting bigger by the second under the scratchy wool of de Vere's pants. I look at him and he smiles at me. The smile's so dirty I can see the butter dripping off of his lips. His mouth suddenly turns into Marie-Thérèse's pussy and her jug handle turns into Picasso's dick and when I look closer at de Vere, I see that his eyes are on the wrong side of his face. I see a minotaur with buttocks and muscles and bulbous breasts and a bouquet of green and violet genitals . . .

'Oh, give me your dick, please give me your dick, please stick it in and fill me up, please let me milk your huge hard cock—'

'Carmen . . .'

I grab hold of the black velvet arm and try and drag him to the floor. The fabric's so soft because he buys his jackets from Savile Row with the 128 individualised vents that work better than liposuction and the 'Established 1803, by appointment to The Prince of Wales, HRH King Edward VII' on all the labels.

'C'mon Freddie, nobody's going to find out. It'll be our little secret!'

I close my eyes and there's a blur of monogrammed suitcases and white opera gloves and PBS Masterpiece Theatre re-runs of *Upstairs Downstairs*. And as I start stroking myself, the cherry-tit girls slip over my back and a bunch of slippery nipples cram inside my mouth and cigar-smoke rings float out of my Fragonard-waxed pussy and I want the big, long signature I know de Vere is hiding inside his scratchy wool pants. When he pulls away from me, it makes me crazy because I *knew* he was going to do that because I've read how Picasso got his kicks from never letting his women come. And, oh boy, that turns me on.

'Oh God, oh yeah Freddie, please say your stuff.'

'My dear Carmen, you really must—'

'Y'know . . . the sales pitch stuff . . . the accent . . . oh God . . .'

I wake up in the bathroom and there's a towel around me. My skirt's still on but not my blouse or my bra. My mouth tastes familiar. It tastes of puke. When I get up and look in the mirror, there are congealed eggs down one side of my mouth and a crust of orange film down one side of my Lupe Vélez hairdo. I groan, although it strikes me that I'm luckier than poor Lupe. Her attempt at a beautiful suicide was foiled when the Mexican last supper she ate didn't agree with the seventy-five Seconals she wolfed down afterwards. At least de Vere didn't have to fish me out of a toilet bowl, drowned in my own vomit.

Still, when I finally stagger out of the bathroom, I'm mortified. I've never failed at sex before. De Vere is sitting at his desk, writing.

'Are you feeling better?' he asks, without looking up.

I rub my head and look round the room. I notice that my blouse is neatly folded up on the couch. Like he wants me out. That's when I start to cry. And when de Vere comes over, I don't think I've ever seen him so sober. Or so troubled. There's a shadow in his eyes.

'I do detest the striking of the clock, Carmen,' he says with a sigh.

'Huh?'

He goes on about how he hates the idea that a relationship should be consumated at a pre-determined moment.

'Picasso believed that love affairs end all too quickly. Like an hourglass that is turned upside down. It is only a matter of time until all the sand has gone.'

It crosses my mind that he's a fag. Come to think of it, he *does* do that gay guy thing of looking over your shoulder when he's talking to you – like he's always on the search for someone better. But then I figure that's what all businessmen do.

'You're just not that into me,' I blurt out. 'Right, Freddie?'

I hate the bitter sound in my voice. De Vere picks up the empty champagne bottle, seems to study it for a while.

'My dear Carmen, everything exists in limited quantity. Would you not agree?'

I shrug.

'Happiness does not exist in the abundance that people believe. And I have always taken the greatest precautions not to destroy the beauty of what one has. There is a kind of beauty in our relationship, is there not?'

I can still feel encrusted puke on my face but I think I understand what he's saying: that he wants a *Bonnie and Clyde* kind of thing as opposed to a *How to Marry a Millionaire* kind of thing. It doesn't seem as though I have much of a say in the matter.

He takes a thick envelope from his jacket pocket.

'A little thank you for your work,' he says, passing it to me. 'And a foretaste of what is to come.'

He turns on his heel and walks back to the desk.

'Now, I suggest you get dressed and return to your digs. Tomorrow, you will terminate your contract as a chambermaid at Claridges. On Monday morning you will arrive here at my suite at 9 a.m. sharp and our relationship will move into phase two.'

And you know what? Not fucking Charles Frederick de Vere was one of the best moves I ever made.

CHAPTER EIGHT

I was to be Freddie's 'amanuensis' which, he explained, encompassed a variety of concepts including secretary, researcher and confidante. It didn't take me long to work out that I'd been chosen as his chief grifter.

He wanted me to learn the whole business. I was introduced to dealers, collectors and the key players of his espionage network. These went from agents (the guys chasing up various paintings around the world) to informants (small-time hustlers who could live for a year on just one of de Vere's 'finder fees'), to hotel concierges who would tip him off when important collectors arrived in town and let him know if any rival dealers were trying to poach on his turf. Last, but not least, came the group of miscellaneous foot soldiers that included critics, museum directors, restorers, art experts, architects, decorators, waiters, butlers, doormen and chambermaids.

My day would start by knocking on the door of de Vere's suite and entering with a pile of newspapers. He explained that he needed to keep tabs on the lives of the people he was trying to cultivate and so I'd underline all the things I thought were important: political situations, international exchange rates, birthdays, anniversaries, deaths.

De Vere would spend a fortune on Christmas presents for his 'pupils'. He'd find out if they preferred to receive chocolate or liquor, hampers of fruit or a donation to their charity of choice and he made sure he knew the name of everyone's favourite flower. He never forgot a birthday, a wedding anniversary or a bar mitzvah because everything was meticulously recorded in leather-bound ledgers in his steady, neat handwriting.

'My pupils,' he'd tell me, 'must be unable to function without me,' and part of my job was to make absolutely sure of that. I bought the cigars he chose for them (6-inch Rafael González 'Lonsdales'), I sorted out invitations to stately homes and Buckingham Palace garden parties, I hustled for seats at sold-out plays. To men who'd won posts in the British government, I mailed letters of congratulation, to his 'ladies', I sent a copy of de Vere's hand-written guide to the Louvre beginning with the thirteenth-century Florentine school (basically a cram course in art appreciation), to Mrs Jennifer Lacey, the housekeeper of a grand old mansion, I sent an electric blanket for her rheumatoid arthritis, to Lady Merriwether Frost's daughter who seemed to be showing an interest in art, I sent a set of expensive oil paints.

By the early afternoon, my secretarial role would be over. I'd straighten up the walk-in closet that de Vere had converted into an office for me and go discuss plans for the evening. If we had an important party to attend, de Vere would hand me five crisp twenty-pound notes that he'd take from a fat envelope in the drawer of his desk. The envelope was sent over daily by special delivery from his accountant and de Vere creased each bill in what he described as 'The Rothschild manner'. This meant that it was folded lengthwise and then folded lengthwise again into a long, crisp torpedo of paper because, he claimed, 'It lasts longer that way.'

Not that the money lasted very long in my hands. De Vere liked me to dress for the part and the look I'd chosen was a *puta* take on the tony British fashion of the time they were calling 'Sloane Ranger'.

With my body shape and my colouring, sexy clothes just make me look like a hooker. Prim clothes, on the other hand, make me look like a high-class hooker and I soon realised that this was the perfect image for the people I was trying to appeal to. By day I'd wear a Liberty-print dress or a simple skirt and a lambswool sweater with a lace collar and an Alice band. By night, I'd take a leaf out of the book of the new British prime minister, Margaret Thatcher: a lot of pussy-bow blouses with cuffs and collars, a lot of pencil skirts with flirty pleats to emphasise calves and ankles as erogenous zones. My best look was a Jaeger suit one size too small so I'd be literally busting out all over, while round my neck I'd be wearing a single strand of Chinese freshwater pearls, given to me as a present by de Vere the day I made my first sale. I deviated a little on the shoes and the hair. I substituted black stiletto daggers for low-heeled Gucci pumps and I back-combed my thick black tresses until you could hardly get me through the doorway.

We got into our stride in the New Year of 1980 and from then until the end of August 1981 we were unstoppable. It was a strange time in London. The Yuppie thing hadn't taken off yet and the city was a mass of seedy pubs and ugly shops and the art scene was a mess. The few contemporary galleries were run by a bunch of public schoolboys who started drinking at midday, got on to the gin and tonics by three so that when the time came to sell any of their provincial English wares, they'd have fallen into a stupor or become unbearably pompous. Meanwhile, over in the auction houses, medieval suits of Italian armour and pieces of fancy French furniture were making more money than Jasper Johns, David Hockney and Andy Warhol put together. However, one fire that'd been kindled in the seventies was starting to get real hot: the Japanese and their interest in the Impressionists and post-Impressionists. Naturally, these were the flames that de Vere and I fanned.

The evenings were when we'd get most of our work done. We'd meet at a variety of places: the bar of the Westbury hotel, an opening at a gallery in Cork Street, an evening auction at Sotheby's or Christie's. There was always a lot of information flying around: words carelessly discarded as a fresh glass of champagne was swiped from a tray, indiscretions whispered in the line to the coat check. With the Japanese, I learned that you had to be prepared to talk about the weather for the first three meetings ('*Nihon bare, desu ne*' or 'Ah, Japan's fair skies' was a good opening line) and to remember that if one of them said, 'Yes' it didn't necessarily mean 'Yes'.

But it wasn't what you'd call tough work and my information collecting was helped by the fact that men don't generally have an eye for detail. They never noticed, for instance, that I rarely drank from the champagne glass I always held in my hand, whereas they drank like fish. It didn't take me long to discover which pieces of new art were about to come on to the market, which of de Vere's agents had fallen from favour in the eyes of an important collector and which hungry new hound I was going to replace him with.

'Knowing what is going to happen before it does,' de Vere once told me, 'must always be your point of pride.'

I listened to a lot of things de Vere said. The guy was a trip. Talk about exaggeration. A work of art was either the most divine object he had ever seen or the most execrable, it was the most shameful, ridiculous or hateful thing he had ever cast his eyes upon or it was the most extraordinary. His enthusiasm was catching. When he was around, everyone behaved as if they'd had a couple of drinks. There were a few scandals, a few lawsuits but intrigues and betrayals are all part of the high stakes game of art dealing. Besides, a part of his nature relished a little law suit and nothing very serious ever came of them. Persuading reluctant officials to bend the rules was child's play to him and even when things didn't go his way, he always managed to turn misfortune on its head; after one customs case that cost him a bomb, de Vere boasted that no dealer in history had ever paid such a gargantuan fine.

I was truly glad we'd never become lovers. I now found him endlessly exciting, and he'd given me a confidence I didn't know existed. Sure, sometimes I got jealous; chicks were all over him, gay men cruised him and when men with wives and kids flirted with him, he flirted back. He could have had anyone he'd wanted but he didn't seem to want anyone. I knew he was married; I'd met his wife, Eleanor, on the several occasions I'd been invited back to their Holland Park mansion. She kind of blended in with the wallpaper, so I guessed he must have a secret vice. But even I, Carmen Costello, the greatest amanuensis a man ever had, never got the skinny on that one.

What I loved most of all was that in spite of being platonic business associates, I got to taste the pleasures of being the woman in black. The scarlet woman. See, the idea of being a 'social outcast' has had a bad rap. But I liked it. I liked going out into that refined world and having society hostesses and aristocratic heiresses feast their eyes on me – because that's what they did. All those piggy little eyes in those stretched faces, crawling all over me, sucking me up like a nasty little kid sucking up the last of the foam from a Coke float. Sometimes the stare was so quick that you almost missed it – it was just a brief laser incision, the flick of a knife.

It turned me on if you want to know the truth. I'd be standing in front of a Van Gogh with a reserve price of four million bucks, and the broads with the piggy eyes and the stretched faces, they'd look at it like it was last season's shop window. What they'd be looking at was me: Carmen Costello from the wrong side of Boston whose dad sold beers and shots in a dive bar and whose mom wore Maybelline eye shadow and had plastic fruit on her table.

I guess that's why I did so well with the guys. If de Vere had success with his 'ladies' then my 'gents' couldn't get enough of me. I developed my own sales patter: a shake of my rack, a flutter of the eyelashes, a carefully placed hand on a dandruffy old shoulder. That was all I had to do. I learned pretty quick that British guys never got over losing their nanny and when, at the fall 1980 Conservative party conference, Mrs Thatcher announced, 'the lady's not for turning', that became my catch phrase when the time came to talk money. Most of them assumed I was just a dizzy American slut who de Vere happened to be balling. But I got them to buy a bunch of pictures. As de Vere used to say, 'A man always has two reasons for the things he does: a good reason and the real reason.'

De Vere even encouraged me to go 'off piste', as he called it. He figured it would help me lay down more trails for the string of blue chip rats in my Pied Piper of Hamelin act. And so, on the nights when there wasn't a party to schmooze in Mayfair, I'd leave the marble halls and the liveried doormen and I'd go eat cheap spaghetti in a smoky underground restaurant in Soho filled with old men and art students and poseurs in fake Westwood bondage suits. I'd sit there on my own, studying The Story of Art by E.H. Gombrich, half-listening to drunken goths talk about the new records they'd bought or eaves-dropping on Derek Jarman and his latest court of boys. One night I saw Francis Bacon in a tight white jeans suit and a hint of make-up walking down Old Compton Street. Another time I saw a bunch of Japanese journalists trying to interview Malcolm McLaren about the Pistols while he kept getting them to buy him cigarettes and free bottles of champagne.

Man, I thought I was living the life. I'd go from clubs where you had to turn up in tin foil to get in, to clubs where denim was banned and the dance floor was filled with old guys in pinstripe, slow dancing to Stevie Wonder with nineteen-year-old escort girls. Sometimes, I'd be up until the early hours, drinking 'lager', as they call it here, and smearing speed onto my gums at a Siouxsie Sioux gig in Camden Town, but by nine the next morning I'd be taking the papers into de Vere's suite before heading off to Holland Park to hang a painting at the residence of the Sultan of Brunei.

I was a piece of work. I wasn't just Carmen Costello, I was filled with genius, with more than 200 years of art. I was shot through with Sickert and Van Gogh and you fucking name it. I had the whole of the Blue Period going for me. I had the balls of Frida Kahlo and the guts of Paul Cézanne. I was making out in the bushes with the *Demoiselles d'Avignon* as the whole of the Salon des Refusés looked on and if I needed, I could switch right back into my pink petticoats, get on my swing and give the timid ones a more eighteenth-century good time. Man, I was a hot little number, I was 'It' with bells on.

And so what did I do?

I married a schmuck and threw my life away.

CHAPTER NINE

Back in the attic room, Cosima has finished drawing. The river has stopped but a dam has broken in Carmen's head. When Cosima tells her that she's finished sketching for the day, Carmen hardly hears her. She sits on the edge of the sheepskin mat, hugging her knees.

'De Vere vanished one day. I was used to him going off for business trips, but this time it was different. After two months I started to get worried. The art gig didn't work so well without him. I guess I got scared.'

She starts to rock gently.

'Six was sweet. He was safe. It turned out that our daily chats at Claridges had touched him more than I'd realised. When I finally decided to make a play for him, the fiancée didn't stand a chance.'

Relaxing back in the chair, Carmen smiles to herself.

'After two years of being mentored by de Vere, I found myself being a teacher to a Texan hillbilly. On our honeymoon in Europe, I taught Six which coffee to order, which outfit to wear, which pictures to look at in which museum.

'And you know what? I loved that my new husband wanted an over-cooked steak with a glass of milk at five thirty every evening. A glass of milk was a relief after life with de Vere. All that high society bullshit. "The Cage", he used to call it. "You can look into the Cage," he'd say. "Observe the creatures playing, admire their exotic plumage but you must never, never go inside."'

'The Cage?' Cosima sounds surprised.

'Yeah, but the trouble was, he'd already shown me the way

in. I thought I'd escaped it by marrying a mediocre guy. But the truth is that you're always drawn back to the Cage.

'I escaped all the way to Dallas. At least, that's where Six told me we were going to live. In fact, his mansion was in a small town two hours away. My "social" life revolved around making quilts with local church groups and chairing a lot of charity bake sales.'

Carmen picks up the dainty glass and drains the last of the dark liquid.

'It was a nice break to start with. See, the art world's not all glamour. There's also a lot of red tape. While de Vere was out dining with his dukes and his earls, I was the one dealing with the invoices and the import taxes and the commissions owed to various spies.'

She shrugs.

'Weighing the pros and cons of dulce de leche cupcakes versus fruit and nut zucchini muffins was a day on the beach after that. Besides, I have a ton of relatives in Texas. I used to go visit them sometimes . . .'

She looks sheepish.

'But after a while, I started dreaming of the Cage again.'

'There must have been some parties in Dallas,' Cosima says, beginning to roll a cigarette.

'Six was what they call a "homebody",' Carmen tells her. 'I mean, sometimes he'd take me to a university fundraiser in Dallas. But that's not the Cage. That was more like a plastic pet carrier full of cats with all their claws pulled out. See, the thing about the Cage is that it has to scare you when you go inside. The fear's half of the excitement.'

Her eyes begin to sparkle.

'It's gold inside, naturally. Even the jackals are gilded. Especially those. The Cage is very unfriendly, as a matter of fact. But it's hard to resist for long. The bittersweet thrills kind of grow on you. So does the gold dust. You soon notice it glittering on your skin.'

Carmen looks nostalgically at the empty glass of medication.

'Meanwhile, back in Texas in the mid-eighties, Six and his friends were reminding me more of Rain Man every day. Six's idea of a good night's entertainment was a chummy game of Bridge with some friends from the church, followed by a tour of what he called his "art museum". He'd had this vault built underneath the house. Had the builders put in a Precious Moments-style Sistine Chapel ceiling. Man, I won't even begin to tell you about the art he had in there. Let's just say he had more schlock than he'd originally told me about. There was this one guy he loved who I figured wouldn't even cut it with the Precious Moments people. A lot of blow-up flowers and rabbits . . .'

'Sounds terrible,' Cosima says, lighting her cigarette.

'Yeah.' Carmen sighs. 'Thing was, the artist was called Jeff Koons.'

'Oh.'

'I mean, that guy got to be Andy Warhol big. And Six got in there right before the rush. He'd met Koons in New York in the late seventies. He was just another loser wannabe in those days making vacuum cleaners in Plexiglas cases and a lot of inflatable crap . . .'

Carmen holds her empty glass up to the light.

'When Koons went stratospheric and made it OK for clever people to dig pink poodles and porcelain statuettes of pop stars, Six made the headlines too. "Hick Texan Hits the Art Big Time", that kind of thing. I know I should have been glad for him, but it just felt like a huge blow to my self-esteem.'

She sighs as she puts the glass down on the floor, as if she suddenly remembers the nasty taste.

'Not that I can complain.'

She smiles.

'We started getting invited to a lot of art parties on the West Coast. Pretty fancy some of them. I hooked up with some fun people. One guy in particular. He convinced me to go into a joint business venture with him in Los Angeles. He wasn't interested in doing business. He wanted to disguise the fact that we were spending most days screwing each other. That's how Perky Parties was born.

'Perky never got off the ground. But when the guy ditched me, I decided to make a go of it. I told Six I was excited about using my brains again, but the truth was I was gasping for the Cage. See, Cosima, you kind of hate it when you're in there, but if you're out of it for too long, the gold on your skin starts to fade. It's like losing your tan . . .'

She watches Cosima's white hand hover in the air with her cigarette.

'I mean, I guess you don't go in for the sun. But take it from me: when your tan goes, you look like shit.'

She slumps back in the chair.

'I was only in my early thirties, and after years of captivity in small-town Texas, I was raring to go. I'd had it with the warm, friendly people, the over-cooked steaks and the glasses of milk. I wanted the exotic birds and the dazzling plumage. I was ready for the stink of the wine.

'Perky Parties started out small. A few stag dos, some milestone birthdays. Within a matter of months I was doing celebrity endorsement breakfasts and big charity gigs. I offered the whole nine yards: food design, marquee hire, DJ booking. But mainly it was about big names. Famous people. I used the same principles I'd picked up from de Vere and it wasn't long before I had a bunch of actors and rock stars and fashionable transvestites buzzing round me. Dealers too, although they weren't the kind who sold paintings, if you know what I mean.

'It wasn't an ideal environment for me. There weren't only fabulous people; there were a lot of coke heads and hangers-on. I started getting a taste for hard liquor, other stuff. I kidded myself it was part of the job territory. I started slipping up. We went bust a few times but money was never a problem, not with Six bankrolling me. Poor guy. He finally had a breakdown in '95. I guess his therapist convinced him to divorce me.'

She folds her arms suddenly.

'The settlement kept me going. And I had a lot of affairs. Love became my new drug. The rush of an early relationship was better than the thrill of a sugar high.'

'But weren't you happy now that you were back in the Cage?' Cosima asks.

Carmen makes a bitter laugh.

'I'd forgotten the rule.'

'The rule?'

'When the chick in the James Bond movie got sprayed with the gold paint, she had to leave a little hole at the base of her spine so she could breathe. Me, I used up every bit of skin. Every particle. I got suffocated by the gold.'

She laughs again.

'I turned into one of the naked fat people from the Louis XV corner cabinet. I got crusted over with gold like a lot of ornamental eczema.'

'So what happened?'

'By the time I met Larry, I was forty-three years old and too afraid to leave the goddamn Cage.'

She makes a half-hearted smile.

'Dying is something that happens very slowly. One minute you're grinding your butt into your seat in a classy oyster restaurant, you're drinking the sea, he's drinking your eyes, it's all kicking off – the crunch and the suck and the rush. And the next thing you know, you're too scared even to order your own drink at a bar. Suddenly he's booking you appointments at Peter John – where all the hookers go to get the best Hollywood wax in town. The one that's supposed to make you look like a schoolgirl. Or an oyster. That's when you know you're in the Cage. When you're worrying if your pussy looks enough like an oyster. You're in the Cage and you're too scared to look out any more.

'Of course, you can kid yourself you're not inside at all. You can pretend you're just skirting around outside, accepting a few treats here and there. First it's shells from the beach. A little expensive lingerie maybe. Then you don't want any more shells from the beach. The lingerie, you're over that too. You're over him telling you how exciting you are. God, that's all anyone tells you these days.'

'Yes,' Cosima murmurs, stubbing out her cigarette.

'You want to be legit. You want to show off your big man in public, right? So you get your big man, and what do you know? He's already looking for someone else to eat oysters with. Actually no, he'll still eat oysters with you but now he wants the waitress to join in too. Suddenly he's telling you the waitress looks like an Egyptian cat. He's telling you to flirt with her, to ask her for a knife. To do your thing of getting a knife so you can open the oysters in front of him. The suck and the crunch and the rush. Yeah, yeah.

'Then you could give a shit about oysters. Poor fuckers, you're thinking. You break into their nice house with the mother-of-pearl insides, you rip them off their foot and you chuck them down your throat to go swim in a sea of deranged bubbles. They call it champagne in those strip joints but those grapes had an urchin's life and after death they got a poor man's burial. Couple of months in a metal vat, tops. Dispensed into cheap bottles, laid in the cellar of a tacky night club. Not so much a "masculine" or a "feminine" wine. More of a vicious old tranny. Swimming with oysters is probably as good as things have ever gotten for it.

'And anyway, oysters remind you too much of yourself. Of the way you used to be. Salty sweet. And clear. Oysters are pretty insubstantial. Like eating thin air. You need something else with them. Love preferably.'

She folds her arms again.

'Earl P. Johnson VI discovering Jeff Koons. That's fucking hilarious, right? A stroke of luck someone like Charles Frederick de Vere would have envied.'

She looks at Cosima. 'I tried to forget about de Vere, and I pretty much succeeded. I mean, I hadn't known the guy that long.'

She glances around the attic room. 'But now, it's weird. It's like he's all over this house. And it's as if thirteen years with Six lasted a single afternoon. What's up with that?'

She smiles suddenly.

'You know, I *am* glad I never slept with de Vere. Being a mistress can fuck you up. Look at Marie-Thérèse Walter. Suicide case, right?'

A splash of black ink glows under Cosima's cheeks then slowly fades.

'Yes,' she says. 'I believe she hanged herself shortly after Picasso died.'

Carmen nods. 'It's like Lupe. She never recovered from divorcing Johnny Weissmuller.'

She sits back in the bottle green chair, stroking the velvet of the arm.

'Hanging yourself or pigging out on enchiladas and then collapsing into a petal-strewn bed with seventy-five Seconals and a suicide note. It's all the same, right? Women being stupid over men.'

She shrugs. 'But who am I to talk? Suicide threats are the trump card of every love addict I know.'

Cosima puts her pencil down on the table. 'Lupe Vélez didn't do her research very well,' she says.

'Huh?'

Cosima studies her sketch book.

'If you're going to take an overdose, you should drink something like Dramamine thirty minutes beforehand.'

'Why?'

'So your body doesn't vomit up all the pills.'

Carmen narrows her eyes. 'Yeah?'

'Suicide has always intrigued me,' Cosima goes on, inspecting her drawing more closely.

'Right,' Carmen says, uneasily. 'I guess I'm too much of a coward. Maybe I'd do euthanasia . . .'

She thinks about this for a few seconds before heaving a sigh.

'Poor Lupe. I mean, it's never even been proved that she drowned in her own vomit. It's just guys trying to put down another loudmouth woman. They wanted to give her a bad ending.'

'Sounds like rather a good ending.'

Carmen does a double take. She squints at Cosima. 'I never thought about it like that. But yeah . . .' She starts to nod. 'You're right. It was a pretty dramatic final scene, wasn't it?'

'Beauty is such a flimsy idea.' Cosima sounds bored. 'I like a little grotesquerie.'

Carmen detects a smile on the face of the art-therapy teacher as she gets up and takes the sketch book over to the window.

'I like it a lot,' Cosima says, moving the book as close as she can to the dim orange light. 'The last pictures are always the best.'

'The last?'

'Yes.' Cosima closes the pad. 'I shall be leaving soon. I don't really want to.'

'Where will you go?'

Cosima doesn't answer. 'This is definitely the best I've done,' she says, rolling down the sleeves of the man's paint-splattered shirt and calling Fido and Phèdre to heel.

'You're preparing a show?'

Cosima stops and looks at Carmen as if she's only just noticed her.

'You could say that.' She hesitates. 'It's been quite a long run. I shall be glad to finish.'

Carmen watches fascinated as a choppy sea of emotions swirls under Cosima's delicate cheeks without ever bringing any colour to them. Suddenly, she remembers she is sitting butt naked with a stranger in a freezing cold room. She jumps up, embarrassed, and hurries behind the screen to get changed. It is only when she comes out from behind the screen that she sees it is painted with Diana having Actaeon ripped apart by his own hounds.

CHAPTER TEN

There is shuffling outside the attic door and when Cosima opens it, Franck is standing there shoving sandwiches into his mouth.

'Cheese,' he pants. 'Very calming, cheese . . .'

There is a film of sweat over his face. 'I'm ready for you to come and look now, Cosima,' he says, in his cracked voice. 'Some very elegant buttons I've drawn. Very smart.'

When he turns to hobble down the creaking corridor, Cosima picks up a glass and the wine bottle and follows him. The dogs trot after her as does Carmen, who notices that Franck accelerates as he walks past her bedroom door. But she doesn't have time to wonder why this should be, because as they are passing room 54, the door opens and Kenneth Sketch comes out. He is wearing a stripy blue shirt with a navy blue jersey draped over the shoulders. He seems delighted to see them. 'Hi, you guys,' he says and follows them into a bedroom where they watch Franck kneel down on a worn-out cushion. He picks up a chewed pencil stub and starts to flick through a drawing book.

'Oswald Mosley,' he announces, flashing them a clumsy sketch. 'Black shirts with buttons on the collar. Do you see? Inspired by fencing costumes.'

He turns to another page. 'And this is Goering. For the Beer Hall Putsch, Hermann Goering made an outfit in kid skin.'

He hobbles up from the cushion to show his cousin. 'They said it was pink but it was oyster grey. A light taupe.'

As Carmen peeks at the illustration over Cosima's shoulder, she finds herself moving closer to the bare neck that smells of lady's furs and bitter almonds.

'Franck likes to design clothes,' Cosima murmurs.

'Uniforms, darling,' Franck corrects.

'Oh, I love uniforms,' says Kenneth Sketch. 'I always wear the same thing. Then I know that people like me for who I am rather than for what I'm wearing.'

Franck eyes Kenneth Sketch nervously.

'The Hussars had beautiful jackets,' he tells him, turning to a page of red, blue and yellow crayon. 'Five rows of horizontal cord across the breast, do you see? Loops and tassels and lots of gold braiding.'

'I used to have one of those!' Kenneth Sketch exclaims.

Franck flinches.

'My New Romantic period,' Kenneth Sketch tells him. 'I had a thing about Adam Ant.'

He taps the drawing and turns to Carmen. 'It's the Prince Charming jacket, right?'

Franck purses his lips. 'The Prince Charming jacket was a Regency design,' he says, snatching his pad back. 'Adam Ant wore the Hussar jacket in *Kings of the Wild Frontier.*'

'Wow.'

'Hussar horsemen were the dashing adventurers of the army,' Franck tells him haughtily. 'Brave and amorous and terribly reckless.'

'That's so great,' Kenneth Sketch says. 'Soldiers don't have colourful uniforms any more, right?'

'Colour was very important in the days of smoky set battles,' Franck informs him with a smirk. 'And you might be interested to know that it was colour that made our family name . . .'

He launches into another of his school play speeches about how Franck and Cosima's great grandfather, Sir Josiah Stokes, built Summer Crest Hall on some land granted him by Queen Victoria.

'He developed an interest in ornithology while he was at Cambridge,' he begins his bland sermon. 'And when, in 1847, he was offered the position of gentleman's companion to the captain of HMS *Athena*, he was overjoyed . . .'

Indeed, it was a stroke of luck that had yet to be bettered by any member of the Stokes family. The purpose of the expedition was to chart new islands in the South Pacific and it was Sombrero Island which proved most fruitful to the twenty-one-year-old Josiah. He spotted a bird he had never seen before and named it the 'Summer Crested Owl' because of its large eyes and because during mating season its brown speckled plumage erupted into flamboyant life, covering the bird in a crown of gaudy yellows, purples and pinks.

Two years later, the bird was extinct. This was partly due to the inhabitants of Sombrero Island using the striking feathers to make warrior headdresses, although prospects for the bird were not helped when dogs, cats and pigs from HMS *Athena* were allowed to run wild on the island, plundering nests and destroying forests.

Luckily, Josiah had already sent two specimens of the formidable Summer Crested Owl back to Britain. One went to Queen Victoria, who was apparently unmoved by the exotic bird, although Prince Albert's enthusiasm was sufficient to spur her to knight Josiah for services to ornithology, and to confer him a small plot of land in Gloucestershire. Here he drew up plans for the construction of Summer Crest Hall, which was completed in 1850.

'The other bird used to be kept in a bell jar here at the house,' Franck says with a sigh. 'But it was lost.'

Carmen points to a patch of yellow mushrooms on the Hussar drawing.

'What's that?' she asks.

'Toggle buttons,' Franck says, wounded.

'Oh.'

She feels bad. 'So, like, where did you get your talent?'

'From my father.' Franck beams. 'Wonderful artist. Very gifted.' He smirks at Cosima. 'You didn't like him, did you, Cosima? "Uncle Ellsworth" came rather a cropper at your hands . . .'

'As you keep reminding me,' Cosima replies coldly, removing the cork from the pre-meds bottle.

'Be careful of Cosima,' Franck says to Carmen with a ridiculously camp wink. 'None of us is safe in our beds!'

Carmen wonders why Cosima doesn't *just swat the little dick*. But then she sees her pour some of the feel-good wine into the glass and it strikes her that maybe Cosima isn't as self-assured as she'd thought. Carmen wonders why Franck keeps insinuating there's something dangerous about Cosima. But she feels tired of trying to understand everything. Her own share in the Summer Crest Hall medication has tipped her into a state where she feels happy just sitting in a frayed chair watching Franck kneeling on the worn-out cushion. As he munches hurriedly on another of his cheese sandwiches, explaining the dramatic visual achievements of Wehrmacht uniforms in World War II to a very attentive Kenneth Sketch, Carmen takes in the plump lips and the pale skin and the cloud of flies swarming over his head. Franck definitely reminds her of the Burne-Jones tapestry boy. She feels as though she's met him before, although she knows she never has.

She closes her eyes momentarily, and when she opens them she can't see Franck any more, just a group of flies dragging themselves along the edge of a discarded crust. She wonders if she drank too much of the funky wine.

'When did you last see him?' Cosima asks.

Carmen jumps.

'Huh?'

'De Vere. You said that he vanished.'

'Oh, de Vere. Let's think. I guess it was . . .' She counts on her fingers. 'Like, 1981? I remember it was a very hot summer. Sweltering. He said he had to take some paintings back somewhere.' She yawns. 'That was the last time I saw him.'

She is surprised to see that Franck has reappeared when she

looks back at the cushion. *The living dead.* She smiles to herself. *That's what aristocrats are. They can't live in the present because everything in the present belonged to someone in the past. So they're only half here.*

She sinks down into the chair.

That cushion's probably been in the same position for a hundred years. And it'll probably be in the same position in a hundred years' time . . .

She closes her eyes and is instantly treated to a slide show of writhing bodies covered with fruit and aerosol-propelled whipped cream. Then comes the screen of Diana and Actaeon – first in de Vere's suite and then in Cosima's studio. But Carmen doesn't care what she sees any more. Strange how sleep feels so good here. Delicious. And such intense colours. *Like the first time you smoke pot, only better.* Big chunks of primary colours, just the way Carmen likes them. She yawns again. Such pleasure even in a yawn. She prepares to slip into another soft abyss when at the end of a very long tunnel, she hears Cosima's voice asking, 'Which paintings did he take?' She hears someone reply, 'A Boucher with a missing nipple and . . .'

Her head drops to one side.

The shadow of a cloud passes over Cosima's face as she watches Carmen sleep.

'The Dead Stuff,' she says, finishing her sentence for her. 'The tethered hare, the bloodied peacock.'

Cosima heaves a sigh and sits down in the worn chair next to Carmen. She puts her glass on the arm and traces a cold finger around her lips as she watches Franck on the threadbare cushion. She can still see him there, plugging away at his terrible designs. She can always see Franck, even though he appears and disappears for other guests at Summer Crest Hall.

She swallows the dark contents of her glass and is not surprised, when she closes her eyes, to hear a boy's voice reciting something that sounds like, 'Slow, slow, quick-quick, slow,' like a shrill choreographer hammering out a dance routine.

Thanks to the powerful effects of the cordial, she has found heself back in the spring of 1981 – the year that set her life on a whole new course, just as it did for Carmen. Of course, she was much younger than Carmen back then. Only twelve. She pulls the sleeves of her painter's shirt over her hands as she feels the euphoria of the medicine start to rush through her body. She sits back in the chair and smiles as she is transported upstairs to the attic room. The attic in the Easter of 1981 when it was still a playroom. As she looks around at the shelves of neatly stacked toys, the mini chairs, the rocking horse, she remembers that the house was much cleaner in those days, slightly more shiny. Leaning leather-patched elbows on the polished floor is an eleven-year-old boy with a pale face and jet-black hair. He is shouting a set of rhythmic drill instructions to a group of plastic men.

'To arms! To arms! Advance, advance, advance!'

The round bottom poised high in the air sways from side to side as it accompanies the high-pitched ditty. There is a dramatic pause. Franck takes a deep breath and snaps orders at two of his most trusted men.

'Forward, Lartius! Forward, Herminius!'

The chewed hands falter. The glass marbles grow damp in his palms. The sight of the battle brings a lump to his throat. A tight formation of knights and Cossacks and gladiators, the 1st battalion of Her Majesty's Grenadier Guardsmen, some German paratroopers, Davey Crockett and Sitting Bull. Serried ranks, a half inch apart, rifles and spears and furry racoon tails.

'*We are the family! The wild nobility!*' comes the half-hearted cheer, but it is no use. Franck shudders as he stares at his beautiful battle. He feels the spray descend, the paralysing cocoon. The marbles drop to the floor and roll away to the rocking horse. His mouth falls open.

'But who will save the town?' he whispers, sadly.

Footsteps and scampering on granite stairs. The girl enters the attic room with a riding crop. The young dogs pounce on the battle and lick it up. Franck looks horrified. 'No, Fido! No, Phèdre!'

Too late. He looks at the mess of mashed soldiers.

'You can't have a battle if nothing happens,' Cosima tells him, stroking her dogs as they come to heel. 'Nothing ever happens in your battles.'

'My boundaries, my territories . . .'

His voice cracks.

The door bangs open again and a feline form bounds into the room.

'Tigris!' Cosima cries, her face lighting up. 'My trusty Tigris.'

She turns to Franck, explaining that Tigris is, 'Strong as a wild boar, the swiftest hound in the pack.'

Franck looks at the small blonde child with the arched back who is sniffing round his soldiers on all fours.

'Looks more like a cat,' he says sulkily.

'Silence!' Cosima commands. 'Or I'll have you ripped apart.'

Franck knows he's cornered. He sighs and sits on a tiny wooden chair, propping up his head in his hands. 'Cosima, darling, do we have to play the hunting game today?'

'What's wrong with hunting?' says Cosima, making herself even taller. The human hound starts to growl as it approaches Franck's chair. Franck looks as if he's about to cry.

'But Cosima, darling, what about the party?'

'You have to play hunting. You know what your father thinks.'

Franck purses his lips.

'You know why he wants a girl to play with you . . .'

'Cosima, darling . . .'

'We'll go to the tree. Come, Tigris!'

She chooses the place. A patch of sticky mud by the tack room. She lies down and rolls through it, back and forth like a rolling pin over pastry. Tigris squeals with joy. Franck's eyes bulge.

'Cosima!' he pleads.

'Fido and Phèdre don't mind,' Cosima shouts back. 'Fido and Phèdre love me!'

She rolls out of the mud and stands up, looking approvingly at her white shirt and cords, now covered in patches of glistening sludge.

'Our spears are clogged with the blood of a glorious hunt,' she announces.

'Glorious hunt!' echoes the blonde dog by her side. She turns to Cosima. 'I'll go and get the tack, shall I, Mistress of the Beasts?'

It was only recently that the children had been able to get into the tack room. The huge barn in the grounds of Summer Crest Hall contained ten horse stalls and a large open space where racks of wizened saddles, bridles and musty blankets still hung from the walls. Ellsworth's father, Bertie, had stabled half a dozen horses here in the 1920s, but lack of funds soon forced him to ship them out. The tack room now functioned as Ellsworth's painting studio. He guarded it fiercely and secured the door with several heavy padlocks.

Except now he seemed to have abandoned the place. When she'd arrived back for the Easter holidays, Cosima noticed that the door was banging in the wind. When it was still banging three days later, she decided to venture inside. She climbed high up into the rafters, made a secret nest in some bales of straw and spent the afternoon spying down at the forsaken studio, imagining her uncle working there. She knows he is a successful painter. A man in London sells his work. 'The Dog', Uncle Ellsworth calls him.

Eventually, she told Franck and Tigris about the tack room and they set about exploring. They hadn't found any paints yet. No paintings, either. Just some rags and brushes, some empty whisky bottles and a huge pile of books.

Cosima gives Tigris permission to bring some tack outside and then she turns to Franck, raising her crop in the air as if she is about to knight him.

'Strip!' she commands. Franck hesitates. 'Go on,' she says. 'You have to play. Your father said.'

Cosima lets Franck keep his pants on. He shivers in spite of the warmth of the April afternoon.

'But why must you always hunt *me*, Cosima?' he complains, getting down on all fours. He makes a coy smile with his rosebud mouth. 'You're like the Iron Lady!'

'Silence!' Cosima commands. When Tigris returns with a bridle and two martingales, Cosima is merciless. She wraps the bridle round Franck's throat and gives him a thwack with her crop.

'Darling!' he protests. 'Let's do some dressage.'

'Mistress of the Beasts!'

'Mistress of the Beasts, please can we do some dressage? Very elegant, dressage.'

'Dressage is boring,' she pronounces. 'You've already had dispensations.'

'Dispensations!' Tigris cheers, jumping even higher.

The dispensation is an Hermès silk scarf with an equestrian print that belongs to his mother. Franck likes to roll it up and slide it into the back of his pants for a tail.

But Cosima soon tires of riding her cousin's pale, sweaty back. She gets off, ties him to a tree and tells Tigris that it's time for the flaying. Tigris's eyes light up. She runs back to the tack room, to the horse stall containing a rubble of discarded magazines and old books. She grabs a hardback and brings it outside to lay on the grass in front of Franck. She opens it up so that the writing is exposed to the day and watches in delight as Cosima flays the pages again and again until all the words are dead.

Tigris goes back for another book. She considers an old Bible and a crumpled paperback with a picture of a lipstick kiss on the cover. Her favourite is the book that never dies. It is large and red with no spine on any more, just a loom of grey threads and pages all shredded and tissue paper-fine. Then she sees something new.

'Look!' she says, dancing out into the sunny afternoon. 'Impostors!'

Cosima comes to inspect the new victim: engravings to accompany the 1789 Dutch Edition of the Marquis de Sade's *The Story of Juliette*. She picks it up and flicks through the ancient pages. She stops at an image of a naked man in a powdered wig being sodomised by a gang of grinning monkeys. She hesitates then walks up to the prisoner, brandishing the page in his face. Franck flinches.

'You have to look,' she says. 'They're your father's books.'

'But the party!' he wails. 'What about the party?'

'The enemy.' Cosima glares at him.

'It'll be all right, Cosima. There'll be pop and cakes!'

She looks at him strangely. 'You think . . .'

The disobedient hound Tigris is already scampering towards the front lawn, howls of, 'Yum!' erupting from her muzzle.

'All right,' Cosima relents. She shouts after Tigris, 'But we'll just spy!'

'We'll have some decent conversation now,' Franck says, excitedly, as Cosima cuts his ropes.

He hurries back into his clothes, tying the Hermès racoon tail around his neck. 'Sophisticated people,' he tells Cosima, as she flogs a page of naked men pissing into each others' mouths in a Palladian drawing room. 'Nice dresses!'

Tigris is waiting for them by the Sycamore tree. 'There's the camp,' she hisses, pointing to a long table covered with a white cloth and laden with champagne glasses and iced cakes. 'Look, Cosima. We can hide under there.'

Cosima grabs the collars of Fido and Phèdre and crawls over to the table on her hands and knees, closely followed by Franck and Tigris. Soon, all three are under the cloth, sitting cross-legged on the grass carpet with the two obedient whippets. Cosima opens the leather hunting bag strapped round her shoulders and takes out her pencil and sketch book. Slowly, she parts the white linen walls. She puts her hands over her face and looks out through the bars of her fingers at the cage of creatures on the lawn. She sees a screaming crow and a flamingo with a sawn-off wing. A parrot is spewing sick into one of the flower beds and there are hippos with pecky birds on their backs. There are birds of paradise, tattered butter-flies and lizards wrapped in jewels.

Cosima grins. With short, light strokes, she sets to work with her pencil and only stops when the walls start to tremble. It is Franck, announcing that he's going out to the garden party. 'So pretty. So elegant . . .'

Cosima feels her heart beat faster. The ceiling might not hold at this rate. Through the bars she watches him lollop to the middle of the lawn and then turn round to the cloth-covered table and start mouthing something.

'Look!' Tigris gasps.

'The idiot,' Cosima mutters.

They watch him collide with a hippo puffing on a cigar.

'Terribly sorry, sir,' Franck apologises. 'My name's Franck. This is my father's house.'

At the name of the father, the hippo and his two friends, break into guffaws. 'How is the old boy!' he says, spluttering into a glass of frothing pink. 'Still daubing away?'

Franck is about to tell them.

'Where is Ellsworth anyway? Someone should go to the Nag's Head – drag him back to his own damn party!'

Franck is about to tell them that his father needs love or the good grape. 'Love or the good grape,' he'd told him the previous week. 'The only way to bait the muse.'

They'd been dining in the Long Room that day. It was pigeon again. It was always like that when his mother went away on her modelling trips. There was good news though. His father had told him that his masterpiece was nearly finished. 'A symphony in crimson . . .'

But the hippos don't want to know anything about his father. Nobody even comments on the silk foulard around his neck.

Then Cosima sees her. Her mother reminds her of the most beautiful bun in the world. Like a sweet yeast bun that has risen and risen. Her bosoms always spill out of any dress she is wearing. She is surrounded by her usual cortège: crabs and crayfish heaving themselves across an aquarium floor. Mainly, her mother loves her Pekinese dogs. One of them starts to yap and Lady Merriwether Frost bends down and strokes it, cooing into its face, letting it lick her cheeks as the other dogs vie for attention and she chuckles and cries, 'Darling Goosie! Such a handsome young fellow! Sweet Hubert! Such a polished coat!'

More creatures come. There are hands in the air, eyes in the sky, cheers from the gentlemen, coos from the ladies, the yapping of Goosie now buried in the warm brioche of her mother's breast.

Cosima comes out because she thinks that maybe it's all right after all. Flanked by Fido and Phèdre with Tigris running behind, the huntress scuds across the grass towards the only thing that exists. Frank's face lights up as she passes him. 'You see!' he's saying. 'It's fine here. Marvellous conversation!'

But she doesn't stop, she goes on, heading towards the only target.

Her mother stiffens when she sees her.

'Cosima,' she nearly shrieks. 'What on earth have you been doing!'

Cosima knows then that she's made a mistake. They want to turn her back into a girl. They've already turned Tigris, who now stands next to Cosima, her head hanging, all the dog washed out of her. They've made her into Susan Lacey, ten-year-old daughter of the housekeeper. *And won't Mrs Lacey be upset when she hears about all of this?*

It is only when Cosima sees her mother looking at her clothes that she remembers about the puddle. An old lady with white gloves looks kindly at her. 'I say, Lady Merriwether Frost, your daughter looks as though she's been with the pirates!'

'Indeed, she does,' her mother says. 'It's high time she started acting in a more lady-like fashion.'

'But Mummy,' she protests, suddenly. 'They don't want me to be lady-like. You said that Franck's father invites me to play because he's afraid that Franck might become a homosexual.'

She hears a gasp and a titter and then she doesn't hear anything more.

Back at the tack room, Franck flicks her a look of hate. 'It's all your fault,' he says. 'They won't ever love us now.'

'You said it would be all right,' she says. 'You said there'd be cakes and pop.'

She walks over to the flaying ground and stares down at the punished *Juliette* book. A torn monkey, a dog-eared penis, a crumpled scrum of bodies. She tells herself it's just as well that she has to spend most of the school holidays at Uncle Ellsworth and Aunt Spike's house. There are places to hide at Summer Crest Hall. Nobody knows what you're up to.

'Things would be all right if I were a goddess,' she says. 'If I were a goddess I wouldn't have to be lady-like. I could destroy whoever I wanted. Have them ripped apart by my hounds, have them dead all over the floor.'

She turns to Franck, her eyes flashing. 'I'd fill bridal chambers with snakes and turn my enemies to stone and . . .'

She is surprised by the sight of a man standing near the tack room. His back is turned but she can see an arc of pee spurting all over the stone wall.

'Never pee on the lawn,' the man says, turning his bright eyes on her. 'V'ry bad for the grass.'

He reminds her of a magician. Cosima knows he's not supposed to be here. He's supposed to be back in the Cage with all the rest.

Tigris is the first to giggle. She scampers off, closely followed by Franck and then Cosima, who looks back at the strange creature in the black velvet jacket still standing by the tack-room wall. At the ditch, Tigris stops dead. When Franck and Cosima come nearer, they find her poking a piece of wormy meat sprawled in a pool of muddy water. It snores and it has crimson paint over its fingernails.

It is dark in the tack room. She tells Fido and Phèdre to stay, plucks a special bridle from the wall and climbs high up into the rafters. She walks along a narrow beam like she imagines a tightrope walker from a circus might move. Reaching her secret nest, she takes off her muddy clothes and lies naked in the cradle of straw. Her nostrils twitch at the approach of the leather. She slides it over her body, slowly to begin with, the soft threads tickling her skin. She breathes in an incense of Rolls Royce seats and the shoes of Miss Hamilton the history teacher, and midnight feasts when Carlotta the circus girl puts her thigh around her neck and picks up sardines with her toes.

She passes the reins between her legs and then there's the struggle, the spasm of whippet bones, the noose pulling taut on her tiny breasts. She tries to escape, but wriggling is hopeless; the leather tongue lashes round her flesh, rubbing it hard, pinching it white. And now the smells grow sour and the world is prickly as straw and needles sprout from hands and sugar tongs have claws.

She thrashes around in her fevered nest, pulling the bridle, winching her flesh. 'Hopeless Cosima! Hopeless girl! Now you've done it! Now you're bad!' And still she wants more of it, more and more of it, until finally she plummets, she gasps and topples over, but she's caught by the arms of Carlotta, the circus girl Carlotta, and safe in the bear hug of leather, she rocks herself to sleep.

CHAPTER ELEVEN

She is woken by the sound of barking. Untangling the mesh of reins, she peers through a gap in the tack room wall and sees four wolfhounds on the lawn, tall as ponies, lean as hares. Franck's father is staggering behind them, still wet from the ditch. He is only forty-three, but the four handsome dogs make a mockery of their deadbeat master in his mud-clogged brogues and his stained black coat. Lucky for Ellsworth that he is grasping a handful of dead birds. The housekeeper, Mrs Lacey, is the only loyal one left. She tells her daughter, Susan, that for all his faults, there is always meat at Summer Crest Hall – pheasant and partridge and the never-ending pigeons.

When Cosima is certain that he is heading back to the house, she scrambles back into her clothes, tightropes back across the beam and climbs quickly down to the ground. She finds Fido and Phèdre waiting patiently in one of the horse stalls. As she strokes them, her eyes are drawn to a large pile of smashed paintings. When she goes to have a closer look, she discovers a suitcase behind the heap of broken frames and canvas shards. She opens it and finds a cache of paints and brushes.

She unscrews a tube that says, 'Prussian Blue' and tastes cake and clay on the back of her throat as the fumes hit the air. She squeezes out a worm of paint and soon there are warts of stewed blue all over her hand: a scab you pick and blue comes out. She smiles as she rummages deeper into the suitcase. There is a bottle of clear liquid with a label that says Windsor & Newton. When she smells the contents, it makes her eyes water and she wonders if it is something that Uncle Ellsworth likes to drink. There are sheets of paper at the bottom of the case. She takes one out and carefully squeezes another worm on to the top right-hand corner. Then she takes a paintbrush and sinks it slowly into the oily blue softness. She likes it much better than the poster paints at school. She skids the brush around on the page and in her excitement, knocks the bottle of Windsor & Newton over. Soon there are long, blue tears eating into the paper. She stares at the marks, wondering what they could mean.

A shadow falls over her and she jumps. The smell of smoke. Cigar smoke and oranges and somewhere she's never been before.

The magician.

She assumes she's landed herself in trouble.

'I found it,' she tells him, standing up and nodding to the suitcase as she hides her hand behind her back.

'Your uncle used to keep this place locked,' the man says, looking round the tack room. 'What do you suppose happened?'

Cosima scowls in the gloomy light. Grown-ups always asked stupid questions. They wanted to know how school was going, if you were taking dancing lessons yet.

'Maybe he paints in his bedroom now,' she mumbles. 'He's always in his bedroom. Or in the ditch.'

She wonders if she's gone too far, but then she sees a smile on the man's face. He's looking at her picture.

'A happy accident,' he says.

'What?'

'Involuntary marks on the canvas. It's how all the best pictures start.'

He turns from the painting with a smile and nods to the hand behind her back.

'Syphilis,' she snarls, flashing the crop of blue spots at him. She starts to edge out of the horse stall.

'Oh, don't go,' he says. 'It's so boring out there.'

'The animals,' she mumbles.

'Quite.'

'The Cage.'

'That's a good name for it,' he says. He stares at her for a while. 'They used to call me "Dog" at school.'

'Why?'

He doesn't reply. He squats down to look at her picture more closely.

'Why did they call you "Dog" at school?' she asks again.

'I suppose they didn't like me very much,' he says, standing up and sinking his hands deep into his trouser pockets. 'My friends call me Freddie.'

'How old are you?'

She's sure he'll leave now.

'Forty-three,' he says, without batting an eyelid.

'Are you the one who sells the pictures Franck's father paints?'

She is surprised to note that this is the question that tips him off balance.

'How do you know that?'

'Sometimes Uncle Ellsworth talks about, "The Dog" coming.'

'Not the most flattering of names, is it?'

'Depends what sort of dog you are.'

He smiles again. 'You must be Cosima.'

She shrugs.

'What sort of dog would you be?' he asks her.

'What do you think?' she says impatiently, stroking Fido and Phèdre. She's surprised he hasn't gone yet. She sees him look again at the marks she's made on the paper.

'Normally, I only do pencil drawings,' she says, quietly.

'What do you draw?'

She shrugs. 'Animals.'

'Yes?'

'And then I hang them.'

'Excellent.'

'I tie them up.'

She wonders why he hasn't told her off.

'I'll send you some proper paints,' he says, suddenly. 'I think you should do another.'

98

Cosima hesitates. She supposes he must still be drunk from the garden party. They always get drunk. He won't send her any paints. He'll be like all the others.

'Do you think these paints belong to Uncle Ellsworth?' she asks, pointing at the suitcase.

He doesn't reply immediately. She watches colour blot into his face like the turps into the blue.

'Why do you think he's getting rid of them?' she insists. 'He says he's nearly finished his masterpiece. Says it'll be ready any day now.'

'Masterpiece, eh?'

De Vere inspects the pile of broken canvases. He frowns as he unearths a bent frying pan and two blue-rimmed enamel plates.

CHAPTER TWELVE

Now even Franck has abandoned his cold bedroom. Carmen too. She woke up, observed Cosima sleeping not-so-peacefully in the battered chair next to hers, drained the dregs of the art teacher's empty pre-meds glass and crept back to her room to 'freshen up'.

Cosima won't wake for a while in spite of the draughty conditions of Franck's room. Under her trembling eyelids she is in Franck's bedroom also, although temperatures in the dream world version are much higher. The clement spring of 1981 has given way to a clammy summer and Cosima is almost thirteen. It is almost midnight and she is about to initiate a ritual she makes sure happens at least twice during the holidays. The first one took place the night before the royal wedding at the end of July. This one is a wake for the end of the summer holidays. There are only six more days of August left.

Cosima looms over her cousin's head, watching him snore in his bed. She knows he's afraid to wake at midnight in spite of the promise of chocolate mini rolls. She glances at her watch then rips off his covers, dragging him from the shallows of an agitated sleep.

'Come on, Franck!' she hisses. 'It's time.'

There's a bang and Tigris charges into the bedroom. 'Look here, Cosima,' she cries. 'They've got Chum in the kitchen. I found the one with rabbit and chicken!'

'Susan!' Franck yelps, jerking up in his bed. 'We mustn't wake my father.'

Tigris puts her hand over her mouth but Cosima dumps her hunting bag on to the carpet with an unapologetic thud. 'Don't worry,' she reassures Tigris. 'Franck's father's run away again.'

'He has not run away!' Franck says, indignantly.

'Then why haven't we seen him for three days?' She turns to Tigris. 'He drank three bottles of claret at dinner on Saturday.'

'He's finished his masterpiece,' Franck protests. 'Anyone knows you need to relax after you've finished a masterpiece.'

'Actually, it's nearly four days,' Cosima tells Tigris. 'We last saw him on Saturday and now it's just turned Wednesday.'

Tonight is an even more secret midnight feast than usual because Tigris isn't supposed to be here. Her mother, Mrs Lacey, handed in her notice a week ago.

'She won't tell me why she left,' Tigris says, passing them mugs of orange squash.

'Maybe it was because Franck's mother ran away as well,' Cosima suggests.

'She did not run away,' Franck mumbles, looking at the picture on his royal wedding mug. 'Models have to travel. She wears lovely dresses.'

'She only eats lettuce leaves,' Cosima says, opening a can of sardines. 'Makes her all spiky.'

'Yes,' says Tigris, fixing a tin-opener to the can of Chum. 'And since she left, your dad's been going . . .'

'What about my Pa?' Franck erupts.

Tigris looks to Cosima who glares at Franck. 'The dribble's getting worse in case you haven't noticed. I'm not surprised your mother left.'

Franck gets out of bed and sits on the carpet. He looks again at Prince Charles's hand resting lovingly on the royal-blue shoulder of Lady Diana. He knows something's wrong too. His father has always been bad-tempered. Sometimes, Christmas and birthdays are cancelled altogether. But since he abandoned the tack room at Easter, he always seems to be shut up in his bedroom playing his Marlene Dietrich records late into the night.

It wasn't always like this. When things were good, he'd be the best father in the world, jumping down from the dinner table on all fours, growling and chasing them round the room. Even Cosima had liked that when she was younger.

But now there was less and less of Ellsworth and more and more of Marlene Dietrich. Sometimes, when he turned up for dinner, he'd be cheerful to begin with. He'd crack jokes, rude ones. And then the tears would come, the glasses of wine and the dribble down the side of the mouth. The slurred speeches about life and death, the hammering on the table, the shouting at Franck. If he and Cosima were lucky, he'd tell them both to, 'bugger off', or he'd slope back to his room and start the record player up really loud. Sometimes they couldn't be sure where he'd vanished to.

Franck suddenly feels furious with Cosima.

'It was you who set Pa off in the bad mood!' he explodes. 'That last time he came down for dinner. You were the one who knocked over the bottle of wine. A mess all over the tablecloth and no Mrs Lacey to clear it up!'

He looks hopefully at the can of condensed milk he sees her opening. 'It's all your fault that he's disappeared,' he mutters.

Cosima decides to pretend that she can't hear Franck. She pretends to be the girl from the circus. 'I'm Carlotta who's staying at Saint Clare's just for a term while the circus is in town,' she tells Tigris. 'I wrap my leg around my neck and I get sardines from the tin with my toes. I dip them into the condensed milk and then I eat them.'

'You're always going on about Carlotta from the circus,' Tigris smirks, loading morsels of dog food into her mouth. 'Maybe you're a lezzy.'

Cosima picks up a sardine with two prehensile toes. 'There's one of those dykes in our dorm at school,' she says, dipping it into the can of condensed milk. 'She wants to do it with me.'

'Why don't you?' Tigris asks, licking jelly from her fingers.

'She's spotty.'

'Yuk.'

'Spots and grease.' Cosima lifts her toes to her mouth. 'I do it on my own, anyway. Under the sheets.'

She munches on the milk-coated sardine but frowns when she sees Tigris and Franck looking at her. She wipes her toes with the hem of her dressing gown, grabs her hunting bag and prepares to reveal her latest scalp.

The tack room smelled dangerous now that it was summer. The brambles growing around it sent off steamy wafts of dog shit and cow parsley and overheated plastic bags. One day, Cosima found a stack of porn magazines hidden in a clump of stinging nettles. One of them was called *Honcho* and had a picture of a naked black man on the cover. Its pages were stuck with paint and she couldn't open them but she could open some of the others, the ones with photographs of naked women on the front.

She pulls *Deep Crack High* ostentatiously from her hunting bag as Franck and Tigris look on with open mouths. She flicks through the magazine as if it bores her profoundly although the truth is that the dark holes and the greasy lips make her feel inexplicably ashamed. She always suspected she was being hunted – it was bad enough when her breasts began to grow and when the Curse began – but now she knows there is worse ahead. She liked the engravings in the flayed *Juliette* book. They weren't realistic. You could make things up in your head. But this is different. She makes herself look at the garish photographs. She reads from one of the pages. 'He pushed me against the dish-washer and rammed in his throbbing piece of meat . . .'

Tigris is spellbound and Franck whinnies hysterically before choking on a mouthful of sardine. Cosima slams the magazine shut and uses it as a fan. 'Too bloody hot,' she says, angrily. She tells them she's going down to the kitchen. 'You know I only eat Winalot,' she scolds Tigris. 'I hate the wet stuff!'

She flounces out of the bedroom and storms down the hall, past Franck's father's bedroom, past the table with the brass goats' legs where a plate of fruit has turned syrupy with the heat. She wrinkles her nose. The stench. It seems that everything in Summer Crest Hall has started to rot. The rubbish bags have been abandoned and the flies are everywhere. She's given up trying to stop things from spoiling. Since Mrs Lacey left, there have been no regular domestics. Cosima doesn't care. They've been left alone and that's what counts.

She goes down the stone back stairs that lead to the kitchen. The back stairs are freezing in the winter, but with the unbearable heat there's no escape to be had even here. Once she gets to the kitchen, she slams the door in relief. The kitchen is cooler and she knows the cupboard will be stocked with tins and packets.

At the midnight feast at school, she and the dyke took half a tab of acid each. Cosima grabbed her new box of oil paints and the two of them ran out to the woods. She was surprised that Charles Frederick de Vere had kept his promise and sent the paints a mere two weeks after the garden party.

In the woods, in the early morning light, she'd crouched down and squeezed out worms of red, yellow and blue from the tubes on to a fallen trunk. As the dyke talked to one of the trees, Cosima stared at the paint until the blue and the yellow started to move. The blue worm turned into a snail in front of her eyes. It retreated into its shell just as the yellow worm jumped up into the air, sticking its tongue out like the mad old man she saw once outside the chemist's in the village.

Cosima gasped and stepped back from the trunk.

'What's wrong?' the dyke asked.

'Can't you see?' Cosima panted, pointing at the mad lemon goblin who had now become a squawking canary.

But the yellow canary soon bored her. It was the blue which disturbed her the most. There was something mysterious about the blue. The longer she looked at it, the more she realised that it was retreating – inwards and downwards, ever so slowly. It beckoned her in and she saw that she would have to be careful or it might drag her with it and she would be sucked down into a very seductive whirlpool.

When she turned away, she saw that the dyke had painted her face and arms with red stripes. The dyke had been Cosima's secret best friend for two years now. She always played the male roles in the plays at school – Sherlock Holmes, or Algernon Moncrieff in *The Importance of Being Earnest*. Cosima had even called one of the whippets after her. But Phèdre's red bored Cosima. She rubbed a tiny amount of blue into the vermilion stripes on Phèdre's arm and the red was quenched immediately.

It was blue that had the power. Cosima went back to studying the snail. She watched it going down, disappearing deeper and deeper into its shell.

'Blue is a snail!' she whispered.

'Huh?' Phèdre was giving herself a red moustache now.

'The snail will kill that stupid canary!' Cosima announced, picking the blue snail up with her finger and dropping it on to the screeching yellow bird. Paralysis. She realised then that mysterious blue stopped lunatic yellow in its tracks, turning it to contented green. A calm, unmoving colour that made her think of Franck.

When they found them the next day, Cosima and Phèdre were lying naked in the grass – fast asleep, hand in hand, their bodies smeared with mud-coloured splodges.

Cosima stands on a kitchen chair, delves inside the emergency supply cupboard and is pleased to locate a small tin of Alphabetti Spaghetti. She puts it in the pocket of her dressing gown and when she turns round she sees two white slits staring at her through the darkness. She gasps and stumbles from the chair, only to be caught by the velvety arms of Charles Frederick de Vere.

'My dear Cosima!' he exclaims in his huge voice. 'That's the second time I've caught you unawares.'

She jerks away from him, feeling silly and worrying he'll think her a kid in the stupid pink dressing gown her mother bought her to make her more lady-like.

'Why are you here?' she asks, backing towards the door.

'Yes, it is rather late,' he says. 'My car broke down. Damn weather overheated the engine.' He sniffs the air. 'Rather fruity in here.'

'Mrs Lacey left,' Cosima says. 'There's been no help here for over a week.'

De Vere smiles at her. She hopes he didn't feel the tin in her pocket.

'I take it Franck's father has gone to bed?' he says, going to the sink and opening the cupboard underneath. 'I was supposed to be here a couple of days ago but I was detained on business . . .'

He bends over to inspect a series of wine bottles and chooses a red.

'You were right,' he adds, taking the bottle over to the dresser. 'What you predicted at the garden party. It appears that your uncle Ellsworth's masterpiece is finally ready.' He removes the cork from the bottle and pours himself a glass. 'I usually send a van to pick up his paintings, but this time he wanted me to come myself.'

Cosima watches him drink. He doesn't drink like Uncle Ellsworth. She wonders if she should tell him about the painting she did after she took the acid at school. After she'd discovered the things about colour.

'You are a woman of mystery,' he says, running his hands through thick layers of silver-flecked hair.

'What?'

'Last time we met you were trying to hide your Prussian Blue hand and now you seem to be hiding a tin of . . . ?' He looks towards her dressing gown pocket. 'Would you, by any chance, be having a midnight feast?'

Now she feels stupid again. 'You're making fun of me,' she says.

'Not at all,' he protests. 'I adore midnight feasts. Although something delicious is best.'

She watches him open the fridge door and start to pull food out.

'Pigeon,' he says. 'Not at all delicious. Partridge and . . . hare and . . . what's this, do you think?'

He turns around, holding a plate with another dried-up piece of game on. She wrinkles her nose. She thought he was a magician but he offers her soily meat just like Uncle Ellsworth.

'If oysters are a choral mass,' de Vere asserts, 'then game is a black mass.' He puts a box of eggs on the table. 'Nothing wrong with a black mass, of course. And the blackest mass of all is Ortolan.'

'What's that?'

'Tiny song birds from France. Illegal to eat. You lock them in a box, gorge them on figs and then drown them in Armagnac. You roast them. You eat the whole thing. Bones and all.'

He expects Cosima to flinch but she doesn't. He smiles as he picks up his glass. 'You're supposed to put a cloth over your head when you eat them. To keep in the fumes.' He drinks. 'But mostly to hide yourself from the eyes of God.'

A red tear dribbles from the side of his mouth. 'The French are Catholics,' he explains, dabbing his lips with the red foulard. 'Very big on guilt, the Catholics. But guilt is a pointless emotion. If you feel guilty about indulgence, then it takes the cream off the indulgence.'

He delves back into the fridge, emerging with a small jar. 'The devil!' he mutters. 'I brought this back from Saint Petersburg for your uncle. Sevruga caviar. He hasn't touched it!'

He puts the jar on the kitchen table next to the box of eggs.

'The bigger the grain, the better the taste,' he tells her, adding that he's going to make scrambled eggs for them both. Then he jumps.

'Thoughtless of me!' he exclaims, picking up the bottle of red wine. 'Would it be indiscreet to enquire your age?'

She smirks, remembering Easter and how rudely she'd asked him the same question.

107

'Thirteen in October,' she tells him.

'Old enough for a little wine, then,' he says, starting to fill her glass.

She thinks of Franck and Tigris upstairs. She hopes they don't come down. He's hers, the man in the black velvet.

'Your uncle Ellsworth once told me that the night before he died, he'd like to drink a bottle of Mouton Rothschild 1945.' He glances at the bottle in his hand and raises his eyebrows. 'Tonight we must make do with more modest delights.'

He chinks her glass and then she can't get out of drinking. She doesn't like wine. It makes you mad like Uncle Ellsworth. She doesn't like eggs either. Disgusting.

She feels a splash in her guts, a dirty red glow. She sits hunched in the chair, watching him crack eggs into the bowl. She has never seen a man cook before. Butter sizzles on the Aga. Funny. A man in a black velvet jacket and a red scarf stirring eggs in a pan.

'I took acid last term,' she says, scowling.

'Any good?'

She thinks of the blue snail and the yellow canary.

'It was all right,' she says, spotting a new painting propped up against the back door. A turquoise peacock with its guts ripped open. A rope cutting viciously into the flesh of a dead hare.

De Vere turns and asks her what she thinks of it. 'An American friend of mine, Carmen, calls it, *The Dead Stuff*.'

Cosima wonders if Carmen is Freddie's girlfriend. Uncle Ellsworth sometimes makes rude jokes about the Dog's 'ladies'.

She goes over to inspect the painting. She feels something like excitement as she takes in the limp plumpness of the gore-smeared animals, the bowl of plums splitting with ripeness next to the soft white underbelly of the hare.

'A banquet of death,' she finds herself saying. 'I like that the animals are all bloody. Makes it look quite . . . opulent.'

He squints, looking at her as though he's trying to remember her.

'Yes,' he says slowly. 'I suppose it is rather a lavish morgue.'

'I like when meat hasn't become meat yet,' she lies. 'When it's still hot flesh in the pan.'

He's still looking at her, rubbing his neck, as if something's just bitten him. 'That's settled then,' he says at last. 'You will have to become an artist now, Cosima. Because art's blood is filthy.'

She looks puzzled.

He picks up the caviar. Throws it high in the air and catches it. 'You know the story of Medusa?'

'Of course,' she snaps. 'It's on the tiles in Uncle Ellsworth's bedroom.'

'Then you'll know that when Perseus hacked off Medusa's head, he tossed the bloody stump away. And where it fell, a fountain sprang up and gave birth to the Muses.'

He turns back to the Aga. 'Which means that under the skin of every great painting, behind every celestial-sounding piece of music, the blood of the monster is stinking away.'

She watches him cooking. She wonders why someone like Freddie would want to work with a monster like Uncle Ellsworth.

'I'm a bit scared of blood,' she confesses.

'Then you will be heroic,' de Vere announces, placing two silver egg cups on a tray. 'To face something that frightens one is heroic. At least, that's the message I've always drawn from Greek mythology.'

He picks up the tray and turns to face her.

'What do you think?'

She thinks of the greasy lips and the dark holes in the copy of *Deep Crack High* upstairs. Then the eggs arrive at the table. They don't look like scrambled eggs. They look like boiled eggs. They're perched in the two silver egg cups and on top of each is a small patch of black spawn.

She watches him pick up his spoon.

'I do *believe* in caviar,' he says, licking his lips.

She looks into the blue fountains, the sparkly eyes. She picks

109

up her spoon and glides the tip into the black. It passes through the darkness, descends into a soft yellow foam and when she puts it in her mouth, she gets kidnapped for a few seconds. For a few seconds her mouth is electrocuted with the monumental shock of egg and sea, hurtling her into a subterranean cave where creatures crawl on fattened bellies, where breasts fall out of dresses, where monstrous porn glares from every wall. Her mouth becomes a brain and the rest of her body ricochets around the kitchen until she wants to roar for all the world to hear.

That was when he entered her body. He took up residence at that very moment. The eggs were in her. Even when she went to get the painting, to show him what she'd done with her painting, even when she went into the room and saw what was in there, it didn't matter because the eggs were in her.

Part Two

CHAPTER THIRTEEN

A large warehouse in the East End of London, October 2004.

Charles Frederick de Vere is rounding up the animals. It's the art safari, the feeding frenzy.

'I'm a member of the cinder club!' croaks a gargoyle, pressing a smoking cigarette into the naked skin of his forearm. A girl sticks out her tongue and licks the end of her nose. 'I can make girls ejaculate!' she shrieks at the lawyer who's been telling her about vaginal hysterectomy lawsuits. 'This is so shocking,' someone's wife drawls. 'It's like the end of the Weimar Republic, you know?'

The Emperor, the Hermit and the High Priestess sit at the top table, waiting for the time to come. 'It's hard to like a painting that's not expensive, nowadays,' the Emperor confides. 'Oh, for heaven's sake,' the High Priestess snaps. 'Shall we take the cocaine now or after coffee? Hurry and decide!'

They are moved momentarily by The Fool who prances through the room in a moth-eaten Hussar's jacket, brandishing a glass of wine aloft.

'Darling!' he whinnies, commanding armies, winning battles, slicing down enemies left and right, now borne up on the shoulders of his faithful men, now talking of boundaries and territories, of gallantry in action and medals of honour. By the time he arrives at the top table to lay the handbag at the feet of the Spike, he sounds like a general on his death bed. His glass is empty and a piece of frayed gold braid has caught on the back of a chair.

'Pom-poms, darling,' he moans. 'Gigot sleeves and tea-tray hats. Lugers and ribbons and black Panzer wrap tunics . . .'

He peters out as a set of sparkly white teeth fills the gallery and it is Charles Frederick de Vere ordering silence in the room. As the Magician rises from his seat, the photographers rush forward in a flurry of bulbs: a blinding glare followed by the brief abyss of darkness.

Liberated from the constraints of the pink and the blue and the froth, Charles Frederick de Vere has found a new seat at the high table of Contemporary Art. Age has not bothered him. Indeed, it has improved him. The salt and pepper hair has turned to a lustrous silver fox and the tan looks more natural than it did in his forties. He looks at ease in his sixty-six-year-old skin while avoiding the unattractive dangers of appearing 'contented'. His eyes still sparkle, although the constant glare of limelight has tinged the periwinkle blue slightly. He still wears his black velvet jacket with the jungle-red foulard which conveys just the right amount of individuality for the contemporary art world of 2004. The young ones like him, finding him sufficiently eccentric to complement their desperately extrovert ways. He is no longer an art dealer, he is a 'gallerist'. He has learned the new language of conceptual art: he talks about a 'great new piece', he tells collectors how, 'the installation lends itself well to the space'.

His metamorphosis was not necessarily planned. A circumstance arose late in that summer of 1981 which ensured that de Vere could no longer comfortably remain in England. Lesser talents might have perished from such a rude upheaval and yet his move to America proved serendipitous. New York was beginning to be dazzled by a handful of impudent 'art stars' who had ambushed the moribund gallery scene of the late seventies. A short-order cook, a graffiti-spraying disco queen and a Voodoo-inspired drug addict had spun on to the stage like bulls in a china shop, breaking crockery, scrawling on subway stations, spraying mayhem as far as the eye could see. Nobody wanted prettiness any more. Plump nymphs in a wood?

Ladies taking their pleasure in a lace-draped boudoir? *Passé*. What people wanted was commotion, gossip, break-dance poses for the photographers.

In the beginning, they called it 'Bad Art', or 'Enfant-garde'. Some hailed it as an artistic renaissance akin to Florence in the late fifteenth century, others saw it as a perfect mirror for the coked-up, sensation-seeking eighties. Whatever it was, it signalled a new Eldorado, a Klondike for the modern age. Living artists had never made so much money in their lifetimes and they began to act like pop stars. They painted in Armani suits, ate in expensive restaurants, resided in luxury hotels, had heroin habits and monogrammed slippers, chucked hundred-dollar bills at Bowery bums. There was a fake Schnabel as a stage set for the new Musical, *Cats*. Donald Trump talked about the 'numbers' that art was getting to justify his valuation of the Plaza Hotel. Artists began appearing all over the glossy magazines.

They basked in the limelight until the limelight started to roast them like tiny spiders writhing under a sunny magnifying glass. Like pop stars with a hit record, their careers rarely spanned more than eighteen months. They were washed up by twenty-five. Some died of drug overdoses, some went back to being short-order cooks. Even when people became tired of Schnabel, Haring and Basquiat, it didn't matter because Koons, Sherman and Prince would soon be rolling right up.

To start with, de Vere observed the hoopla from the sidelines. His belief was that the bulk of art contains neither transcendence nor significance, that most collectors are shoppers who want pictures that will match the colour of their sofa. This was borne out by figures in the New York auction houses. The economy was fizzing and while the hip new art was the talk of the town, the Impressionists and post-Impressionists were proving an even steadier bet. In May, 1981, a Picasso self-portrait became the most expensive art work of the twentieth century to date when it sold at Sotheby's New York for $5.3 million. In 1987, Van Gogh's *Irises* would go for an incredible $53 million.

De Vere took an apartment on the Upper East side and set to work. He was not devoid of contacts, and his change of circumstance had merely sharpened his wits and hardened his mettle. He became an avid reader of obituaries. He would locate the number of the deceased in the telephone directory and through his manner on the phone or perhaps the 'numbers' he promised, he would often be invited to homes in Connecticut and Long Island to make his case, alongside agents from the major auction houses, for being the best man to sell off their valuable collections.

His performances were impeccable and he rarely left without securing sizable portions of the treasure. He never failed to make heirs and estate trustees feel sufficiently important and his *sang froid* was at its best when he knew that some of the work was damaged. News of a peeling Monet, a chipped van Dongen would send his pulse racing. He would solemnly lay the picture out like a patient on an operating table. He would contemplate the neglected body for a full two minutes, until tension had risen to a pinnacle and the hopeful eyes of spouses and children would turn to focus on the only possible saviour left to them: Charles Frederick de Vere. Only then would he signal for his restorer (a former shooting friend from London) to enter the room dressed, as de Vere stipulated, in a spotless white coat and always moving with the gravitas of a Harley Street surgeon.

As his fortunes improved, de Vere began to be seen in public. He didn't introduce himself as a dealer to start with. He was a collector. In spite of the fading interest in European artists, de Vere found that Americans were as thirsty as ever for the cultural cachet offered by an upper-class Englishman. He was elegant and soft spoken in a city that was irreverent and wise-cracking. His fingernails were always clean, he used French words in his sentences, he never patronised the Americans as he had seen his compatriots do and he never succumbed to the art dealer fashions of the eighties: the baggy Comme des Garçons suits, the witty bow ties, the flashy braces. His foulard and his black velvet jacket continued to serve him well and something in his sparkling blue eyes even spoke of sincerity.

The new young artists took to the strange English gentleman. 'But Freddie,' they'd confide in anguished tones. 'Do you think I should *believe* in all this success?' Charles Frederick de Vere would smile, puff on his cigar and, as he watched the smoke dissipate upwards into the tall gallery ceiling, he would reply: 'My dear boy, success is like wine. One does not believe in wine, one drinks it.'

Even when they came back to him a few months later, washed up on all the wine they'd drunk too quickly, de Vere would point out that fashions in art must always be shaped by the vagaries of politics.

'Think of eighteenth-century France, my dear boy. It begins with Boucher's *The Toilette of Venus* and ends with David's Marat stabbed to death in the bath.'

De Vere tried not to think too much about life back in Europe, in spite of the irritations he found with New York. The informality. The cutting up of food with knife and fork and then eating with the fork in the right hand. Like babies in the nursery. Often not using cutlery at all. Serving oysters with vodka and tonic. 'Tex-Mex' and pitchers of beer. The 'you guys' this and 'you guys' that.

He shudders now at the thought of it. And yet he took to the life, slipped into it like a man getting into a warm bath. He was soon a fixture at all the art parties. There'd be Andy, Julian, Keith, Jean-Michel and Charles Frederick de Vere. Before long, people began inquiring if he had anything to sell himself.

Contemporary art was a pool that de Vere had resolved not to plunge into. And yet, he couldn't help but notice the exalted positions in which New York 'gallerists' were held – they often seemed more important than the artists themselves. True, de Vere knew very little about contemporary art, but almost any sale, if dangled enticingly enough, aroused his instinct for the chase.

He began secondary dealing or 'resale' as it was sometimes less glamorously called. It involved no visits to studios or nursing the egos of neurotic artists. He started with the minimalists: Judd, Flavin. De Vere relished the challenge of selling artists whose prices had been damaged by the coming of the new young gods. Not being hot off the press meant they were easier to acquire and seemed more of a safe bet to some of his more conservative buyers.

He speeded up his game. His practices became more swash-buckling. He offered collectors work still owned by other collectors. He bought pictures at auction, put down a deposit and then sold them at a profit in the ten-day period allotted to come up with the rest of the money. If the picture failed to sell, he would complain that it was not as described in the catalogue and demand his money back. He took to dining in the more fashionable restaurants in town: Odeon, Le Cirque, Ballato's on East Houston.

'Do I need a Richard Serra?' an influential publisher would inquire from a nearby table.

'Most definitely,' he would reply, drowning them in a sea of blue.

He bought a beach house in Montauk and invited young crowds to come and stay. In October 1987, on the weekend of Black Monday, he threw a party to celebrate the fact that art was immune from the mundanities of commerce. Art hadn't even winced when everything else had plummeted. Its health was as buoyant as the lily pads which were only becoming more numerous in de Vere's fantastical trip through life.

The following year, Jasper Johns became the first living artist to make more than 10 million dollars for a picture when his *False Start* sold for $17 million at Sotheby's. A week later, a Blue Period Picasso sold for $24.8 million and when, on 15 May 1990, the gavel came down to thunderous applause on Van Gogh's *Dr Gachet* – sold for a record $82.5 million – it seemed as though the champagne would never end.

It was in November that the first trace of blood appeared. A broken plate painting by Julian Schnabel (the man who, in the early eighties had declared his only peers to be Caravaggio and Giotto) failed to sell at auction. Then a number of corporate tax scandals began to seep out. It emerged, for instance, that many of the Japanese art lovers of the eighties had not been seeking a cultural Elysium after all. A loophole in the law meant that if your company owed 500 million yen to the taxman, then the purchase of a 500 million yen painting by, say, Renoir, would mean you owed the taxman nothing at all. The only catch was that you had to turn your board room into an 'art museum' for one morning of every month. On this day, a lady or a gentleman with a megaphone would travel up to the twenty-seventh floor of your business tower to extemporise to a party of school children on the sensual warmth of the Impressionist brush stroke in the one and only painting in your 'art museum', while next door, a room full of product managers would be discussing innovations for low-risk, cost-effective car engines.

When US bombers struck civilians in Baghdad in February 1991, the carnage in the American contemporary art market began in all its fury.

Charles Frederick de Vere remained unscathed by the turn of events. On the contrary, he smelled spring in the air and the musky perfume was blowing from the direction of London. A clutch of new spiderlings were emerging from their cocoons, a generation of young British artists nourished on the cold air of ambition breathed out by Margaret Thatcher. Their fangs were sharper than their predecessors' and they were cocky, entrepreneurial; in particular, one hooligan from Leeds who had made his name with a colony of maggots and a skinned cow's head. The biggest collector in the world had started to buy them up. De Vere recognised the signs and returned home to London in time to witness the hysteria of the shark floating in a tank of formaldehyde and to snap up real estate while property prices were rock bottom.

In 1992, from the comfort of his former suite at Claridges, he bought a warehouse in Hoxton in the East End of London. He fashioned the place into a temple of Brutalist chic: 12,000 square feet of poured concrete floor, high ceilings and frost-white walls. He organised a gala evening in aid of a charity he knew was dear to the heart of many of his old 'pupils'. When he persuaded several famous New York artists to donate pieces for auction at the party, the new London spiderlings became animated. Several of them even offered to donate examples of their own work.

De Vere forgets now the name of the African orphanage that received the proceeds from the evening, but he remembers clearly how the gala relaunched his career as master of hounds in the great blood sport known as taste. He ended the night with many fresh pupils who came to understand that whereas people used to buy art because they loved it, the thing to do now was to buy art to make money from it. It was not only a good night for his British clients. He could not deny that his New York coterie of shopping-centre billionaires, taxi-fleet magnates and Puerto Rican garment-district barons might have been burned by the crash in America. But he smiles now to remember how quick they were to re-open their cheque books once they saw the art pastures fresh he was offering them via a live TV link-up of the party to New York.

The following morning, de Vere was woken early in his four-poster bed in Claridges by a phone call. The phone never stopped ringing and it wasn't just collectors who were pursuing him. The new British artists were drawn to him like moths to the flame, and he to them. Whenever he came across someone he liked, he would declare their work to be an 'epiphany'. He was rarely proved wrong. He took pleasure in taking on what were known as, 'difficult' artists. His eccentric *savoir vivre* became a talking point. His artists marvelled at his demeanour of entitlement and were wont to talk of his Mayfair suite with a frisson of excitement in their voices.

Things were speeding up again. He needed to expand his

operations. In 1997 he married again, his bride a lady he had known for some time. It was a felicitous arrangement.

And now, here he stands in his magnificent white gallery, in front of the gathering of 500 people, the most influential and successful in their field. The boom in what came to be known as 'Brit Art' has exceeded even de Vere's expectations. So many new collectors, so many new opportunities. All eyes are on him: the legend. A cigar smoulders in his hand, veiling him in a miasma of smoke.

'You're the man, Freddie!' the gargoyle shouts from the back of the room. 'Freddie's the man!' he slurs again, turning to the other people on his table, his glass of champagne wavering in the air.

De Vere smiles, tightly. Unruly behaviour. One of the snags in the world of contemporary art.

'I propose a toast,' he intones. 'To one of the most creative men I know. An incredible talent, a new chapter in the history of art.'

He raises his glass to the artist, thinking how much larger will Charles Frederick de Vere's place be in the history of art. 'Since I discovered him, he has taught me much about life, art and . . .' He pauses for comic effect: 'Caviar!'

The assembly roars with laughter.

The whole room is crawling through a sludge of the stuff. It is even on the walls. The party de Vere is throwing tonight is for an artist from Brazil who specialises in society portraits done in jam, peanut butter and caviar. It is undoubtedly clever. His ladies seem to like it. And yet it scarcely moves him.

He picks up his knife and fork and prepares to lose himself in another dainty dish. And yet he finds it hard to enjoy the salt-cod tart while talking to the woman with the cheek implants. The cod is good. Tender, succulent flakes soaked in water long enough for the excess salt to leave but not left too long to lose all the flavour. Yet he finds the cheeks of the woman next to him troubling. Like carelessly inserted stuffing in a roasted chicken breast. Too much on one side and a dent in the other. Charles Frederick de Vere feels his stomach shrink as he looks at the Spike. The eyes are dead, the bone structure fragile as if a single touch would make her crumble to dust like an Egyptian mummy exposed to daylight. He feels the delicate fish flesh against his tongue, under his teeth. He feels a pang of regret as it slithers, only half-enjoyed, down his throat.

He looks at the framed black eggs on the wall and when he looks at the Spike he sees shit smeared all over her, over the little creases in her tailored trousers, her tiny feet in heels as thin as pins, her little steps.

'Are you feeling all right, Freddie?'

He jumps in his seat. Sitting next to him is a man who looks like a boiled egg and his wife, who resembles the spoon.

'Couldn't be better,' he exclaims. With a flourish, he plucks the red-silk square from his top pocket.

'I think your Brazilian kid is so talented,' the Boiled Egg is saying, pointing to Greta Garbo in maple syrup on the other side of the room. 'I mean, the pictures are so much fun . . .'

'Yes,' de Vere murmurs, wiping the palms of his hands with the red handkerchief. 'My discoveries rarely disappoint.'

'I'm really excited about seeing our caviar portrait,' the Boiled Egg drones on.

De Vere's lips twitch waspishly. 'An incredible piece,' he mumbles, his eyes suddenly fixated on his hands twisting at the square of red silk.

'That's so great,' the Boiled Egg says, nervously.

De Vere looks up to see the eyes of the table on him. He tucks the handkerchief back in his pocket and breathes in deeply. 'Incredible!' he repeats dramatically, reaching for his champagne glass.

'Do you think . . .' the Boiled Egg says. 'I mean, now that it's finished . . .'

'What he wants to know,' chimes the Spoon, 'is can we see the picture tonight?'

'We'd love to see it,' the Boiled Egg ventures.

De Vere takes a long drink of champagne before turning to the Egg and Spoon.

'I would be delighted to show you the portrait,' he announces, filling the room with a bracing draught of Alpine air.

'Oh, you're a good person,' the Spoon says and de Vere smiles strangely. As if he has spent time with the notion crossing his mind that he is not a good person at all.

'A very good person!' Franck pipes up from down the table. 'In fact, my mother's been wonderfully lucky with her husbands. My father, Ellsworth, the great artist. And now my stepfather, Freddie, the virtuoso salesman!'

He turns to the Egg and Spoon and informs them in a dramatic stage whisper: 'Freddie will probably sell you some of my father's paintings, if you ask him nicely!'

The icy stare of the Spike turns Franck's rosebud mouth sulky. He pulls his sketch pad from a patched pocket of the worn-out cavalry jacket and flicks through the pages, dreaming back to the time before the fire. The golden owl above the fireplace and *Dum Spiro Spero*. The dining table always formally laid for dinner. A housekeeper to look after them. Pigeon, partridge and hare. And marvellous conversation with the guests.

De Vere stands up. Bowing briefly, he excuses himself from the table and begins to move through the crowds, smiling and accepting the pats on the back with good grace. He goes upstairs to his white-walled office, opens the door, closes it behind him and sits at his desk with a huge sigh of relief. He can still hear the safari downstairs, the rutting and the screaming. He chuckles to himself. He sits back in his chair and casts an eye over the sketches on the wall – the Picasso bulls, the Boldini *flâneur* – some of the fruits of his earlier years of labour, more stirring than anything his Brazilian could have come up with.

He takes a Lonsdale from the cigar box on his desk. Next to

123

the box is an owl in a bell jar. The owl is old now, born two centuries ago. Strange, he's been meaning to throw it away, yet he can't quite bring himself . . .

He clips the end of the cigar, lights it and goes over to the wall where a number of his client's commissions are leaning. A group of children in jam, the Egg and Spoon in caviar eggs.

Eggs. He glances to his left. His office appears to be a simple, sterile white box but at the very end of the room there is a tiny corridor, a kind of hidden alcove that can only be accessed by a white door to which only de Vere holds the key. He thrusts his hands into his pockets, jangles the key chain for a while and then strolls almost idly over to the small door. He hesitates as he stands in front of it before suddenly taking the chain from his pocket, finding the key and inserting it into the lock.

A smell of oils wafts out. De Vere's face clouds momentarily but then he smiles as he sees the stack of canvases. He closes his eyes. He shivers as he touches them. When he opens his eyes, he sees a huge flying horse with tiny children on its back. He moves quickly through the stack in a flash of white rabbits fierce as wolves, haunted children and strange ghostly shapes.

He savours these moments. He doesn't come often to look at the pictures. Too painful. He doesn't even try to sell them any more. They were never fashionable, even at their height. Dreamy, surreal images, although there was definitely something to them. He sighs. His fingers stroke the different paintings. More horses, a frightened faun, an emerald sea horse larger than all the fish around it.

He stops. He looks at his hand. His cigar drops from his mouth. He staggers back from the cupboard his eyes bulging. He has a spine chilling thought, *no, it's impossible*, and is rubbing furiously at his hand when suddenly the door of his office opens and there is a drunken voice wailing, 'Too complex! Too fucking complex!' like a wounded Robinson Crusoe crawling up the beach after escape from the ship.

Quickly, he retrieves the cigar from the floor. He shuts the alcove door, locks it and walks swiftly back to the front of the office.

'Nobody is allowed in here,' he snaps.

It's the gargoyle. He slumps into the swivel chair, apparently oblivious of de Vere.

'Prosecco,' he wails. 'Why can't they serve us prosecco? It's champagne every fucking time!'

De Vere heaves the boy to his feet and leads him towards the door. He makes sure to lock the office when he closes it. He walks down the stairs and back into the main gallery where he takes his place at the dinner table. It strikes him that his life has been flicked through quicker than he thought. That the pages of his diary are nearly used up. He leaves it to the Spike to make small talk with the assembled guests. His mind is filled with a pool of red and he notes with alarm that his champagne glass is soon stained with smears of Madder Lake.

CHAPTER FOURTEEN

The paintings keep coming. He can't deny it any more. The small, white alcove sends him one a week. Washes of red paint. Formality and chaos all at once. Like red water with something floating on top. Or rather, something emerging from the bottom of a container of liquid scarlet.

He tried to convince himself that the paintings weren't new. After all, it had been so long since he'd looked at her work. And yet, in his heart he knows he has never seen these pictures before, even though he recognises them. There are no animals any more. The paintings move him. They make him not able to sleep and if he does sleep he spends the night in the thrall of blood and pale white skin and starched maid's pinafores and dark, cold rooms that don't feel safe.

He wonders how they got there. Did he disrespect her so much that he didn't even catalogue her work properly? He knows they are painted by her. Why shouldn't they be? It is her cabinet after all, the special place he keeps for her. They frighten him. The reds become more shadowy in each new picture he finds. Each week, an intermixture of blue seems to deepen the coldness of vermilion and scarlet, subtly altering its nature. The active element of the red is gradually disappearing, the inward glow increasing; crimson becomes old wine and ruby turns to the last glimmerings of a burgundy dusk.

De Vere is drawn to the glow. Drawn into it. To the silence and the space. The threat.

He sits in the tea room of Claridges, his arm never far from the bottle of champagne resting in the ice bucket. His heart is thumping. It is six years since he set foot in Claridges. He vacated his suite after Cosima died in 1998. He moved back to his old house in Holland Park with the Spike. He hardly dares look around now. The whole of the tea room seems to have turned to sponge cake. The men were always stale but the women at least used to be moist: fruit-filled and soaked in brandy. But now they seem to have dried out, turned into slivers of yokeless sponge. Just stiff whites and air, a little flour. A dusting.

By the time the waitress comes with a pot of tea, Charles Frederick de Vere can already feel the great wave of apathy start to roll in. The sponge particles gather above by the snaky chandeliers like a cumulo nimbus that will rain down on those who have escaped so far and smother them in a cloak of *ennui*. He has come to dread luxury. The butter and the cream of it all. Thick and oozing and slow. Always withered freshness. The lips go first. Lips that tremble if deprived of bone china cups with sides as thin as wafers, brains that are lulled to sleep by the gurgle of tea, the whiteness of linen, the piplessness of jam, the warm air everywhere.

It would be easy to disappear into the softness. A tempting idea but he stops himself. With a shaking hand he tops up his glass of champagne. He must keep awake. Once you fall asleep you are lost. He must stay vigilant.

He feels more lively once he has drained his glass. Thank God for the champagne. Although he finds that no matter how much he drinks, he is not capable of blotting out what the white alcove sent him this morning. It was clear. She had revealed herself at last. A trace. Insect husks risen to the surface, or the faint outline of a human being. Swimming in a dirty red sea: a black-eyed satyr, a head of glossy curls, a memory of drinks cabinets raided in numerous stately homes.

It had been a sunny morning in the East End. It made the discovery of the painting even more shocking. De Vere squinted at the canvas, wondering if he really did see these things. He staggered back from the alcove, hurled the monstrous apparition across the office, watching in dismay as it impaled itself on a corner of the filing cabinet. He went to stare at the rip with something like regret, finally throwing his head into his hands, although all he could see when he closed his eyes was Sir Philip Lampton. All those years ago.

'Damned fine woman,' Sir Philip thunders, passing de Vere a miniature of a woman with a hooked nose and a gold-brocaded gown. 'Did a lot of good works for the poor. Got a painting of her mother upstairs.'

'Christ,' Ellsworth chuckles when Sir Philip has left the room. 'Let's hope the mother's more of a good time girl than the daughter.' He pours himself a glass of wine from a nearby decanter. 'Alas, knowing Sir Philip, she's not going to be the kind of woman you'd want staring down from the wall at your fashionable London dinner party.'

'She does look rather . . . stiff,' de Vere says, frowning at the miniature.

'Stiff! You could chop wood on that face!'

At that moment, Sir Philip re-enters the room. 'Young rascal!' he roars, giving Ellsworth an affectionate slap on the back. 'Always did have a quick tongue.' He turns to de Vere. 'Drawing cartoons of us all when he came to visit. Couldn't keep his nose out of the wine either!'

He beams at Ellsworth, 'First taste of Mouton '45 in this very room, wasn't it, old son?'

A peal of laughter from the alluring woodland creature.

The snakes in the ceiling of the Claridges tea room twitch over the head of Charles Frederick de Vere. He pulls the wire top from the champagne cork and starts to twist it in his fingers. He turns to the string quartet and watches the black-haired cello player collapse and die on the floor while the waitress flays her with a bunch of thirty red roses. Thorns intact, stamens big as cocks. Blood all over the buttocks and black petals and blood drops on the white skin. She has fur on her inner thighs, a patch of soft feathers. Part bird, part woman. The claws. Sharp claws and tender skin of inner thigh . . .

'More scones, sir?'

'What?'

'Or sandwiches? We've got crab on today.'

De Vere pulls himself together and turns, with a pained expression, to his wife, the Spike. She sits there, limbs like spines, jaw like nutcrackers, jabbing her knife into the cream pot, talking of spas, of the difficulty of getting staff on Saturdays. She has the laugh of a little girl and a finger that she points at you and a spike shoots out. She aims it at the waitress. 'No scones or sandwiches,' she says, revealing a flash of lipsticked teeth. 'Just hot water with lemon.'

She opens de Vere's birthday gift. Fifty-two pearls on a silver string; one for each year of her life. She stabs at the necklace. Little, pecky movements. Fingers small as wishbones. When he'd first introduced her to Ellsworth she'd moved like a bird. She still appears to be draped in the lightest of sponge cake, but underneath there are spikes – a tangle of wire and hooks. A lead shot in a breast of grouse, a needle cluster in an iced bun, a dagger in the bed. Because nothing can ever be perfect: the hair in the cheese, the fly in the soup. Another trial, another cup of suffering. Savages and blacks and people who have unclean corners in their house. The knives begin to whir.

His eyes glaze over and he turns to look at the remaining cakes on the stand. One is stale-looking, a cunt that never had an orgasm. Next to it is an obscene maggot of Danish pastry, sticky and shiny with buttery labial folds. His hand reaches for it, a black crab gauntlet, a chain-mail glove that climbs up inner thighs, nipping at tits, cracking off cherries like nutcrackers. He squashes the pastry in his hand as he turns to watch the dead cellist crawl like ants around the room, pulling her skirt up, shaking her hungry arse at all and sundry. He can smell her. Dirty bitch.

He has to stop.

Filth speeds things up but he knows he cannot carry on like this. The Glitter Gulch, Mary's, Ginger Tiger. He's been to all those places, using as an excuse the tedium of a life of business trips. But it has to stop. Those women bore him anyway. What they offer. Indeed, in the six years since Cosima died, he has proved incapable of finding a substitute. For nearly his whole life, he'd thought that all the windows were sealed tight shut. And then she'd come along and shown him a chink of air. The memory of it still scrambles his senses.

As he wipes his fingers with a napkin, it occurs to him that it is time to summon the lift again. It has been a long time since he used the technique. Not since New York. But since she died, he's only been able to see Cosima in still images. His memories are frozen and he wants to see her move again.

'Too white!' The Spike snaps the box shut. 'The pearls are too white. Who sold you these?'

He takes a scone from the stand, pulls it in two and buries his tongue inside. At least his tongue can hide. It is warm in there, peace and quiet. Ten hundred leagues under the earth, stone on stone lying on his chest.

He jumps in his seat. Tosses the scone to his plate. He must keep alert. Once you fall asleep you never wake again.

'Bill!' he snaps at the waitress with a click of the fingers.

He watches her rush back to the kitchens. He considers how the waitresses have changed since he lived here. Carmen Costello. Poured his best champagne into the plant pots and thought he didn't notice. The chase so exciting, the kill so dull. Nothing more depressing than an awestruck fuck. It was true, she had read a lot about Picasso but she'd obviously never found out that the great artist made all his women read the Marquis de Sade.

He sits back in his chair, frowning. A talented secretary, though.

The best he'd ever had. It was Carmen Costello who helped make him what he is today. A twenty-three-year-old Mexican American from the rough end of Boston making an honest man of him. He smiles.

Happier memories trickle into his mind, but then Ellsworth's black eyes bob to the surface. He'd had to curtail his working relationship with Carmen at the end of that hot summer, nearly twenty-five years ago. He'd had to leave London and go far away to New York. But of course he couldn't escape. You never can from these things, he supposes – the most unlikely of people can have a conscience. Cosima's death six years ago must have been the catalyst. Her suicide must have caused the dramatic circumstances of 1981 to gradually open up inside him, like a malignant black bud that can't be dormant any more.

Cosima's death in the early spring of 1998 had set off a chain of events. Summer Crest Hall burned down. He moved the Spike back to Holland Park. He quit his suite at Claridges. And yet, he now sees that there are passions he has still to catch up with, rot he has neglected for too long.

He thinks back to the Andy Warhol party in New York. To the young artist who'd first told him about the lift. The Le Mesurier Meditation Technique.

'It's like mind control, Freddie. It heightens your levels of inner peace, you know? It can heal the deepest emotional dysfunction. Take my word, man. They even say it evolves your untapped ESP . . .'

So many promises. At first, de Vere thought it sounded like so much American nonsense. The Le Mesurier Meditation Technique was on the radar of all fashionable New Yorkers in the early eighties along with Brooke Shields and 'Gay Cancer'. Fashion designers and film producers and ex-models were all taking the course.

And yet it turned out to be a lifesaver during that terrible autumn of 1981. At the core of the technique was creative visualisation: you take the lift to the basement, you walk along the corridor and you turn into your room. You can talk to anyone you like down there. Dead or alive. You summon them to the chair in front of you. You got things off your chest, put your life back in order. It was true that the technique brought him considerable inner peace, and yet he was afraid to stay down in the basement for too long. He talked to his father sometimes, his mother came. But there were people he always kept out of the room. Sometimes he thought he'd seen a shadow of Ellsworth hiding behind the door but he'd never let him come any closer. Not Cosima either.

And yet he can't go on like this.

A young man with dark hair and pale skin comes up to the table carrying a handbag. 'Mummy!' he complains. 'I've been looking for you everywhere!'

The Spike snatches the bag and turns back to de Vere.

'Some lovely Hermès scarves they have here,' the young man goes on. He points to a glass cabinet. 'Do you see?'

The Spike takes no notice so Franck takes out his pad and pencil. He attempts to copy the swirling silk arabesques, smiling as he thinks wistfully back to a world of midnight feasts and dressage lessons outside the tack room.

He is pulled from his reverie by a sharp poke in the back. The Spike is preparing to leave. The birthday tea is over. She flicks de Vere a smile, takes Franck's arm and the two of them hobble towards the revolving doors.

De Vere watches them pass a framed picture. Another painting that started out as love, a smear of shit on a sheet, now embalmed in a tea room scented with flowers that smell like the current of air left by the flopped-down petticoats of a woman kept in too much luxury.

He frowns again.

He crushes the metal wires from the champagne top in his fingers. He drains his glass, composes himself and walks over to the lobby. The sight of a silver deer embedded in the wall makes him stop. Funny, he never noticed it before. Art Deco.

Lithe and impatient. Beautiful. He thinks of Cosima again, although since the paintings, she's always on his mind.

He feels dizzy. Damn champagne.

'Anything the matter, sir?'

De Vere jumps. He sees the concierge standing next to him.

'Nothing the matter, thank you,' he says and walks briskly towards the revolving doors.

Once he is in Brook Street, the cold air refreshes him. There are no signs of the Spike or Franck and he is delighted to recognise one of the liveried doormen.

'Flip!' he exclaims, his face lighting up. 'I haven't seen you in an age.'

'That's right, sir,' says Flip, tipping the edge of his top hat. 'Not since the good old days.'

'I have been rather a stranger.'

'That you have, Mr de Vere, sir. Does me a heap of good to see you again.'

De Vere chuckles. He is gratified to see tears well up in Flip's weak blue eyes.

'My dear Flip,' he says. 'You were an indispensable part of the battle plan.'

'Ladies and lolly. Makes the world go round, don't it, sir!'

The two men laugh.

'You'll be wanting a cab, I should imagine, Mr de Vere.'

'You would imagine correctly.'

With that, the doorman steps forward, puts two fingers to his lips and summons a taxi with an impressive whistle. A black cab screeches to a halt and de Vere, relieved that Flip has put the world to rights, digs in his pocket for a tip. As Flip holds the door of the taxi open, de Vere passes him a couple of crisp notes.

'You cut yourself, sir?' Flip enquires, pointing to de Vere's hand.

When de Vere sees the splash of dark red smeared down the side of his thumb, he stumbles into the taxi. He slams the door and is only half aware of the muffled voice of Flip, apologising wildly on the pavement outside.

CHAPTER FIFTEEN

The taxi is slow. The traffic is clogged. Charles Frederick de Vere daren't look at the red mark on his hand. It will be a while before he gets back to Holland Park and he starts to feel something like panic.

She was never good with blood. Even when she grew up into a rather competent artist. She was forever trying to find the right colour. Obsessed with it. At the doctor's for a routine blood test, the nurse had told her that sometimes, when there wasn't enough haemoglobin to turn it red, you got pink blood.

'She says it looks like fizzy drink in a test tube, Dog. Like bubble gum water!'

And yet she never managed to pin it down. She tried all the shades but nothing seemed to satisfy her.

'Flesh is so easy,' she'd complain when she came round to the Claridges suite. 'But blood is so hard.'

Sometimes, she thought she might have hit upon something. The right way to do it. She would disappear for days and then there would be a knock at his door and he'd open it to see the misty young woman with the delicate skin. A trace of a smile would be on her lips, but he could tell that she'd failed again. And watching the moon white creature sleeping on his pillow afterwards, he'd wonder what kind of blood might possibly flow in her veins.

He tried to help her forget. He told her the myth of Blodeuwedd, the girl created by the gods from flower pollen. He told her how, after Blodeuwedd murdered her husband, she was transformed into an owl, to haunt the night in loneliness and sorrow, shunned by all other birds.

She needed the trances he offered, the escapes he showed her. At least, that's what he told himself afterwards when she'd left and he was clearing up the suite, hiding the evidence.

She'd lived her childhood as an adult, and it was only when she grew up that she could finally live as a child. And how thrilling he found it. Yet he suspects now that being exciting wasn't enough for her. Or maybe he hadn't realised that the excitement was slowly overwhelming her.

He knows it is time for the lift. The Le Mesurier Meditation Technique has saved him before now. He can go down in the lift and sit for hours in the room if he wishes, stare at the hairs of dust on the slats of a blind. Nobody can disturb him in the room.

He rests his hands on the cold seat of the taxi, closes his eyes and takes a deep breath: one floor, two floors, three, four, five . . . all the way down. The lift is plain and metal. Stainless steel. The darkness grows as de Vere plunges downwards, away from the taxi, away from the chaos of Oxford Street, the blur of bill boards for DVDs and new albums: The Scissor Sisters, The Libertines. Lower and lower he goes . . . six, seven, eight, nine, ten. When the lift reaches the basement it stops. The doors open and Charles Frederick de Vere walks along the dark corridor. A sound of wet concrete on shoes with metal taps. When he comes to the fifth door on the right he stops. He opens the door and goes inside.

The room is plain. There is a desk like a teacher's desk with a high-backed chair behind it and two wooden chairs in front. The brown walls are bare. There is light but it's not clear where it comes from. There is a green couch in the middle of the room.

De Vere wonders who will come today. Sometimes, you don't know who will come. He sees his first wife, Eleanor, lying on the couch. She is surprisingly friendly. *Dear Freddie, I have missed you*. He talks to her about London in the Seventies, about the people they knew. She disappears soon after that and he can't say he's sad to see her go.

135

He smiles with satisfaction when he sees his meal waiting for him over on the desk. A pear poached in claret, stuffed with blue cheese. Juniper roasted wild mallard with *pommes de terre Dauphinoises.*

He frowns at the *pommes de terre Dauphinoises.* He closes his eyes and when he opens them he is pleased to see a mound of mashed potato. It's what he used to eat at school back in the fifties. Four or five scoops of the stuff. He needed his energy back then. The maid.

He lights a Lonsdale and puffs at it quickly between two fingers as if he is expecting one of the beaks to apprehend him at any moment. He jumps when he sees that the meal has suddenly disappeared, leaving in its place a tin of baked beans. A whole tin next to a blue-rimmed enamel plate.

He glances round the room but sees no one. He gets up from the couch and goes quickly to sit behind the desk. He waits for a few moments, as if he expects someone to appear in the wooden chair opposite. When nobody comes, he stubs out his cigar, looks back at the empty chair and begins to speak.

What you must understand, Cosima, is that a whole can of beans was too much for one person.

In the beginning, I'd leave the rest of the tin in the fridge but when I came back the next day to find that nobody had stolen it, the horror of my situation sunk in. I was a pariah. I was 'Dog de Vere' or just plain 'Dog'. I was Charles Frederick de Vere, the boy who messed alone.

It was rather unfortunate. My mother had always encouraged me to be honest and so two weeks into my first term I told the Dame that I didn't get on with my allotted messing partner. Finch was nice enough but too much of a swot for my taste. The Dame granted my request but then I found myself messing with Ellsworth, a wiry, faun-like creature whose penchant for sticking compasses into random bodies I had already heard about from the boys who had been at his prep school. When I told the Dame I'd rather not mess with

Ellsworth, she flew into a rage. She declared that as I was so fussy I'd be better off messing on my own for the next four years. Four years.

Messing is supposed to be something to look forward to. We didn't have dormitories; each boy had his own tiny room consisting of a bed, a chair, a desk, an ottoman and a fireplace from the time he arrived at the age of thirteen to the time he left at eighteen. But during mess time you could enjoy camaraderie with another boy. Every evening from 4.45 to 5.45 you returned to your house and met up with your messing partner – either in his room or your own. You both made a light supper in the kitchen and then you went back to the room where you did what you wanted before regrouping at 5.45 for prep and then bed.

I never got used to messing alone. The loneliness got larger rather than smaller. I tried my hand at drawing because I'd heard you could lose yourself with paper and pencil. I'd sketch away for hours, concentrating on one cup, one book, a lone shoe. But my drawings were mediocre; they were precise, tight. I soon realised how foolish I had been to denounce Ellsworth. I confess, I developed rather a crush on him. He reminded me of some nocturnal sprite with his black curly hair and his enamel black eyes and a small mouth that seemed to twitch with spite.

He wasn't a scholarship boy but his shirts were always slightly off-white, there was grime under his nails and he got his uniform second-hand from Tom Brown tailors in town. And yet he was the most glamorous person I had ever met. He'd saunter to class as if he were approaching a social event he didn't much care for and then something would amuse him and he'd spring to life, bringing the whole world with him. He was at his most exciting when he had a pen in his hand. A streak of madness would flash through his eyes and he'd draw a brilliant caricature of whichever beak was teaching us. He'd boast about the phrase, 'able but idle' which inevitably found itself scrawled all over his reports.

I marvelled at Ellsworth's ability to lose himself in pleasure. And he was all the more attractive because he seemed unaware of his

137

talent. It never struck him as odd, for instance, that on the evenings he chose to cook the pigeons he had brought back to school with him, the house kitchen would be completely deserted.

In shooting season, boys would return from Long Leave with braces of pheasants, partridge and grouse that they'd shot on their fathers' estates. The poorer boys would come back with pigeons. The thing to do was to tie one end of a rope around the birds' necks, the other end to your bed post, and then to hang them for a couple of days out of your window. The sight of entire stretches of red-brick wall hanging with dead birds was a bizarre one, but the corpses dangling from Ellsworth's bedroom window were the most macabre of all. He used to hang his pigeons until the heads turned green and the bodies fell off. And unlike the other boys, who would usually sell their game to a butcher in town, he even dared cook his.

It was a given that boys would know how to make rudimentary meals during mess time, even though most of us had never had any cookery lessons. At home, when you walked into the kitchen, the cook would immediately stop what she was doing because her job was to listen to what you had to say. Mostly, we lived off beans and scrambled eggs but Ellsworth loved to experiment. Everyone was aware when he'd brought pigeons back to school because when he deemed them sufficiently high, he would clean them, pluck them and cook them, gradually filling the whole of our house with the hot vapours of putrefying blood.

Ellsworth was endlessly hungry for sensation and whether it was pain or pleasure, he didn't seem to mind. He would initiate games of naked midnight cricket in the summer half, or invite boys back to his room, letting his blood into a beer glass and inviting them to help him drink it. At the beginning of the second half he invited me to a communal wank session but it was a disaster. The other boys seemed to have choreographed the whole ritual and I didn't know the steps. I lost my head and my erection and my memory culminates with Ellsworth, tugging away with a manic smile, jeering: 'Dog without a bone! Dog without a bone!' until all the other boys joined in and I slunk out of the room determined to erase Ellsworth from my thoughts once and for all.

But I could never avoid him completely. I'd bump into him at Chambers, in Divs, by the river, in the kitchen. I'd find myself with a group of boys who'd beg him to re-tell the story of how his grandfather had turned bird excrement into gold. He'd throw his hands dramatically into the air before finally agreeing to explain how, even when the Summer Crested Owl became extinct, Sir Josiah hadn't given up the ghost (hence his family motto: *Dum Spiro Spero* – while I breathe, I hope).

He would inform the crowd of admiring faces that Sir Josiah soon realised how the dowdy birds of Sombrero Island could be even more precious than the exotic ones.

'Bugger pretty feathers!' Ellsworth would chuckle. 'Bird shit was where the money was!'

The Peruvian locals called it 'guano' and it was like a miraculous fertiliser. With no rain, the nitrates never washed out. Victorian Europe and America couldn't get enough of it.

'He went to oversee the crap harvest every year. Fifty metres deep in some places. Had Spiks chipping it off the cliffs!'

We would roar and Ellsworth would add how his grandfather's guano was shipped to Liverpool, Antwerp, Hamburg and Bordeaux. How, even though it was known as the 'dirty trade', Sir Josiah was treated like a god and the natives of Sombrero would adorn him annually with the Summer Crest head dress of honour.

It was only in 1910, when a German company discovered a way to produce fertiliser synthetically, that his luck ran out. We learned that Sir Josiah's only son, Bertie, had neither the talent nor the strength of character to make wise investments with the considerable wealth his father had accumulated.

'By the time I was born, Pa had frittered the lot away,' Ellsworth would conclude with a wanton shrug of the shoulders. 'An empire of dirt spent on casinos in Monte Carlo and tarts in Shepherd's Market!'

It impressed me that Ellsworth would reveal such intimacies, that he seemed willing to go to the very tip of the gangplank just to see what was at the end of it. He seemed almost disappointed

139

when nobody pushed him over the edge, so he took to making his own dangers. He got into scrounging, swapping – he had the best wine and the best 'sock', as we called 'tuck', of anyone in our house. And then there were his scrambled eggs. I'd try to remain inconspicuous as I watched him put three eggs into a bowl and use the white of a fourth. He'd whisk them up, put them in a pan and thirty seconds before they were ready, he'd take them off the heat and stir in the remaining yolk so that the finished dish would look golden and succulent.

I kept Ellsworth's scrambled eggs to myself. Even when I found myself alone in the kitchen I'd never dare make eggs as splendidly as he. But when I went back to my room I'd think of them as I lay on my bed. When I closed my eyes I was swimming in yolk, it was all around me, all under me – it became warm, slippery air that glistened like the black curls on Ellsworth's head. And soon I wasn't in the yolk, I was the yolk. Except I was hard too. I was hard and soft.

One night I dreamed of a hooded figure in a black cloak who was beckoning me. I knew it wanted to touch my cock and I felt compelled to go towards it. I moved so close that I got a glimpse of an elfin face inside the hood and then the figure ripped back its cape and I saw with horror that it was Death. I woke in a spasm, ejaculating all over the sheets. (Due to my segregated status, it was not until some time later that I discovered this was known as a 'wet dream'.)

For four years, I lay suspended in time, spreadeagled on the bed. The free-falling eventually came to an end and I started to live in caverns under the sea. Each night I'd hide under the bedclothes and make myself go further down. I imagined deeper and deeper: ten feet, twenty feet, a hundred feet, three hundred, a thousand. A tiny confined space with the weight of the earth on my back. It was dark and frightening. I couldn't take it every day. Sometimes I'd wake up, breathless. But I made myself go back. I always made myself go back. I was in training. Making myself stronger.

And then, one day, my life changed. It was the first day of third half and I'd just turned seventeen. It was lunchtime and I was sitting stoically at the refectory table, preparing for another interminable eight weeks in my own company, when I became aware of softness on my back and a smell of what I can only describe as femininity. It was a fullness, a seductive pressure different from that of the fat, whiskery dames who normally served us food in the dining hall. A forearm appeared holding a serving spoon piled high with mashed potato. It was a young arm. Naked. And such slender wrists.

When I turned round I saw the bosom of a girl straining from behind a starched white pinafore. She had a ponytail of blonde hair and she looked about my age. She was smiling at me. I turned back to my plate in shock.

It was as quick as that. I was suddenly a hero. I was 'Freddie the Fox', the chap who knew how to get his leg over. For the first time in my life I experienced the thrill of power. Life was suddenly good. My skin became clearer and my tight drawings became larger.

'Our little secret,' Dorothy called it, although it didn't remain a secret for very long.

'Go on Foxy,' the other boys would say. 'Let us have a go!'

Most boys of my age had very fumbly beginnings with the opposite sex but it wasn't like that for me. Dorothy was as up for it as I was. I spent hours in bed with her, inspecting parts, using the names. It began a lifetime obsession with sex although it took me years to realise that the more pleasure you give a woman the more you'll get back. Still, it was extraordinary. Her bedroom was even next to mine. She'd rap on the wall at 11 p.m. and in I'd go.

She was from Croydon. She was what we'd call, 'downstairs material', but she was game. I used to buy her little presents. Perfume. Some jewellery. Screwing a bunch of public-school toffs. She couldn't believe her luck. When I told her about Jefferson and Davies, she agreed to see them as well.

The height of my glory came the night Ellsworth invited me to his room.

'Come in, Dog,' he said, flashing me a smile. 'Come and taste victory!'

He was holding a bottle of wine. On the label I could see a large

letter 'V', a golden laurel and the words: Mouton Rothschild 1945
– *L'Année de la Victoire*.

'They blather on about Château Pétrus,' he said, starting to open the bottle. 'But the day before I go to hell I shall drown my sorrows in a bottle of Mouton '45.'

When he'd pulled the cork out, he smelled it.

'Still a trace of death,' he said, tossing it into the fire. 'Dirty bandages. A burning Jew or two.'

He filled a glass, held the dark liquid up to the light then closed his eyes and brought it to his nose. As he inhaled, his lips twitched and I watched arousal seep slowly into his face. He seemed surprised to see me standing there when he opened his eyes again. He poured me a glass and we both drank.

My stupor at the richness of the taste was heightened by the fact that there was something almost disgusting about the wine.

'Horrible, isn't it,' Ellsworth said, his eyes filled with glee.

'Funny that they call it victory wine,' I observed.

'Why funny?' He frowned. 'Why should victory be a pleasant flavour?'

He filled his glass again and proposed a toast to 'The horrifying taste of victory!'

He turned his back on me and went to sit on a chair in front of the fire.

'Pa's stony broke but Ma comes from a family of minor blue bloods who find the idea of a badly stocked cellar utterly inconceivable.'

He stabbed at the flames with the poker.

'They're broke too but they've always kept us going with some excellent clarets. Stroke of luck when Pa got gout last year. Can't touch a drop now!'

A peal of laughter momentarily drowned the crackle of the fire. Ellsworth hadn't invited me to sit down yet. I knew why he'd invited me to see him and, in fact, I'd planned to lord it over him a little. But now, I was feeling confused and the overpowering wine wasn't helping matters.

I hovered around behind him, feigning interest in a picture on his wall, a tattered print of Hieronymus Bosch's *Garden of Earthly Delights*. Ellsworth told me he'd found it in a shop in the Charing Cross Road.

'Too much sweetness bores me,' he explained, finally strolling over to fill up my glass.

He graced me with a purple-stained grin before adding, '*A propos* of which, Dog, when do *I* get to try out the Croydon tart?'

Ellsworth was the only one to dare carry on calling me 'Dog' during those weeks of glory. And of course, he was the one to whom I offered the best conditions. Not that he seemed overly interested in Dorothy. She thought there was something strange about him and admitted that a lot of the time he didn't even screw her, preferring to paint her instead. One time he made a version of Courbet's *L'Origine du Monde*. It was incredible. Almost photographic in its accuracy. I used to think of that painting even as I was fucking her. Ellsworth's cunt.

Then the captain of the house found out what was going on. Someone told him you just had to knock on Dorothy's door then go in and screw her. One evening he organised for the whole house to be out at a debating event so he'd have her to himself. He knocked at her door and announced, 'House Captain here, open up!'

'You what?' she barked.

'I said, "This is the House Captain here", and . . . I'd like to come in.'

'House Captain?' the voice came back. 'Sorry love, Freddie never told me about you.'

That was it. He went straight to the headmaster.

I was sacked. They didn't say 'expelled'. Something too dramatic about expelled. A little *ordinaire*. 'Sacked' sounded nice and casual, like the sloppy toff-English our parents had instilled in us so we didn't stand out from the crowd too much.

'You ain't coming back then?' Ellsworth drawled one day, stretching his muddy shoes on my ottoman. 'Damn bad luck, Dog old chap.'

It wasn't casual, though. It was a devastating blow. The shame was impossible to digest, I was clogged with it. It chugged around my body like coagulated fat. I was sent to a new school in the wilds of Scotland where I was surprised to discover that the biggest humiliation was the shorts. I had been used to wearing bespoke trousers and now that I was nearly eighteen years old, I was forced to expose my legs. I could put up with most of the inconveniences at the new place: having to sleep in a dormitory, not being treated like a little gentleman any more. A face scrubbed red with coal tar soap, the endless sport and the cold. But the shame of wearing shorts. Like a skirt.

I buckled down for my father's sake. Apart from the night when I ran away. I caught a train to Glasgow and ended up in a coffee bar. They were new in those days. Formica tables and ketchup and a juke box. I'd never seen a juke box before. A boy with grease in his hair put a coin in and I heard Elvis sing 'Blue Suede Shoes'. So exciting. 1956.

Before you were even born, Cosima.

That was when I felt myself expanding. I thought of shiny corners, the thrill of skin, the feeling of wind blowing through my hair: adventure. A coffee bar, chips and a song. It gave me strength, you see.

CHAPTER SIXTEEN

When I told my father I wanted to be an art dealer, he said, 'I thought all art dealers were Jewish or homosexual. You, to my knowledge, are neither.'

But I was twenty-one and he thought it was time for me to start earning a living. So he had lunch at his club with a couple of friends from the House who told him there were only two galleries of any worth. One was a place in Bond Street specialising in Impressionist paintings. It was called Sévigné and was run by an acquaintance of theirs, a Mr Stanley Cheeks.

And that was how I ended up spending one week of every four at the Hotel Bristol in Paris. The year was 1959 and I would accompany Mr Cheeks to Paris and arrange a series of meetings with the aim of procuring paintings at a good price. At 10 a.m. we'd have a meeting with a quick-witted dealer without a gallery – known as a runner – who would show us a Degas ballet rehearsal. He'd tell us it was from a private collection in Lyon which had never been seen and that it could be ours for £30,000. Two hours later we would go to a *hôtel particulier* off the Champs-Elysées to see a 'collector' who would show us exactly the same Degas ballet rehearsal. He would assure us it had never been seen by the public, that it was a masterpiece and that it could be purchased for £40,000. An hour later we'd go back to the Bristol for a meeting with another runner who would have the same ballet rehearsal to show us. Naturally it had never been seen by the public, it was a jewel among Degas masterpieces and this time it could be purchased for £50,000.

I would spend the rest of the afternoon tracking down the original runner and trying to work out whom the Degas really belonged to.

It was a relief to be in Paris after my shame with the maid. Back in England I was still invited to country houses for the balls but the mothers made clear that I was NSIT: Not Safe In Taxis. In Paris, I felt like an adult for the first time in my life. The Bristol was done out in French Empire style which is designed to make it seem as if a duke lives there. My junior room measured ten foot by twelve and the window looked out on to a wall, but there were gilded mounts on the desk and a bed that looked as though it had been made for a grand château. I bought a pair of blue jeans and a pair of gym shoes and after an early dinner with Mr Cheeks I'd spend evenings in cavernous night clubs that played Sidney Bechet and Django Reinhardt, drinking gallons of cheap wine and gyrating the night away with girls who were a lot more liberated than the ones I'd met in England. I'd become friendly with the night porter at the Bristol. He was always reading *Paris Match* and if I came in late at night with a girl, he'd pull the magazine closer to his face and pretend he hadn't seen me.

The following year, I made friends with a rather sombre French couple, Emile and Jacqueline. They liked to practise their English on me and one day a friend of theirs called Benoît came to join us at our café table. Emile and Jacqueline always introduced me as the English boy who'd been expelled from school for having sex. Benoît found it amusing that I could have been punished so severely for heterosexual sex while boys who committed buggery were merely flogged by the headmaster and allowed to stay.

I warmed to Benoît immediately. He was a little older than us, in his early thirties, and obsessed with the idea of *le chic anglais*. He told me that he was throwing a party to celebrate his second wedding anniversary and that he wanted the men to dress like English gentlemen. When he said he was considering evening black tailcoat, I tried to dissuade him. As you know, Cosima, evening black tailcoat is the highly formal costume worn for state banquets or adopted by gentlemen attending the Scottish Highland Balls who are unable, by nationality, to wear a kilt.

But Benoît was convinced it was the most romantic attire a man could possibly wear, and so I tried to answer his questions as best I could.

'How is the black coat looking?' he wanted to know, taking a pen from his pocket.

'An evening tailcoat is twin breasted,' I told him. 'And *never* fastened, even though there are three buttons on either front.'

'It is the same as a morning coat?'

'Certainly not. A morning coat has straight sides and is single-breasted with one button which *does* fasten.'

He made a note on a napkin. 'And a white waistcoat is necessary, *n'est-ce pas*?'

'A cummerbund is a possible alternative to a waistcoat,' I suggested. 'Remember that it's not good to have the waistband on trousers showing.'

'*Ah bon*. A belt is possible?'

'Never a belt, always braces. But the braces must never show.'

He nodded.

'And a watch in the waistcoat pocket,' I said. 'A gentleman feels undressed without a watch-chain in his pocket.'

I added that the white shirt must be stiff-fronted and wing-collared, that there must be no buttons on it, only gold studs and cufflinks, and that patent black shoes must be worn at all times.

'And the bow-tie?'

'White *piqué*.'

I leaned towards him.

'And no clip-ons, old man.'

He thanked me profusely and invited me to his party. When he'd left, Emile explained that Benoît was an artist who had recently become very successful. He made a lot of money, liked to spend a lot and his *soirée* was likely to be *trés amusante*.

They were right. When I arrived at Benoît's huge apartment on the rue Saint Honoré I saw that the men had all adhered to his strict dress code, with some even sporting top hats and black cloaks. Luckily, the girls had been left to their own devices and I found myself sitting next to a captivating redhead whose outfit I do not recall but whose manner reminded me of a Klimt *femme fatale*. The evening passed in a golden blur that was only interrupted when Emile and Jacqueline came up to me at midnight and Emile said, 'It's time for us to go now.'

I said, 'Must you?'

He replied, 'No, we must all go.'

I couldn't think what he was talking about. Things had just started to hot up. They were starting a game of musical bullfights in one corner of the room and there was already talk of going upstairs for '*l'autre fête*'.

'This is not a place for you now,' Jacqueline insisted. She annoyed me. Who was she to accuse me of being square? Besides, many of the guests were in the art world. I might actually learn something, make some contacts. Mainly though, I reckoned that my chances were good with the *femme fatale*.

'I think it's a very good place for me,' I said, surprised at my rudeness.

'Freddie,' Emile sounded quite stern. 'Please will you come with us now. I do not like to leave you here.'

'Really Emile, you are very kind but I am old enough to decide when to leave a party.'

I must have sounded very arrogant. But I didn't care.

'So be it,' Emile snapped, turning on his heels and leaving the room, closely followed by Jacqueline. I turned to a young girl draped in a feather boa who had come to sit on the lap of the Klimt redhead.

'Some people don't know how to enjoy themselves,' I said.

'*Pas grave*,' she said flirtatiously, introducing herself as Benoît's wife. 'All the more fun for us!'

People started to go up a narrow staircase in single file. When I saw my Klimt friend and Benoît's wife following them, I grabbed a bottle of whisky and went too. After two flights of stairs, the men and women separated: girls went to the left and men to the right. Naturally, I tried to go to the left but a plump girl with short hair informed me, '*Mais non*! It's that way for you.'

I started to protest but I felt a hand on my arm and the next thing I knew I found myself in a large room sparkling with gilt-edged mirrors and crystal chandeliers. There was a scratchy American jazz record playing and a cluster of men lounging round a drinks cabinet on an elegant array of furniture.

A young boy had entered the room just in front of me and I watched one of the men get up from his chair and go over to offer him a glass of champagne. The man watched the boy drink until suddenly he grabbed his hair, confiscated the champagne and kissed him full on the lips. When he let him go, the boy didn't run away. He stared defiantly back as the man touched his pale cheek in a gesture that was half-slap, half-stroke. Then the man began to pull the boy's starched shirt open, revealing the bloom of young, naked skin.

The record had stopped. The only sound in the room was of gold shirt studs raining down on to the parquet floor. Others approached. Soon there were groups of men kneeling on the ground, white shirts skimming naked buttocks, hands and mouths over groins and thighs, fingers up arseholes, stiff cuffs and saggy scrotums, strips of firm flesh spread on velvet couches, half-fucking, half-fighting, to groans of, 'Putain . . .' and supplications of, 'Oui, monsieur, je vous en prie . . .' from boys with cherubic faces and twisted mouths running with streams of piss.

I slipped behind a curtain with the whisky bottle. I'd never come across grown-up homosexuals before. If this had happened now, I would naturally have joined in. I like nothing better than to be a stranger among groups of people who are getting into their own thing. At Claridges once, I found myself in my suite with someone I'd mistakenly believed to be a woman and it hardly mattered.

But that evening in Paris, I mistook my excitement for fright. I spent the night hidden behind the curtain, drinking myself into oblivion, occasionally peeking out at the filthy collage of glistening cocks and clawing hands, and the wooden floor covered in pools of semen and clip-on bow ties.

I was woken in the early hours when the curtains were suddenly ripped back. My eyes focused on a pair of hairy thighs, and when I looked up I saw that they belonged to Ellsworth.

*　　*　　*

149

The thumping of my head almost dulled the shock of seeing him again. Ellsworth himself showed no signs of embarrassment. Looking now at the subdued battlefield in front of me, I realised that I was the only person in the room wearing any clothes. I blushed.

'It's the Dog!' he exclaimed. 'Back in his kennel!'

His eyes were gleaming. I hadn't seen him for over four years and he'd grown even more delicious-looking than I remembered. We were both twenty-two now, and while he was still lean, he'd become more muscular. The curly black hair was radiant under a slick of pomade and his mouth had a new redness to it. Half-man, half-boy, half-beast, I thought, watching him play with a glass phial in his hands. The glass suddenly snapped and the air filled with an overpowering smell of dirty socks. He brought the broken phial to his nose and as he took a fierce snort, I watched his black eyes turn blacker and his smile contort into a beatific grimace.

'Bloody good stuff, Dog,' he panted. 'Take you to Never-Never Land!'

And so I waited outside in the cold for the Lost Boy to emerge. When he did, an hour later at ten past four in the morning, he was bristling with life.

'Bloody starving, Dog!' he exclaimed. 'How about you?'

'Actually . . .'

'Let's go to the Pied de Cochon. Only place you can get a decent meal at this hour.'

He was wearing a shabby, ill-fitting tuxedo that looked as though it had come from a cheap hire shop. He didn't seem surprised at seeing me again. Nor did he comment on the fact that he appeared to have spent the night having sex with a room full of men. As we walked along the rue du Louvre, he told me how he was studying at the Beaux Arts.

'Pa's in his eighties now,' he said. 'Starting to loose the plot. And Ma died. Left me a bit of cash.'

'You'll do well,' I said. 'I remember your stuff from school.'

'Bloody school,' he scoffed, lighting a cigarette. 'So serious.' He exhaled a mouthful of smoke. 'I know much more now: there's no life after death and we're living in an Absurd universe . . .'

'A what?'

'An ordered delirium, Dog. And the only way of triumphing over it is to find as much diversion as we can.'

'An interesting theory.'

He looked surprised. 'Do you think so?'

I was glad when we arrived at the rue Coquillière and went into a warm, brightly lit *brasserie* tucked behind a row of neatly trimmed bushes. *Ouvert Jour et Nuit,* it said on a flapping red awning outside and even at this early hour, the place was bustling with waiters serving onion soup to market-stall holders from Les Halles and huge platters of seafood to bleary-eyed revellers. The waiters seemed to know Ellsworth and two or three tipsy men wandered up to our table to say hello. I was impressed but not surprised. It seemed completely reasonable that the world should be as seduced by Ellsworth as I had been.

He summoned an older, portly waiter who proceeded to take a plastic pig's nose from his pocket and solemnly strap it to his face. I glanced over at Ellsworth who was looking equally earnest until suddenly, both men burst out laughing and began to congratulate each other. Ellsworth made a theatrical aside with his hand.

'*Cochon,*' he said. 'House speciality.'

Still chuckling, the waiter asked him if he'd like his usual. '*La Tentation de Saint Antoine. C'est ça, Ellsworse*?'

Ellsworth lit a cigarette and waved his hand dismissively. 'Yes, one of those for me, twenty-four *claires* to share with my friend here, a bottle of Puligny Montrachet and a *rouge de la maison.*'

He turned to me. 'You've got a bit of cash, haven't you, Dog? You know how it is with students . . .'

I had no objections to footing the bill. I'd almost expected it. I was about to ask Ellsworth if the Temptation of Saint Anthony he'd ordered had anything to do with the Bosch painting of the same name when he suddenly walloped the backside of a young woman

151

who was walking past our table. She turned furiously but broke into a smile when she saw who it was.

'*Ellsworse*!' she chided. 'You are bad boy!'

'*Mais,* Hortense!' he protested. '*C'est toi qui m'as abandonné*!'

'You are inviting me, *Ellsworse*?'

'Tomorrow, Hortense! Come to my studio.'

'*Peut-être,*' she said, nonchalantly.

I could tell she'd be there.

He blew a line of smoke up to the ceiling and flopped back into his seat. '*Ellsworse,*' he repeated, a languid smile on his face. 'I think my French name rather suits me, don't you?'

'Your French is very good,' I said.

'I have my little helpers,' he grinned, gesturing to an invisible Hortense.

When the waiter brought the oysters and the wine, Ellsworth poured us two glasses each, one of white and one of red.

'You should read some Camus,' he suggested. 'Help you get laid.'

'You think?'

'Everyone loves Camus. When his car crashed into that tree in January, they loved him even more.'

He smiled, dipped his finger into his glass of red wine and made a deft cartoon of a coiffed King Charles Spaniel on the linen table-cloth. 'Laughing myself into the grave,' he said, looking slyly up at me. 'That's what I'm planning on doing.'

'Good idea,' I said, looking awkwardly at the dog on the table-cloth.

'Idols of mud,' he added, grabbing an oyster and his glass of white wine and downing both in a few gulps. 'That's what Camus called the objects of all pleasure seekers.'

'Well, it certainly looks like you're having a good time, Ellsworth. My life here's much more ordinary.'

His meal arrived and the waiter explained to me that the platter – grilled pig's tail, pig's snout, and half a pig's trotter served with béarnaise sauce and *pommes frites* – was named after Saint Anthony, the medieval patron saint of sausage makers.

When he'd disappeared in a wheeze of laughter, Ellsworth dug his knife into the mustard pot. 'Damn the patron saint,' he muttered. 'You know me, Dog. I'll have whatever Hieronymus Bosch is having.'

Watching him tuck into the food reminded me of the orgy all over again. The first time he stopped for breath was to announce, 'I love oil paint, you know. It never dries. Like blood!'

He picked up the empty bottle of red wine and waved it at our waiter.

'Like monster's blood,' he said, his mouth full.

'Monster's blood?'

'A theory of mine. Medusa. The Gorgon. When Perseus chopped her head off, her blood poured to the ground and turned into the fountain of the Muses.'

'I see.'

'I'm drinking from the fountain, Dog!' he said, taking the new bottle of wine from the waiter and filling up both his glasses. 'And I intend to drink as much as I possibly can. The orgies, the terrible human passions. You know, the full range of earthly delights.'

He mopped up the last of the béarnaise sauce with a piece of bread and pushed his plate away.

'I intend it to be a sort of alchemy,' he said, wiping his mouth with the back of his sleeve. 'If Grandfather Josiah can turn shit into gold, then I can turn filth into great art. Stir the world from its torpor.'

He picked up his glass and swirled it round under the restaurant's dazzling lights.

'Blood, paint, drink. It's all fluid . . . all part of the circulation of . . . things . . . the holy grail . . .'

'The holy grail?'

The long night of debauchery was finally taking its toll on Ellsworth. I suddenly realised that he was quite drunk.

'Being an artist is the ultimate grail,' he slurred. 'Artists live twice, you know. Once in life and once in art.'

He was silent for a few moments, before confiding, 'Alas, my own genius is yet to surface.' He looked down at the tablecloth. 'Although my teachers here tell me I excel at fabric. Apparently, I paint taffeta as if it were "*une rivière en feu*".'

He made a half-hearted laugh and looked up. 'Talking of fire, Dog,' he said, 'my loins seem to have sprung to life. Fancy searching out some fresh mischief?'

I told him that I'd be delighted to. On one condition.

'Which is?'

'No more "Dog",' I said, surprised by my courage.

He burst out laughing. 'Foxy, is it to be? Freddie the Fox?'

'Just plain Freddie will do,' I said with a smile.

He seemed to sober up. He looked me in the eye. 'Freddie it is, then,' he murmured, putting his hand gently on my arm.

The moment passed. He snapped his fingers, I paid the bill and we left the restaurant with Ellsworth nursing another full bottle of red wine under his tuxedo jacket. As we reeled unsteadily in the direction of the rue Saint-Denis, we soon tumbled back into drunkenness, although it did cross my mind to wonder when Ellsworth found time to do any painting.

'I suppose an artist has to work out how to get at the monster's blood without poisoning himself in the process,' I said.

'Yes,' he replied vaguely, his eyes scanning the shadowy doorways. 'It is a conundrum.'

He began digging around in his pocket, swaying as he tried to keep his balance. 'Thing is,' he said, 'I always think there's a better monster just around the corner.' He began waving another of the glass phials in the air. 'I seem to remember you're not averse to a bit of fun!'

Our eyes met but we couldn't hold each other's gaze. Ellsworth looked away and started to talk about that time. It turned out that the other chaps hadn't thought my sacking shameful at all. He told me how I'd become something of a hero after I left. The other boys had thought I hadn't cared about the expulsion, they assumed I'd taken it in my stride. Ellsworth began to sound as if he were in awe of me. He began patting me drunkenly on the back and then there was the sound of glass breaking and a stench floated on to the dawn air.

I was hesitant as he waved the opened phial under my nose, but then he declared, 'It's your own smells that corrupt you, Freddie. Not other people's.'

And so I snorted and then he did and soon we collapsed hysterical into each other's arms. Through snatched gasps of breath, Ellsworth started to talk about Dorothy. How not only had she lost her job at the school, but that she'd been pregnant at the time.

'We had a sweepstake . . . on which of you got her . . . up the duff!' He doubled up with the mirth of it all. 'Jefferson claimed it was him . . .' he was panting, trying to get his breath back, '. . . certainly wasn't me!' Another explosion. Tears ran down his cheeks.

The rue Saint-Denis started spinning. I felt sick. I wondered if the child was mine. I wondered what would happen to it. Ellsworth raised the broken glass phial into the air. 'I propose a toast,' he slurred. 'To derring-do and dirty sex!'

I hated him then. Thought him low and cowardly. He frightened me too. And I didn't want to be frightened any more. That was all from the old days. From school.

I left him negotiating a price with a prostitute.

'Another vision of hell coming up!' he shouted after me. 'With any luck, eh Freddie?'

And yet I couldn't deny that it was amusing to discover Paris with Ellsworth. We usually met in the Latin Quarter. He knew the best bars and *boîtes* and every evening he was surrounded by groups of fresh lackeys, new admiring faces, urging the defiant genius to further feats of *outrance*. My instinct told me to keep a safe distance, but luckily Ellsworth was usually tight by midnight, enabling me to sneak back to the Hotel Bristol without my absence being noticed.

Apart from one evening. It was my twenty-fourth birthday and Ellsworth had persuaded me to stay out later than usual. I'd drunk rather more cheap champagne than was wise and yet when we finally emerged from the bar on the rue des Beaux Arts, he announced that the night was still young and did I fancy going to his studio to pick up a little 'sustenance'?

The invitation almost sobered me up. Although I'd known Ellsworth in Paris for two years by now, he'd never invited me to his studio. I slurred that I'd be delighted to accompany him and we soon wobbled through the gates of his art school, zig-zagged across a stone court-yard and ascended a flight of creaky wooden steps until we arrived at a corridor lined with doors. Ellsworth unlocked one of them and we stumbled into a large room which looked as though it had recently hosted a chimp's tea party. The large paintings propped against the walls were all scrawled with a series of hectic doodles executed in thick brush strokes clogged with lumpy paint. I stood there swaying, trying to take them in as Ellsworth went to rummage through the drawers of his desk. He told me that he sometimes added crushed glass or sand to the paint to make the effect more 'primitive'.

Mr Cheeks had happened to mention only that week that this was a technique employed by the contemporary French painter, Jean Dubuffet. His paintings were fetching good prices in the early sixties, although his strange graffiti and misshapen scribbles weren't to my taste. Sure enough, when I lurched over to Ellsworth, I noticed a crumpled Dubuffet poster on his desk. I was becoming quite mesmerised by the picture's swirl of red, blue, and black cells when Ellsworth slammed a drawer shut. In a voice filled with barely concealed irri-tation, he admitted that he'd been following the French artist's career.

'He believes that mental patients and children are the world's true artists,' he announced, snapping the glass capsule he'd located. 'The less a work of art has been influenced by culture, the more intense it is.'

He took a snort. 'It's important to break free from the burden of technical perfection,' he wheezed.

When I looked back at his homages to Dubuffet propped against the wall, it struck me that the frenzied splurges of paint might easily have been executed by a child but nothing more than that. Still, I didn't claim to be an expert in contemporary art. I felt safe with the Impressionists.

I left Ellsworth to giggle uncontrollably at his desk and went to look at some canvases at the other end of the room. They were very much burdened by technical perfection – and all the better for it. I saw a meticulous record of the effects of late-afternoon sunlight on a piece of faded silk damask. I was struck by the vividness of a shaft of moonlight gleaming on the naked skin of a female shoulder. I could see why Ellsworth's teachers were so impressed by his talent for naturalism. I was keen to see what was under the sheet covering a nearby easel, but the good humour contained in Ellsworth's glass phial seemed to have evaporated. I was suddenly aware of a figure behind me.

'Come on,' he grunted. 'Let's get out of here.'

And yet I didn't concern myself too much with my friend's mood swings or with his efforts to find his artistic voice. The fact was, Ellsworth was just one part of my life in Paris. It had begun to emerge that I had a real talent for something: selling. I listened eagerly to everything Mr Cheeks told me. 'Remember this, de Vere,' he'd say. 'A good salesman will make you buy a picture. An excellent salesman will make you buy two.'

He pointed out that nobody needed to buy paintings and therefore if someone showed the slightest inclination to purchase something, the important thing was to make it fun.

'Chap doesn't care two hoots about the exquisite brushwork,' Mr Cheeks would say. 'Chap wants to remember that Wildenstein wanted a million for it and he got it for £800,000.'

Finding Impressionist paintings in Paris in the early sixties wasn't difficult and Mr Cheeks had taught me what pictures not to buy: no sunsets (too kitsch), no moonlight (too gloomy), no cows (too rural – the exceptions being Aelbert Cuyp and Alfred de Breanski), no *barques echouées* (anyone who likes boats hates to see one stranded at low tide).

Then suddenly everything changed. In 1963, Mr Cheeks died of a heart attack and his successor, Mr Julian, decided that while Paris's art star was waning, New York's was beginning to shine bright. My new job was to come back to London and take care of the Impressionists at the Sévigné gallery while Mr Julian travelled to New York to see what he could find there.

157

I didn't mind staying in England. London was starting to twinkle as well, thanks to a new young chairman at Sotheby's who had introduced the idea of evening sales to complement the traditional, stuffy eleven-in-the-morning slot. The 7 p.m. auction proved a great success, plugging a cultural gap for those who were bored silly by charity galas, yet who found a whole evening at the theatre too demanding. The event soon became renowned for its glamour. There were men in tuxedos, girls in cocktail dresses, wives sporting some serious jewellery and all of it was captured in the atomic sparkle of the paparazzo's camera bulb and served up the following day in the William Hickey gossip column of the *Daily Express*.

I was twenty-five when I came back, and at Mr Julian's suggestion, I got married. I'd been seeing a woman called Eleanor and although the sex wasn't great, I assumed things would warm up after we tied the knot. An added incentive was that Mr Julian had offered me a thousand-pound per annum increase in my entertainment budget if I found myself a conjugal partner. Eleanor's family were comfortably off and we bought a spacious house in Holland Park which was perfect for *soirée*s with potential clients. Fuelled by some very good wine, I might possibly divulge news of a freshly acquired Pissarro to an expectant man and his wife. Eyes would grow large, ardent longing would be professed, but only after cigars and brandy would I turn to the gentleman and soothe, 'With the greatest of respect, my dear fellow, I don't think you're quite ready yet for a work of such importance.'

The gentleman would protest in the strongest of terms and so, with great reluctance, I would lead them both to the drawing room where the painting might be displayed to maximum effect. The wife would announce that it would look even better in their own drawing room, whereupon I might interject: 'Alas, I can't possibly sell a Pissarro to a lady who owns no other Impressionists. The Pissarro would be lonely . . .'

I amused myself in this manner for three more years and then, in the late summer of 1966, Ellsworth reappeared.

CHAPTER SEVENTEEN

He turned up outside Sévigné one morning on a flashy motorcycle. He was wearing a Royal Hussar's cavalry jacket, a purple paisley silk scarf, a pair of beautifully cut trousers and some zip-up Chelsea boots. Everyone in the gallery turned to watch as the outrageously elegant figure removed his crash hat and a mass of thick black curls tumbled down on to his shoulders.

When I hurried outside to greet him, he announced that he was taking me for lunch. 'In Soho, though,' he warned, wincing at the Renoir family picnic displayed in the gallery window. 'Mayfair's not very Pop, is it?'

That was his new thing. Everything had to be Pop. Pop was why he'd left Paris to go and live in America, although the only inkling I'd had of this was an anonymous postcard that had arrived from New York the previous autumn. A baroque swirl of green ink instructed me to: 'Watch the dancing scenes in *What's New Pussycat?*' and concluded: 'Do you think they got my good side?'

The film had just been released and when I went to see it, I was delighted to catch glimpses of Ellsworth doing the Mashed Potato behind Peter O'Toole and a scrum of photogenic girls in a series of entirely unconvincing scenes in a Parisian night club.

'Dreadful movie,' Ellsworth shouted as we pulled up outside a Chinese restaurant on Wardour Street. 'Although it did help me escape Paris.'

We went into the restaurant and a brusque waiter handed us a menu. When he'd ordered us to our seats, Ellsworth began to explain what he'd been up to for the past three years.

'I missed you when you left,' he declared, lighting a cigarette with a rather fancy lighter. 'And then one night I met someone who wanted

159

me to be an extra in this comedy with Peter Sellers. They kitted us out in suits and ties, herded us into that nightclub, Castel's, and told us to pretend we were having a groovy time.'

'Castel's?' I said with a smile. 'Very grand.'

'Yes,' he replied, wearily. 'I ended up getting in with rather a swanky set. Had to leave the seedy jazz dens behind. Still, I met Balthus's son. He's even more idle than me. "You don't have to do anything to be someone," he used to say. "Simply to scintillate is enough."'

Ellsworth clicked his fingers for a waiter.

'So I did absolutely nothing and sure enough, I was soon on speaking terms with Terence Stamp, Salvador Dalí, Françoise Sagan . . .'

A glaring Chinese waiter arrived at our table.

'You order now!' he commanded.

The place was making me feel rather nervous but Ellsworth seemed to relish the theatrically rude service.

'We'd be delighted to order,' he said, addressing the man as if he were an endearing but slightly retarded elderly uncle. He ran his finger slowly down the menu. 'Now then, we want . . . one duck tongue with shredded jellyfish . . . one . . . oh yes, this looks good: one braised pigeon feet with Yee Hang sauce . . .'

The waiter narrowed his eyes. 'You sure you like this?'

'Oh, absolutely,' Ellsworth replied sweetly. '"Sea cucumber and conch hot pot". What do you think, Freddie?'

'Well . . .'

'Yes, I agree. Rather conservative.'

He threw the menu down on the table and blew a line of smoke at the waiter. 'Bring us the pork intestine with sour cabbage instead.'

Our eyes met. Ellsworth hadn't changed at all. He'd brought me to this side of town not through a lack of money – that didn't seem to be a problem any more – but because he was still keen to turn the most banal experience into a reckless adventure.

When the waiter left, he sprawled back in his seat.

'I got bored of scintillating after a while,' he admitted. 'I started dreaming of rolling around in the mud. But you know how stuffy

Paris is. It wasn't until I got to New York at the end of '65 that I discovered . . .'

He glanced round at the restaurant's greasy walls, the worn carpet, the murky water feature at the back of the room. '*Le* low life,' he whispered. 'Or rather, the high life *and* the low life. Anything but the straight life.'

He brushed some ash from the gold braiding on the spotless blue Hussar jacket and told me how he'd met Andy Warhol and some of his Factory entourage one night at Castel's. They were in France for Warhol's first Paris exhibition.

'Andy pointed out that the French aren't interested in new art — that they'd gone back to liking the Impressionists. That was why he decided to show his flower paintings rather than the Elvises or the soup cans.'

The way Ellsworth said 'Impressionists' made me blush, but he didn't notice. He was busy extolling the virtues of New York which sounded like one big bohemian party. There was Max's Kansas City, a restaurant where sculptors and rock stars and boutique owners mingled with poets and go-go dancers and Hollywood actors; there were the girls in the streets humming 'Get Off Of My Cloud' as they strutted along in fur mini coats with no stockings or underwear underneath. Best of all, it seemed, were the weekend acid trips on Fire Island.

'A friend of mine from the Factory, Silver Tony, warned me that they put acid in your food. So to start with, I only drank tap water and ate sealed chocolate bars.'

His eyes lit up as a curious selection of broths and noodles arrived at the table.

'But then I decided to go with the flow. LSD connects you with rebirth, life after death . . . it's incredible, Freddie.'

His enthusiasm made me smile.

'New York's the place to be. I mean, art is dead in Europe.'

'What about Dubuffet?'

He shrugged. 'I didn't do a lot of painting in New York. Pop art's all about the disposable, the surface. Who needs profundity?'

161

It was only when the waiter slammed the bill down at the end of our meal that he mentioned how his father was seriously ill at his pile in Gloucestershire and that this was the reason he'd returned to England. When I expressed my sympathy, he shrugged again. 'Probably good for me to hole up in the country for a bit,' he confessed. 'Life *was* becoming rather fast.'

Naturally, it wasn't long before the charms of country life began to pale. Ellsworth started coming down to Bond Street to visit me at Sévigné, leaving his sister, Lady Merriwether Frost, to play nursemaid back in Gloucestershire. He wanted things to be like they had been in Paris but when I tried to explain about my changed circumstances — about my marriage, the demands of my job — he didn't take any notice. He started lavishing me with presents: platinum cufflinks, an eighteenth-century opium pipe. Lots of things I didn't need.

It wasn't suprising that he started to look for new distractions. He soon discovered that London wasn't so boring after all. Not only did it have its very own Factory in the form of a notorious art gallery in Duke Street, but it also possessed a home-grown Andy Warhol, a young man known in fashionable circles as 'Way Out Eddie'.

Way Out Eddie was actually a flamboyant art dealer who'd become infamous for daring to exhibit British and American pop artists such as Richard Hamilton, Peter Blake and Ed Ruscha. Like Warhol, Way Out Eddie had gathered about him a coterie of people from both the *beau-* and the *demi-mondes,* as well as cultivating an appearance that singled him out from the crowd. He was tall and thin with a penchant for elegant suits and he had the demeanour of a high-society pimp. Rumour had it that the dark glasses he habitually wore served to hide the effects of the large quantity of drugs he consumed, including the more *recherché* ones of the 1960s: heroin and cocaine.

Funnily enough, he'd been at school with both Ellsworth and me. His real name was Edward Hastings, but back in those days Ellsworth had christened him 'Stink' because of the French cologne he insisted on wearing — Caron's Tabac Blond. He was a year older than us and in a different house, but you couldn't miss him. He was an insufferable show-off and could usually be spotted pouring over *Vogue* or the social diary of *Tatler* in Howard Roberts, the chic place to have your cup of cocoa and your club sandwich in Eton High Street.

Ellsworth considered Stink to be a social climber, indicating that although his father was a successful banker, his grandfather had been the butler to a department-store magnate.

'Old Stink's been chatting me up again,' he drawled one evening as he emerged from his session with Dorothy. 'I think he's angling for an invitation to the haunted house.'

I too was keen to visit Ellsworth's family seat although, as yet, nothing had been said about it.

'Will you ask him up?' I wondered.

Ellsworth snorted as he pulled the cork from a new bottle of wine. 'Why should I?' He jerked his head in the direction of Dorothy's bedroom door. 'It's not as if he can bring me anything.'

And yet, as 'Way Out Eddie', Hastings was in a position to bring Ellsworth rather a lot. Artistic recognition and a glamorous new social circle to start with. Although that didn't stop me having bad feelings about him.

'But it's important for an artist to have his work shown in a good gallery,' Ellsworth reminded me when we next met for Chinese in Wardour Street. 'For the same reason that Yves Saint Laurent doesn't sell his clothes from a counter in Woolworths. You of all people know that, Freddie.'

I had to concede that Hastings did have an excellent eye for art and there was something undeniably stylish about his Duke Street gallery. Perhaps I was just jealous. Now that he was courting London's contemporary art world, Ellsworth seemed to have little time for me. I, who'd been so proud of my entertainment allowance, now felt decidedly square next to Ellsworth. Cowardly too. My theory that Eleanor would warm up in bed had proved unfounded. Sometimes I convinced myself that if I'd stuck things out in Paris, spread my net a bit wider, then I could have been as fulfilled as Ellsworth.

And yet, in my heart, I knew that I didn't want to be like Ellsworth. When we did manage to meet up, I noticed that he was getting thinner and paler and all he could talk about were the Duke Street parties. His monster's blood seemed to come in powdered form these days.

'I've been snorting lines of coke and heroin together, Freddie!'

'Now, Ellsworth . . .'

'Oh, don't worry. Nothing low life about it. It's never cut.'

I still found him irresistible.

'It's all very Sherlock Holmes,' he insisted. 'And what's good is that it makes you feel so euphoric that you don't need to drink for the whole evening. So it's quite economical and healthy in a way.'

I was flattered when he invited me to one of the parties. I didn't even mind when he insisted beforehand on taking me to Mr Fish off Savile Row to be fitted up with a suitable outfit. I was soon the owner of a green velvet jacket with a Nehru collar, which I must say I was rather pleased with. It gave me a taste for velvet jackets that has lasted throughout my life. It was only a shame that Hastings' party didn't fill me with the same enthusiasm. My memory is of everyone sitting round like zombies trying to appear relaxed. I found the whole affair incredibly unfriendly.

But Ellsworth's mind was set and I just had to bite my tongue. Hastings and Ellsworth did, after all, have a lot in common: chiefly, a disregard for authority and the opinion of others. I convinced myself that the gentleman junkie would be good for Ellsworth if he could promote his work in any way. Indeed, I suspected that my friend's art was already taking off; cash never seemed a problem any more.

Towards the end of 1966, Hastings invited Ellsworth to Tangier for Christmas. He wanted to let off some steam after his prosecution for staging an allegedly obscene exhibition of work by the artist Jim Dine. I decided to be positive. I told Ellsworth that the harsh sunlight and the rich textures of Morocco would inspire him. I even made myself start thinking of Hastings as 'Eddie', just as Ellsworth did. And my friend did seem to have his eyes open. He explained that he wouldn't be staying with Eddie, that he was going to rent a crumbling old place in the Kasbah which, according to Silver Tony from The Factory, had once been Francis Bacon's bolt hole.

And so, at the beginning of December, after our final lunch in Wardour Street, I wished Ellsworth a bon voyage and he patted me on the back and told me to 'Cheer up!' He tapped the side of his nose and said he had good reason to believe that he'd have a show at Duke Street before the following year was out.

When I received a postcard a couple of weeks later, I started feeling rather optimistic myself:

Painting away furiously in my studio — mint tea, kif and the queeny shriek of peacocks my only distractions. Some of Eddie's friends (especially one brazen English playwright and his long-suffering boyfriend) are very amusing. Start bidding for my memoirs now . . .

Fondly yours, Ellsworth.

And yet when he returned to London at the beginning of 1967, I could see that something was wrong. He looked paler than I'd ever seen him and his eyes were edged with dark circles. I only knew he was back in London because he appeared one morning at Sévigné wearing a filthy white shirt. I remember it was February because the papers were filled with news of a drugs bust at the home of one of the Rolling Stones. Eddie's name was mentioned. I asked Ellsworth if he was all right but he just mumbled that he was rather 'bummed out'. When I inquired about the holiday in Tangier he started twitching. 'Too many flies,' he said, scratching at the dirty shirt. 'Too many flies all round, Freddie.'

He didn't stay long, although he came back the following week. He started coming by quite often for manic periods of five or ten minutes before stumbling out of the door and disappearing into Bond Street. I got the impression that he wasn't seeing Eddie any more, although the Duke Street drugs had merely been replaced by alcohol from his sick father's cellar. As the weeks went by he started to look

165

puffy and I noticed that his fingers were stained with nicotine. Most days when he came in, I'd have to hurry him out of the back door before one of the clients saw him.

Things didn't get any better as the year went on. In May, Edward Hastings was sentenced to six months' imprisonment for possession of heroin. In August, Ellsworth learned that the playwright he had met in Tangier had been bludgeoned to death by his boyfriend in the couple's Islington flat. By the time his father finally passed away that Christmas, he seemed at the end of his tether.

In the new year of 1968, he came to Sévigné with a present: a bell jar containing a stuffed owl with a crown of brightly coloured feathers. It was one of the rare times of late that I'd seen him sober and I was touched by the gift. I assumed the bird was one of those his grandfather had caught on Sombrero Island. When I protested that he couldn't possibly give me such an heirloom, he shook his head.

'This is the last vestige of success in my family,' he said, looking into the jar. 'All gone now. You're the most victorious person I know.'

I told him not to give up. I suggested that his creativity might help him through this rough patch.

'Creativity,' he spat. 'I'm tired of this fantasy of the inspired artist. An artist's life is deathly. You're always trying to re-invent every experience: where can I use that? Or, How can I convey this? Or, What's the point of being at this boring dinner if the person next to me isn't bringing me anything?'

He lit a cigarette.

'Remember, when I told you that being an artist was like living twice?'

I said that I did.

'Well, now I think that being an artist is only half a life. Actually, no . . .' He blew out a line of smoke. 'Now I think that artists shouldn't exist at all!'

He made a bitter laugh. 'God and I are alike, you know, Freddie. We're both artists.' He gestured towards the street. 'And look at the bilge *he's* come up with!'

166

His eyes were watering from the smoke.

'It's not even the pain of creating imperfection,' he said, angrily brushing away a tear. 'I dream of creating imperfection. But everything I make is fucking perfect!'

I decided that a wife would be good for him. So I introduced him to the daughter of one of Mr Julian's Portuguese clients who'd done very well in the hotel business. She'd started doing some modelling.

Eleanor and I threw a dinner in Holland Park and to my surprise, Ellsworth got on rather well with the girl. She was very *gamine*. Rather capricious. He started to clean up his act. He stopped drinking during the day. One morning, he came to Sévigné and told me that he intended marrying her.

'The more tragic one's condition, the more aggressive one's hope becomes. Don't you think, Freddie, old man?'

On 14 February 1969, thirty-one-year-old Ellsworth Stokes married seventeen-year-old Bárbara Vasconcelos de Souza at the Chelsea registry office. The social pages of *Tatler* enthused that the Portuguese heiress was wearing an embroidered Indian dress of the kind favoured by members of the international hippie jet set. Her dashing husband, they noted, was sporting a hat with a pink musketeer plume and his best man was the lead singer of a popular group of the day.

In November of that year they had a baby, Franck. Also in that year I entered a pact I have since regretted for the rest of my life.

CHAPTER EIGHTEEN

But why am I telling you this, Cosima?

Charles Frederick de Vere jerks back in the seat in his under-ground room. He looks lost as he stares at the wooden chair on the other side of the desk.

I suppose I'm trying to explain why I had to leave England so suddenly at the end of that summer of 1981. I want you to under-stand what lay behind my decision to go away. Although God knows, at the time, it didn't feel so much like a decision as an act of self-preservation.

You were a child when I left for New York and an adult when I returned. I was shocked to find that your presence excited me. You offered the thrill of newness and the comfort of familiarity. I fell very deeply in love with you. It was Ellsworth who created 'Dog', but it was only you I allowed to use it. You didn't know how it had hurt me as a boy, and yet after a while it didn't hurt me any more. You gave it new life, you made the word fresh, you imbued it with hope just as you imbued everything in my life with hope . . .

He stands up and glances around the room.

Cosima, are you here?

He hesitates.

Are you all right, Cosima?

He falls back into the seat, throws his head into his hands.

You made me clean and I tarnished you. Please say you forgive me.
I don't know if I can go on if you don't . . .

When he looks up, he sees his father appear in the chair opposite him but he has no wish to talk to his father today. He glares at the old man who vanishes in a puff of smoke.

Cosima! Why don't you come?

He thumps the desk. He closes his eyes and grips the edge of the table until his knuckles are white. Gradually, he composes himself. He opens his eyes, picks up his cigar and lights it again with a trembling hand.

But why should you listen to me? I never listened to you. Not properly. I knew you'd always been charmed by the idea of death. Sucked on it like butterscotch. When you grew up, the taste seemed even sweeter.

'When we were kids, Uncle Ellsworth told Franck and me what happens when you die,' you announced one day as we tumbled into bed. 'When the Cossacks slayed Haji Morad, crimson spurted from the arteries of his neck on to the ground.'

Your lithe body wound its way on to my back and you whispered in my ear, 'The grass got absolutely soaked, Dog!'

I thought you were taunting me. I grabbed you, pulled you down on to the mattress.

'I suppose one must choose a reason to die,' you mused as you wriggled naked under me. 'But the air is always full of reasons at any given moment.'

'Cosima, please . . .'

You quoted me poetry when I was hard.

'"Suicides have a special language,"' you said. '"Like carpenters, they want to know *which tools*. They never ask *why build*."'

I thought you were talking about . . . I didn't think you were talking about yourself. I pulled away from you, but immediately I wanted you back.

We took our turns with control and surrender. Played around with both without the need for words. Yet I always felt you had the upper hand. I was mesmerised by something in your eyes which I wasn't sure how to translate. Sometimes I was convinced you were going to leave me. I didn't for a second think that you had fallen so far . . .

You came looking for me at Summer Crest Hall, that damned house where I went to live with Bárbara after our marriage. A registry office in Gloucester in the late winter of '97. Such a chill in the air. The Spike, you called her. Thank God I still had the suite at Claridges. The place we spent our year of filthy bliss.

Do you remember?

You were furious when I married her. As a child, you were indifferent to your Uncle Ellsworth but you claimed to despise your Aunt Spike. You were happiest when she was away, having one of her flings on the other side of the world. When she was at Summer Crest Hall she was petty, you said. She told Mrs Lacey off for feeding you too much, scolded you for making too much noise.

You thought I was weak for falling into her clutches, but there was no other way. She knew too much. I'd been married to her for less than a month when you rang. Out of the blue. After all those years. We hadn't seen each other since the midnight feast. You were twenty-eight now.

Do you remember the meeting at the National Gallery?

I wonder, if you'd foreseen what was going to be unleashed in us both that day, would you ever have called me?

If you hadn't rung, you might still be alive. At any rate, you wouldn't have spent your last day on earth at Summer Crest Hall. Were you angry with me? Is that why you did it there? If I'd found you would it have made a difference? Could I have stopped you from . . .

You went to hide in the tack room. You climbed up to the rafters. I should have known. You always talked about the thrill that vertigo

170

gave you. How it terrified you. Always you talked of thrills, excitement. But to take your own life . . .

Oh, my baby.

He looks again at the empty chair, this time with horror in his eyes.

I burned the house to the ground after you died. I left Claridges and went to live with Bárbara at the old house in Holland Park. Anything was better than Summer Crest Hall. I hated it. So many dreadful memories. The house that no longer exists but which will always exist in my head no matter how hard I try to forget.

Charles Frederick de Vere scrapes back his chair and staggers up from the desk. He opens the door of the room and turns left into the hallway. He walks along the corridor until he comes to the lift. He steps inside. Ten, nine, eight, seven, six . . . all the floors up to the surface. He rips the grill open, comes out and opens his eyes. He takes a deep breath, makes a long sigh.

Out of the taxi window it is starting to get dark. A calm night. The lights on the Albert bridge are rippling on the water. Soon, he will be back at the airless house with the Spike. He touches the sleeve of his black velvet jacket, brushing away the salty beads beginning to sink in.

CHAPTER NINETEEN

So I sit in the woods at night and make friends with the monkeys. I can't say it's unpleasant. Cosima's idea of a perfect day is nobody interfering with what she calls her piece of 'private rapture'. By which she means sketching me into the picture of two baboons prowling around a bunch of trees in the pitch dark.

To tell the truth, I've come to like her demented rabbit face and the sound of the pencil river running over the sketch pad. I started looking forward to the sessions: the hairdryer, the faggy Burne-Jones boy on the tapestry, the fauns and the nymphs and the robed goddesses on the old fashioned wallpaper.

Cosima says she was blocked for a very long time but thanks to me she isn't blocked any more.

'You're just who I've been looking for,' she says.

And you, me, I think, although I don't tell her this. See, Summer Crest Hall is the best rehab I've ever been to. It seems as though everybody loves me here, with Sykes endlessly checking me out through the corner of her eye and Cosima gazing at me daily like no lover ever did. Cosima is better than any therapist I ever had because I know that for the duration of the sitting, I am at the centre of her universe. I can relax, go off to some other place in my head where I don't give a shit about fat Carmen Costello with the 55-inch hips and the cheating boyfriend. I go off to some far-away location – I don't know where the hell it is, but it feels a million times better than the place I came from.

Larry leaves me messages but sometimes I don't even return his calls. See, he doesn't fill me up any more. His love is like cream. The crappy spray-on cream that I sometimes get flashes of when I go to sleep. Or it's like a cheap perfume and you don't realise how cheap it is until you're standing next to a bottle of the really good stuff. I like the way Cosima smells and I figure that's a good sign. Every morning, when she opens the attic door in her paint-splattered man's shirt and gives me the European-style kiss – a brush of the lips on both cheeks – I get a whiff of lady's furs and bitter almonds.

I like the way she hovers constantly between melancholy and a kind of childlike glee. And there's something about her that I can't put my finger on. I try to get her to talk some more about love – about the affair where she tasted mortality in the first kiss. But it seems she doesn't want to play. Or rather, she prefers to flirt in a way that's kind of blood-thirsty, if you want to know the truth. Not that I don't understand it. I mean, you have to hand it to these poshies, they even know how to die better than we do. Someone's face is eaten by a tiger, someone's arm is shaved off in a water skiing accident, a guy goes missing off the coast of Zanzibar, another one is shot through the head at a house party in Kenya. Nobody ever seems to get run over by a bus or have an itty bitty bout of cancer.

'The thing about death,' Cosima tells me one day, 'is that it makes you take notice. A dead body looks like it's having an orgasm.'

'No kidding.'

'A rictus of ecstasy in a face drained of blood.'

That, she adds, is the good thing about being an artist.

'Being a goddess. That's what an artist is. You can kill anyone. Have them dead all over the floor.'

I tell her she should have been a good Catholic girl like me. 'You'd have worked that gore thing out of your system,' I tell her.

'How do you mean?'

'Well, you know you're in a Catholic church because there's always a naked guy on a cross with a ton of blood hanging off of his body.'

I take another sip of pre-meds.

'Jesus always wears clothes in the Protestant places. What's up with that?'

Still, I did start to wonder if she really had killed someone, just like Franck kept insinuating. But that only put me off a little bit. The fact is, I can't stop thinking about Cosima, even though I know that sex doesn't solve things any more than food does. I remember that time I picked up a guy from the Internet when Larry was away filming. He was gross but I told myself it would be like gobbling down a plate of greens so you can go on and enjoy dessert. I don't know what I imagined dessert was going to be. I sat on the couch and I said, 'I want to go to bed with you.' Jesus. It came out real intimate. Like I was in love with the guy. When all I really wanted was to get it over with. No kissing, no caressing, just fuck me hard while I lie there and think about my secret stash of dulce de leche at the back of the refrigerator.

The guy must have read my mind. He looked kind of freaked out. Said he had to go pick up a TV for a friend. He called me up later from his car. 'I wanted to see if you were all right,' he goes.

To be rejected.

To be rejected by someone ugly.

To be rejected by someone ugly who feels sorry for you.

To tell the truth, I don't worry too much about my feelings for Cosima because at Summer Crest Hall, I don't worry too much about anything. I don't care that I haven't seen my face in weeks because there are no mirrors, I don't care about the groaning pipes and the single-pane windows that leak with a perpetual mist. I don't care about the cold and soon, I don't even crave sugar. It's fine by me that it's going to be pigeon or partridge yet again for dinner and not even the flies bother me any more. They prefer to sleep rather than fly and that makes perfect sense to me.

See, aside from Cosima, sleep is the best thing about this place.

It makes up for all the hardships. It's so delicious that some-times you don't even want to wake up. And even when you're awake, the days go by in choppy bits and pieces, like in a dream. There's not a lot to do apart from the sittings. There are the fading oil paintings to look at, the piles of out-of-date celebrity magazines that Kenneth Sketch uses for his art, but I lose my concentration before I get to the end of a paragraph.

These days I'm not sure what's real and what's a dream. It's a little like being drunk and a little like all the natural spaci-ness I've ever experienced: jet lag (which can make you feel out of it for days), illness (which makes things more intense), mugging (which sends time into slow motion) and love. In the early days of love, everything is connected and nothing seems insignificant. Not eating for a long time is the closest I've ever come to feeling what you might call 'spiritual'. Getting off on a carrot for two whole days. Slowly sucking out the nutrients and even those feel like pig fat now that your body's turned into a temple.

Cosima tells me not to worry. She says the pre-meds some-times distort patients' perceptions of reality. But with me, drinking that stuff just makes me feel relaxed. As if everything is normal, even though at the back of my mind I know that nothing here is normal at all. Take the picture on Cosima's screen of Diana shooting an arrow at the stag-head guy. One day, I ask her if she doesn't think it a weird coincidence that the screen is like the one in de Vere's suite at Claridges that I'd told her about. She says she doesn't think it's strange. She says that hunting pictures are common in big houses like these.

But there are other things. The artificial glare of the sticky orange light, for instance. And the time. The time is the only thing that's not off kilter here at Summer Crest Hall; whenever you look at the digital clock on the fireplace it's always some-thing like 11.11 or 20.20 or 12 on the dot.

And there's the food. Even though it's always woodcock or pigeon or partridge, it always tastes of nothing, like an itch you can't scratch. But you want to eat it because it feels like cigarettes taste on ecstasy – like you're breathing in fresh air.

Kenneth Sketch seems to understand what I'm talking about.

'How come we never want to do anything?' I asked him one day. He was still working on his collage. It was of two heads. Next to the one made from pictures of sushi and swimming pools, there was a cut-out of Kate Moss's face. It had a bunch more pictures stuck into it: a fried egg, a string of black pearls.

'Well, I know there are yoga classes,' he said. 'But personally, I don't want all that time to think.'

'Yeah, but who gives the yoga classes?'

The staff walk around the house like ghosts. Aside from Sykes who appears at mealtimes, and Mary, whose legs are endlessly exposed by the drafts that whip round the house and under the thin fabric of her maid's uniform, you hardly notice the others. They blend in with the carpet, the walls.

'This place is like a movie set,' I told him. 'The clocks are always at weird times, the people are in period costume . . .'

'Oh, but I love Sykes's vintage wear . . .'

'I'm not convinced that's a fashion statement,' I told him. 'And if I smell her Evening in Paris perfume one more time I'm going to barf.'

'She says it's by Bourjois.'

'Smells like an Evening in Atlantic City to me.'

The flight attendant smile resurfaced.

'And what about the paintings? They're rotting but there's something new about them. Like they've been painted for a mini-series about a haunted house . . .'

'I wouldn't mind if we were in a TV series,' Kenneth Sketch said with a yawn. 'TV dramas make life seem thrilling and believable. When things happen to you in real life, you don't feel a thing.'

And then I go back to sit with the monkeys and suddenly I don't care about anything. I take my clothes off, I sit on the sheepskin mat and me and Cosima go into the woods together. I'm kind of worried though, because she says she's nearly finished the sketching. Soon it will be time for the paint. Not red paint this time. It seems she's decided that red's a one-trick pony that only gets interesting when you add another colour to it. Like blue. Blue, she says, is like a snail going back into its shell because it draws you in the longer you look.

'I'm going to use Prussian Blue,' she tells me. 'Putrification and depth.'

I'm not crazy about the sound of Prussian Blue, although I was pleased to learn that I'd been the one to inspire the colour. Cosima said she didn't really know where she was going with the red and then that first night at dinner I'd changed everything.

'Your talk of blue blood,' she said. 'Of aristocrats having blue blood . . .'

'Yeah?'

'Very apt, actually. Prussian blue has a very high tinting strength. But it's not very permanent to light or air.'

'Sounds like Franck,' I tell her. 'He doesn't seem a very permanent fixture around here.'

'Oh, Franck's more green than blue.'

'Why green?'

'Green is yellow which has been paralysed by blue,' she explains, putting her pencil down. 'It's motionless, the most restful colour that exists. But after a while it becomes wearisome.'

Our eyes meet and she smiles. Then she picks the pencil up and with a small twitch of the nose, she carries on drawing.

I think she did kill someone and I think it was me.

And then one day, there was a new smell in the attic room: a sweet, cakey odour that was sharp at the same time and it made my nostrils tingle. Cosima wasn't there any more. There was just a canvas on an easel in the middle of the room and a pale hand dipping a sable brush into a worm of dirty blue.

The hand would rise up into the air and then disappear into the woods.

The sketching was over. The river had stopped. The rabbit was gone.

The other smell in the attic was hot wax because she'd started painting at night. She said she preferred to paint at night because candlelight subdued the colour yellow and she didn't like yellow at all. 'Too loud,' she said, in a new, hard voice. 'Shrieking. Like a squawking canary.' All that mattered was the Prussian blue.

The truth was staring me in the face: now that I'd led her into the woods, Cosima was going on without me. Sure, she didn't want to hurt my feelings. She still invited me up at night but she didn't talk any more. I just sat there with my clothes on, watching in silence as she disappeared deeper and deeper into her private rapture.

When I realised that my therapy had stopped, I went to consult Kenneth Sketch.

'Have you been having strange dreams?' I asked him.

'Oh, my dreams are always the same,' he droned. 'Nightmares that the doorman at Studio 54 won't let me in.'

He shuddered.

'They had this "tossed salad" door policy. Like, you don't want a salad just made up of iceberg lettuce, right? Or just asparagus tips?'

'What kind of vegetable were you?'

'Oh, I didn't usually have a problem getting in. I always had good Quaaludes.'

'Right.'

'One time, I got in ahead of Burt Reynolds.'

'No kidding,' I said. 'One time I got in ahead of Mick Jagger.'

As I'd predicted, Kenneth Sketch's scissors stopped in their tracks.

'It was at a club in London called Blitz,' I went on. 'Early eighties.'

'Oh, my God,' he rumbled. 'I was a big fan of that club! A bustle skirt and a pirate shirt? Ziggy Stardust eye make-up? You couldn't keep me out of that place.'

'The suburban queens used to bug me a little,' I confessed.

'Oh, I was relieved to get away from the rich guys at Studio 54. Andy used to say to me, "Why don't you sleep with that one and talk him into getting a portrait done?"'

That's when I had another of my déjà vu flashes.

'Dude,' I said. 'Have we met before?'

'Oh, I can't remember much of anything,' he said, with a nervous laugh. 'Which I'm very happy about because it means I can live totally in the now.'

I shouldn't have been surprised that I'd been having strange dreams. I'd stopped taking the pre-meds. Now that Cosima was shutting me out, I figured I needed to keep awake to find out what the hell was going on. But life off pre-meds didn't keep me awake. I kept drifting off into deep sleep just like I always did, only now, the primary colours would get all cloudy and my sleep would be punctuated with endless nightmares about missed buses and long journeys. The brief visions of writhing bodies covered in cream and chocolate sauce and women's voices shrieking 'Take that, Mr Man!' had been with me since I'd gotten to Summer Crest Hall. But until now, the wacky wine had sweetened things and the rest of my dreams would revolve around nice things like cakes with tits and people wanting to be friends with me.

One time I had a nightmare that I was dressing a woman's cancerous breast sores. The stink of the wounds was grossing me out but I wanted to pretend I didn't have a body any more, so to prove I could overcome the impurities of the flesh, I gathered the pus into a ladle and drank it. And then Jesus appeared to me, inviting me to drink the blood flowing from his pierced side. Naturally, the blood was Prussian blue and I drank it, and when I jerked awake I was looking at the tapestry and the squashed cherub was giving me the evil eye.

I panicked. There was just one thought in my head: call Larry. I got out of bed and rushed to get my cellphone. The battery was dead. I panicked some more and then decided to just get out of the house and look for a nearby village. I was sure I'd find a phone box along the way.

I ran down to the Long Room. Kenneth Sketch was working at the art desk.

'Morning, Carmen,' he said in his slow drawl.

It was early. Only 6.06 according to the clock on the mantel-piece. Kenneth Sketch was cutting out dicks from some porn mags to stick into a third head he was making. He told me he'd found the magazines outside of a big old barn not far from the house.

'You know,' he said, 'I think it's weird that when men have big cocks everyone takes them seriously.' He turned his picture this way and that into the gooey orange light. 'When women have big tits, nobody takes them seriously at all.'

Kenneth Sketch's voice was so soporific. I felt the tiredness seep into me all over again. Even without the pre-meds, it still felt as if the walls were spraying out some kind of morphine mist. I couldn't help sinking into one of the tattered chairs, closing my eyes and preparing to plunge into the irresistible warmth of Summer Crest Hall sleep.

But a surge of dread forced my eyes open. I stood up and told Kenneth Sketch I was going shopping. I ran out of the Long Room, out of the house. It was cold outside but somehow it was warmer than inside Summer Crest Hall. There was the smell of wood smoke and nutty rotting and it seemed pretty noisy, like jungle birds, although I figured maybe that was because I hadn't been up this early in a while.

I found myself going down a green, slippery path bordered by hedges that grow the black, seedy, prickly berries that English people eat and that I can't see the point of. In the distance I could see a big house with turrets. A castle maybe. I could see a blur of two men with sticks in front of a lake. Shovelling up

180

leaves? There were a couple of chicks too. Women in big, stiff skirts and old-fashioned hats by a field of sheep and a crumbling wall.

I squinted into the distance until the day became a painting with water sloshed against it. Reality dribbled down the day, smears of colour that blurred into more colour until the day was just a mess of dark, uncertain shapes. I wandered along the road, past twisting flowers and turrets and moats and men in breeches working the fields. And then, through the orange and blue glow, I saw it: a telephone box. I opened the door and once I was inside, I felt not just miles away but, eras and planets away. I stared through the glass but didn't see through it, just into it. And what I plunged into wasn't a sea; I was swimming in a dark place filled with a clutter of black pearls and dusty feathers and a bunch of tarnished silverware.

I'm not surprised to find exactly fifty pence in my pocket but when Larry picks up the phone, his voice could be a tape recording. It gets louder or softer like a sound through a door that keeps opening and closing, an invisible membrane that lets some things through its pores.

And yet it stops talking when I ask it to.

What? What do you mean 'stop talking'? Are you OK, Carmen?

It even tells me it loves me.

Love you, Carmen. God, I miss you, baby.

But it's just a voice at the bottom of the caviar funnel, jostling for space among the debris of bent mustard spoons and blue-and-white soup tureens with hairline fractures.

I frown.

I put the phone down.

I leave the booth and look down at my legs in the sticky light. They look unreal too. I carry on walking. I leave the main road and walk into the wet grass, but then I stumble over a molehill that turns out to be a stack of porn mags. When I get up, I see an old barn in front of me so I pull the creaky doors open and I see a row of cobwebby saddles and shrivelled reins hanging on the wall. There's a tangle of stirrups in a pile on the floor next to a box of old books with the pages all battered and torn. I feel inexplicably moved. Like a kid hearing a chord on a piano. The kid knows that something intense is going on, even if he has no experience of that sadness yet.

I look up to the rafters and think of climbing up. But the wood's all rotten and as I'm stepping back, I trip over a pile of dirt. A shape like a sunbather lying on her front. I fall back into a pile of trash and when I lift up my hands there are pieces of a ripped-up oil painting stuck to them. There's an animal ear, a strip of grey fur tethered with rope. I try and clamber out but new scraps keep sticking to me: bloodied feathers encrusted with moss, a gold wine jug covered in black mould.

There's metal in my mouth, a taste of rust. I can't seem to get to my feet and as I turn to look for firm ground to put my hands on, I see something glittering at the bottom of the pile of broken pictures – a sticky wet body like a primitive creature giving birth, a green crab, undulating and squeezing, a thing with feelers or suckers that makes me gasp. Terror propels me to my feet and sends me running out of the shed, down a narrow path which comes out in a tangle of withered vines and in the middle of the vines there are two slabs of granite, two headstones. Just before I pass out, I register how stupid the noise coming out of my mouth sounds. Like a lonely old lady who just found a spider at the bottom of the bath.

CHAPTER TWENTY

When I open my eyes, I find myself looking at a bowl of crunchy black peanuts. They're scattered all over the blue lake and the broken towers and the flock of sheep. Then comes the splash at the bottom of the well. The movie I'm in. The same fucking movie. I didn't escape at all. The dead flies are everywhere. Scattered on the blue-and-white Spode dinner plates with the pastoral landscape vignettes. And the Long Room didn't change either. The pastel paintings. The rusty cheese toasting fork. *Dum Spiro Spero*. Kenneth Sketch and Cosima. Talking about maids.

'I'm uncomfortable with the idea of someone cleaning up after me,' Kenneth Sketch drawls, cutting away with his scissors. 'I guess it depends how you were raised.'

'I was brought up by cooks and nannies,' Cosima says.

'Wow. I can't even look chambermaids in the eye when they come into my hotel room. Sometimes, I have the "Do Not Disturb" sign on the door for days just so the maid doesn't come in.'

'Sykes and Mary are sweet enough,' says Cosima.

'Oh, definitely,' Kenneth drawls. 'It's actually exhausting avoiding the maid, when I think about it.'

'The thing to do is never sleep with one,' she says.

'Sleeping with the maid!' Kenneth Sketch seems to find this hilarious.

'Happened to a friend of mine,' Cosima says. 'He was terribly traumatised.'

That's when my nostrils start to twitch. I smell him then. Buttered broccoli and cigar smoke. I feel the tremor. Something is breaking through the chipped paint of all the pictures in the house. I know them! The ornate stuff Freddie used to sell before he got in with Picasso and scored some credibility: the pinks and the blues, the rippling chiffons, the beautiful fabrics, the foamy cherry tits. They were the same ones, only now they were all rotted with age, destroyed by time.

I close my eyes again because I don't want to believe it. But when they're closed, all I can see is that night in de Vere's room in Claridges. The Picasso celebration. The Marie-Thérèse Walter painting. The shadow in de Vere's eyes. I remember how horrible I felt. I couldn't believe I'd let myself get so drunk.

'Freddie, I'm really sorry, I . . .'

The finger on the lips. The pacing of the room. Up and down. Up and down.

'The thing is, Carmen, I have always made it a rule never to mix business with pleasure. Not since . . .'

The red foulard whipped from the top pocket. The mopping of the brow.

'I told you about my school days . . .'

'About you getting, "sacked"? Sure I remember.'

The gaze out of the window, down on to Brook Street.

'I was expelled for . . .'

'Yeah?'

'. . . For sleeping with a maid.'

Such troubled eyes. Dregs at the bottom of the blue. Sent away for sleeping with a maid? I tried not to laugh.

My eyes bang open. I spring out of the chair. I start walking around, looking up at the walls. The paintings. He's everywhere I look.

'Hey, Carmen!' Kenneth Sketch exclaims. 'Welcome back to the land of the living!'

Cosima snaps into drawing room mode. 'Are you all right?' she says, coming over. She takes my hand in her cold hand and

184

leads me back to the tattered velvet chair. 'You've been sleeping for hours.'

'She looks pale,' Kenneth Sketch says in his lazy voice. 'It's like when people are having a nervous breakdown. That delicate thing can make them look beautiful.'

Cosima settles me in the chair. She frames my face with her hands. 'You looked like a beautiful corpse,' she whispers.

'Hollywood dying,' Kenneth Sketch agrees. 'Like Ali Macgraw in *Love Story*, right?' He makes a giggle. 'I must have looked that colour myself when I did those mushrooms on that plane from New York! And John Paul tells me that flights in September are longer than summer ones because of the gulf stream . . .'

I shake Cosima off and then I see that the mists in her eyes are thicker than usual. The tang of metal comes back into my mouth.

'You know him,' I say.

She pretends she doesn't understand what I'm talking about. 'Know who?'

'Charles Frederick de Vere.' I can feel my heart beating faster. 'You fucking know him.'

Sykes comes in. I guess my voice must be pretty loud. She glances at Cosima. It's creepy. The look on their faces. I realise they're both in on this. But I won't back down now.

'You said a friend of yours slept with the maid.'

'Did I?' Cosima sighs as if she doesn't care what she said. As if she's glad the pretence is up.

'You were talking about de Vere,' I go on. 'I know you were. About de Vere being expelled from his school.'

Cosima turns to Kenneth Sketch. 'Carmen actually *was* a chambermaid,' she tells him.

'Oh, my Lord!' The beetle brows rise. 'You must have a lot of secrets, Carmen.'

'Not me,' I snap. 'Secrets are Cosima's thing.'

I stand up. Walk right over to her.

'You know Freddie.' I say it slowly. Not a question any more.

185

A statement. There's a long silence. I think she's going to deny it. But then she doesn't deny it. She's pretty stylish about it, as a matter of fact.

'Those paints you sent me from his office back in the spring of 1981,' she says. 'Terrible cheap things. You should have bought Windsor & Newton.'

I can't help smiling. It's the relief.

'I was probably saving the change for a new pussy-bow blouse,' I tell her. 'He liked chicks to dress up. You know Freddie.'

'Yes, I know Freddie' she says, coldly. 'Or rather, I knew him.'

'What do you mean. Did he die?'

'No, but I did.'

That's when the clock strikes thirteen. The room starts closing in on me. All the pastel paintings on the walls, all the pastoral scenes on the Spode tableware – they don't look so innocent any more. There aren't any peasants or sheep or ladies in volu-minous skirts now. There are just centaurs and sirens and demons and demi-gods and the eighteenth-century sea nymphs have warts and blacked-out teeth. They slip out of the baby blue sea to join the gorgons and the goats and the owls who are turning the room into a big scary bacchanal to the point that I'm wondering where it's all going to end . . .

And then it does end because a chill hits my stomach. A chill even colder than the room. Because there's someone else here. Someone apart from de Vere. Another person who's part of this whole story. I look around, as if he's in here somewhere, hiding out. His face keeps popping up in my head and then disappearing. I know it's a guy. And I know I'm getting closer. I know it won't be long before his face comes cracking through the surface like a deformed hatchling from a rotten egg.

I have to get out of here. Except why can't I leave? Maybe I went into a psychotic state. Or maybe this is an out-of-body experience. A parallel universe, although I don't even know what that means.

I collapse into the tattered chair and the next thing I know, Cosima says, 'Meet the maid,' and there's Sykes standing in front of me with her hand stretched out.

'I know she's the maid,' I snap.

'You can call me Dorothy,' Sykes says with a shrug.

'Dorothy Sykes was Freddie's school maid too,' Cosima says, almost apologetically.

'Post-natal depression, I believe they call it now,' Sykes says. 'Still, mum will of brought the little boy up better than me.'

She scratches half-heartedly at a stain on her pinafore. 'Petrol fumes in the garage. It was quite an advanced suicide for the time.' She looks up and strains to smile. 'Not many girls owned cars in 1958.'

'The 1950s!' Kenneth Sketch exclaims. 'That's where your cologne's from, right?'

'The cat as well,' Sykes scowls, thrusting her brooch forward. 'All gifts from his lordship. Young Freddie.'

'How romantic,' Kenneth Sketch croons.

'Woolworth's? I don't think so. You could get Evening in Paris for a few shillings back then.'

'Oh . . .'

'"A girl with a bunch of toffs. She can't believe her luck." That's what I heard him tell his school pals one day. Little twerp. They should have seen him with his boy-scout magnifying glass inspecting my parts like he's dissecting a frog in the science lab . . .'

She starts stroking her marcasite cat.

'Bloody turn-on it was. I mean, I liked James Dean but I liked David Niven and all. I'd had my fill of the rough blokes down at the Ventura in Croydon.'

Cosima's skin starts to talk its troubled language. Jets of black ink spray into the chalk white of her face and then there's another hand in front of me. This time it's Mary.

'Mary's not her real name,' Sykes mumbles. 'I had to change it. Can't be talking French . . .'

'Marie-Thérèse,' Mary says, with a shy curtsey. 'My name is Marie-Thérèse Walter.'

I narrow my eyes. 'Marie-Thérèse Walter?'

I see a flash of colour. A jug, a guitar, a slice of watermelon.

'The doormat?' I go.

Marie-Thérèse blushes.

'He was . . . a great man.'

Sykes snorts.

'So great you had to hang yourself when he died. You were seventy. You might of waited!'

Marie-Thérèse nods submissively.

'He . . . needed me.'

'Needed you!' Sykes explodes. 'Where is he now then?'

She turns to me. 'Every day during the Occupation he made her traipse round to his studio and beg for five kilos of coal. Bleeding millionaire!'

'La rue des Grands-Augustins,' Marie-Thérèse says with a tiny smile.

'He made her take it home on the Underground!'

'On the Métro, yes,' the voice quivers.

'Bloody muse,' Sykes mutters. 'Bloody mug.'

'He wrote me many letters!' Marie-Thérèse protests, her grey bun trembling on top of her head. 'He filled them with drawings of flowers and pigeons. *C'était l'amour fou, quoi*!'

She crumples, sobbing into a tea towel as Sykes rips off her rayon pinafore and flings it to the ground.

'Oh, what's the bloody point!' she says. 'I thought life after death would be better than this. I thought there'd be donkeys and a nice man in a white tunic waiting at a gate.'

She gestures at Franck who has suddenly appeared in the Long Room snaffling at another pigeon carcass. 'It's a bloody swizz!'

She slumps down into one of the dining-room chairs and a bunch of crazy stuff comes out of her mouth: about how none of them know how Summer Crest Hall works. About how there are communities of houses just like this one. And levels. The only thing Sykes has worked out is that the people who look after the patients are suicide cases, that they all killed themselves on earth. And because they committed suicide, the purgatory placement people have deemed that they have to perform a kind of celestial community service as nurses looking after the new arrivals. But they are only ever given brief pieces of information. Sykes insists that all she knew about me was that I was a Latina socialite who once met an art dealer called Charles Frederick de Vere.

'No rhyme or reason,' she says. 'Just "10.10 hijacked plane crash", or "18.18 cocaine-induced cardiac arrest" . . .' She stops. She looks at me, biting her lip.

I decide to go along with their game. Part of me is hoping that Lupe Vélez is going to come rumba-ing through the door at any minute, brandishing a steaming tray of pigeon martinis on the end of her arm.

'So, if you're dead . . .' I say to Sykes.

'Worse luck.'

'. . . and Marie-Thérèse is dead . . .'

'He needed me!' the kitchen maid weeps into the sodden towel.

'And Cosima is dead . . .'

'My own fault,' Cosima grimaces.

'Then . . .'

This felt really stupid.

'Am I . . . ?'

'We can't be sure,' Cosima says, awkwardly.

I ask Cosima how long she's been here but she tells me she doesn't know. 'What is time, after all?' she asks. 'If I looked back over my life and I condensed all my memories, they'd be under five minutes.'

There's more silence and then I hear the musical drawl.

'Oh well,' Kenneth Sketch says. 'If we are dead, at least we got the whole thing over with.'

I look at him more closely. The dull green eyes, the thick

eyebrows. There's something about him. Claridges. The pretty party boy with the swinging blond Bowie wedge. When his boyfriend was around it was breakfast downstairs at nine every morning. A blue stripy shirt and a navy blue jersey draped over the shoulders. When the boyfriend was away on business, he always ordered breakfast in bed as late as he could and the room was a mess. Wasp-striped leotards lying in the bathroom, chandelier earrings under the sheets and yeah, now that I come to think of it, a big, pink bustle skirt shoved in the back of the closet. He never dared look me in the eye when I came in to turn down the room. 'Had a good night, man?' I'd go. 'Oh yeah,' he'd drawl, a sly smile on a mouth that still bore traces of lipstick.

I start to recall the conversations we've had at Summer Crest Hall about his New Romantic obsession, but then I shake my head. I pull myself together. 'Le freak, c'est chic, right?' I say, springing up out of the chair. 'You know, it's been great meeting you all. But I really have to go now.'

I walk quickly through the Long Room into the kitchen. I'm going to make another break for it. Nothing will stop me this time. But as I'm opening the kitchen door, I hear Cosima's voice.

'Not everyone's dead,' she says.

I hesitate. 'There you go with that dead thing again,' I say. I feel a hand on my shoulder and the touch makes me shiver.

'Chinese take-out orange,' I say, softly, looking toward the horizon. 'Funny how it doesn't seem strange any more.'

'You might still be alive,' she says in her old voice. The hiding-under-the-furniture voice. 'You might wake up and remember us as though we were people in a dream.'

I turn around in time to see a wisp of a smile.

'You have to wait and see . . .'

Then her hand drops from my arm and the life goes out of me.

CHAPTER TWENTY-ONE

I follow her up to the attic room. I don't care about a whole bunch right now. I'm on the point of asking her how she killed herself, but suddenly I'm not interested in her suicide because I can see a smear of dirty blue. Out of the corner of my eye. On the easel. She normally hides the monkey painting with a sheet. But now it's uncovered.

I should have been prepared. If it was going to be a nice picture, she wouldn't have gone for Prussian blue – a colour originally made from polluted animal blood. And if the decomposing blue hadn't been a clue, the forest setting should have told me something. The place where civilisation ends, where restless spirits dwell and where regular folks don't go, especially not at night.

There are a few seconds before the scream comes. Before it actually arrives in my throat, all I can think of is the word 'shoplift'. Men go to strip joints when there's a crisis and me, I slip things from the grocery-store shelves into my pockets. I feel bad for Mrs Mendoza at Sparky's, but it pulls me through the emergency and it saves me from the charade of having to pretend I'm buying fifteen candy apples for my non-existent kids.

It's funny because I know the anti-shoplifting spiel by heart now: related to low self-esteem and losing sexual attraction in a relationship. Often associated with anorexia and bulimia.

Meanwhile, Cosima doesn't know about any of this because by now, it has happened. The attic room is filled with a primordial wail of anguish, a chaotic mess of noise that sends her running over to her painting. There's the sound of footsteps up granite stairs and soon Sykes and Marie-Thérèse are in the studio,

191

holding my arms by my side like I'm one of the fruit loop C-Wingers.

'Look at my body!' I'm screaming. 'I'm a fucking skeleton!'

The shock is even bigger because, thanks to the corroded mirrors, this is the first image I've seen of myself since I arrived at Summer Crest Hall. Cosima and Sykes and Marie-Thérèse all look real awkward. They won't look me in the eye.

'What's a fat bitch like me doing looking like a goddamn skeleton?'

They're silent. And that makes me start to cry. Real tears, not just drama queen stuff.

'You're just like all the others!'

They don't have to restrain me. I'm too weak to be able to do very much. I collapse into the bottle-green chair.

'"You're too skinny, Carmen!", "Carmen you need to eat some more!" For God's sake, can't anyone see how huge my belly is? My fat butt? And what about my operation? I don't care if I'm dead or not. I want my fucking lipo!'

Nobody gets it. I like not eating. It feels clean. It makes me feel light-headed. That's what I dig about this place. It gives me that ethereal feeling I get when I don't eat, when I literally live off thin air.

Of course, there's bad stuff: the depression, the endless excusing yourself from the dinner table to go 'freshen up', the making sure you wash the pieces of orange puke from your hair afterwards, the discoloured teeth. But mainly, there's the good stuff: the purity of anorexia and the high-rolling elation of bulimia.

Bulimics are much more fun than prissy anorexics, although anorexia is more fulfilling. It's like the opposite of the genie coming out of the lamp: it's when the wisp of smoke goes back inside, spirals down to who knows where? It's like what Cosima was always telling me about blue: the snail going back into its shell. Withdrawing, taking you with it away from the world.

Except I didn't escape at all. I'm right there in the goddamn monkey painting. Looking like death warmed-up against a tree.

And then another penny drops. Sykes has only been looking me up and down all this time because she wants to check out what she assumes is de Vere's latest conquest. And Cosima? She doesn't have the hots for me at all. She's just an artist who got excited about the opportunity to paint a living skeleton.

It's happened before. I know what they say about me, the girls at the spa, the people in the street. The stares, the gasps, the whispering behind my back.

I get up and start yelling at Cosima.

'OK!' I go. 'So I'm forty-eight, I'm five foot nine and I weigh the same as a skinny sixteen-year-old. But I manage, don't I?'

The appalled look on her face shuts me up. I collapse on the floor in front of the painting, a pathetic pile of nothing.

'That's us in Summer Crest Hall, isn't it?' I say, weakly. 'We're all trapped in the woods and we'll never get out.'

'Don't upset yourself, love,' Sykes says. 'It's better here than the fifties.'

'Dear Carmen,' Cosima says. 'It's only a painting.'

'All portraits are fantasies,' Marie-Thérèse offers.

'Oh shut up,' I cut her off.

Cosima sighs as she looks at her picture.

'It was meant to be quite pleasant but then it turned out to be gothic. Sort of monstrous.'

And then the opium cloud descends. I yawn and Sykes leads me back to the green chair, handing me a glass of pre-meds to sweeten my imminent nightmares. I'm about to drink it when Cosima snatches it back. There's something hard behind the mists. There's something more she wants from me.

I try to stay awake. But the ache of pleasure pulls me into another bout of spastic sleep. I see the Burne-Jones *Primavera* tapestry, the boy with the plump lips, reaching up to pluck a peach from a tree. Only in my dream, it's a candy apple he pulls down and we're in Sparky's in Santa Barbara. Which is also Sotheby's in the early eighties. All the paintings have come to life and creatures are climbing out of them. There's Gainsborough's Blue Boy, who looks like Jayden from the checkout at Sparky's, followed by the primate from Francis Bacon's *Study of a Baboon*. Only this baboon's skin isn't smudged grey and white like Bacon's, this one is velvety black. Jayden rings the bell for the supervisor but a goat turns up instead. He starts hitting the black velvet baboon with the candy apple until the baboon turns into Charles Frederick de Vere. And then the goat pulls out a paper bag and someone tells me to be careful because there's heroin inside. But I'm convinced there's candy in the bag and when I look in, I see blue powder, like pigment. And then the goat shoves my face in the bag and blue dust flies up my nose and chokes me and Jayden starts whispering into one of de Vere's ears and blood comes out of the other one. The goat starts to cackle. He points a broken glass hoof at de Vere and a stream of foul-smelling smoke comes out, and when I wake up, I'm twisting around on the sheepskin rug, going, 'Dog! Dog! Come to see a dog!'

The first thing I see is Cosima's eyes about three inches away from my face. Half of me's still in the dream, but I'm aware of her shouting at me.

'What did you say!' she's going. 'What did you say!'

I try and push her off. Jesus, who knows what the hell I said. I can still see the goat, that crazy fucking face that keeps coming and going.

'Dog!' Cosima insists. 'You said "Dog". As if . . .'

She swallows.

'. . . As if it were the name of a person.'

I know by the look in her eyes that she has to start telling me stuff. It's the point of no return, you might say. I pull my arm away from her, get up from the chair and walk to the other side of the room. I don't know who the hell 'Dog' is. At least,

I probably do, but I don't want to think of anything right now. I turn to the Burne-Jones tapestry and try and forget everything.

And that's when I remember. When I'm looking at the *Primavera* tapestry. That's when the deformed hatchling starts to crack open its shell.

'It's him,' I say. 'The fly in the ointment.'

'What?' Cosima comes closer.

Now I know why that damn tapestry's been bothering me.

'Who are you talking about?' Cosima wants to know. 'What "fly in the ointment"?'

'Mercury,' I tell her, pointing at the tapestry. 'The faggy guy's supposed to be the god Mercury.'

'Carmen, I don't understand.'

I tell her that I need to see the original *Primavera*. The Botticelli version. I need to remember what Mercury looked like when Botticelli painted him in the fifteenth century.

Cosima looks puzzled but she goes over to the pile of art books stacked up on the floor. It doesn't take her long to pull out a large tome. She flicks though it with trembling hands until she stops at a double-page spread. Her body tightens, like a bird shot in mid flight. She's seen it. The strange similarity. When she looks over at me, there's something pleading in her eyes.

She puts the opened book on my lap.

I can't help gasping when I see him again. After all these years.

Botticelli's Mercury.

Ellsworth.

'You knew Ellsworth?' she says, quietly.

She looks at Sykes and Sykes just shrugs her shoulders in that Sykes way of hers. I guess she's right about the purgatory placement people not telling her everything.

'Life's full of surprises, right, Cosima?' I go. 'Or should I say "death" is?'

*   *   *

It's all coming back now. A poster of Botticelli's *Primavera* was on the wall in my little office in Claridges. I didn't really like the picture. The prissy Venus in the middle, the Three Graces on the left-hand side – more chubby chicks and real miserable-looking. The only person who seemed to be having any fun was the guy with a pink robe and the pointy helmet: Mercury. The god of commerce and thieving, de Vere told me. He said he found the picture sexy; that paintings with woods always turned him on.

Botticelli's version of Mercury was worlds apart from Burne-Jones's Victorian take on the god. Botticelli had portrayed him as a wise guy. His brows were slightly too expressive and his lips were slightly too red. He looked like he'd been round the block a few times, done a little too much commerce. Burne-Jones's sugary boy, on the other hand, reminded me of Franck – like Ellsworth with all the darkness bred out of him.

One day there was a knock at de Vere's suite. A couple of weeks before de Vere vanished for good. It was late one afternoon in that hot August of 1981. I remember that de Vere had only just come back from lunch. Some British bird-shooting festival he'd been celebrating with one of his aristo pals. When I opened the door, there was a sleazy-looking guy standing there and he looked kind of familiar. He could have passed for fifty, though I could tell he was probably only in his early forties. He looked like he'd been sleeping outside for a week, and wearing an overcoat in a heatwave wasn't helping him smell too sweet.

And yet I couldn't take my eyes off him. Behind the face of a fat, brooding bull, I could see a trace of the beauty he'd once had.

'Dog there?' he snarled.

I was impressed. Whisky breath so early in the day. And 'Dog'.

He scratched at his matted curls. I still couldn't think who he reminded me of.

'Would you mean Mr de Vere?' I said, like a bitch.

'No, I would mean Dog,' he slurred, taking a bottle from his pocket. *You're the dog, honey*, I thought, watching him take a swig and and break into a choking fit. Then I remembered where I'd seen him: he'd walked out of the painting on my office wall. He was Botticelli's Mercury.

'Tell him Ellsworth's here to see him,' he said, looking at me like I was dirt. 'There's a case of Mouton '45 up for auction at Christie's this afternoon. Tell him he owes me a bottle.'

When he belched, I couldn't help laughing. He grinned, revealing a mouth full of stained teeth. And then suddenly de Vere's office door opened. Even when business was bad, even when one of his 'ladies' let him down, I'd never see him like this. He stared at Ellsworth with a mix of sadness and horror in his eyes and I felt excitement in the pit of my stomach. I'd never thought someone would come one day to challenge him. Certainly not a guy with a whisky bottle and a filthy overcoat.

'I've come to see a man about a Dog,' Ellsworth said to him, not sounding drunk at all now.

That was when de Vere snapped back into life.

'You'd better come this way,' he told the guy who followed him into his office, treading mud into the carpet as he went.

They hadn't been there long when there was a cry, like a howl of pain. I didn't know if it had come from de Vere or Ellsworth. After a while, de Vere opened the door, said he wouldn't need me that afternoon and that I could go home.

I didn't see the Ellsworth guy again but I knew he hadn't gone away. Over the next two weeks, I started recognising a new voice that de Vere would put on for some of his phone calls. 'Yes, Mrs Lacey,' he'd go. 'I know it must be hard. Try and keep him inside. I'll send my men down at the weekend,' and I knew it was Ellsworth he was talking about. Sometimes, de Vere would look physically sick when he put the phone down. Those were the days when he'd had Ellsworth himself on the line. De Vere would try and sound nonchalant as he talked into the receiver: 'I've *told* you I'll come and see it by the end of the month and I *will*.' But he wasn't fooling me.

Afterwards, I'd ask if he was OK.

'Just one of my artists,' he'd go. 'A fly in the ointment.'

That's all he'd ever say. 'A fly in the ointment, Carmen. Nothing to worry about.'

I never found out who Ellsworth was, but de Vere vanished two weeks after he came to visit the suite. I remember circling 25 August 1981 in my diary because it was the last day de Vere showed up for work. He said he had to 'return' some paintings that evening, although he wouldn't tell me where he was going. I remember helping him load *The Dead Stuff* into a white truck.

'That last couple of weeks was weird,' I tell Cosima. 'De Vere kept going on about how everything was fine. But something changed after Ellsworth. It was like a chink in de Vere's armour. I'd thought he was fearless and now I could see he wasn't fearless at all.'

'What do you know about him,' Cosima hisses, suddenly. 'What do you know about de Vere. You don't know the half of it!'

The fierceness of her voice sends me stumbling back into the chair. I'm stunned, or maybe I'm just delighted that she finally seems to have lost it.

And then it hits me.

'Oh my God!' I say it slowly. 'You were in love with him.'

She spins round, stares out of the window.

I can't get over it. 'You were in love with Charles Frederick de Vere!'

She turns back then. The pale, misty girl is shaking with fury. Her eyeballs have turned to steel. Her whiteness has exploded.

CHAPTER TWENTY-TWO

Charles Frederick de Vere watches his hand tremble on the glass. When he lifts it to his lips, the wine spills over, smearing his desk with a dark stain. Her eyes, he thinks. She watches him from above, she wobbles his cup, trips him up.

Even in the sterile office of his East End gallery there is no escape from her. The owl is always on the desk, staring at him. Blodeuwedd. And a new painting has arrived. He hardly dared look at first. The red had gone completely and what remained was the deadliest colour yet: a cauldron of blue. A sky melting like plastic, sinking almost to black, echoing a grief that seemed hardly human. The sooty haze, the prowling monkeys, the tails, the escaped cage creatures, the naked corpse propped against a tree with branches coiling like serpents. His eyes darted to a small clearing in the trees where a pool of milk-blue seemed to bring hope to the sky. But it was too late. The woods offered no escape. A haze was radiating from its murky heart, oozing into the milk, already tainting the edges.

He'd taken the painting back to the alcove and locked the door shut. But almost immediately he felt compelled to go back and look again. The anger. The sadness. He felt something beyond his control pulling him into the picture, beckoning him into the clouds of infected blue.

He'd understood the colour immediately. The meaning. The shade the sea goes when there is nothing but deep water beneath. The movement is inwards and downwards. It pulls him under the waves in a way that red never could, into a night without stars, a darkness made visible.

She has done it, he thinks. She has found her blood.

He'd discovered the painting at the very back of the cupboard and at first he was convinced it was one of her old works. The red pictures he'd come across had hovered between abstraction and figuration but in this, her former style seemed to have returned. She had even painted herself into the woods.

Today, he has brought the picture out again and laid it on his desk. The glass of wine he is holding is to steady his nerves and yet as he looks at the body crouched by the tree, he feels splashes on his hand. He puts the glass down and notices how self-consciously prim Cosima's posture is, how her skin is not so white after all and the hair . . . A vulgar palm tree of black strung up on top of a head in the style of . . . a certain Mexican Hollywood actress? Yet nothing but skin and bone . . .

Surely not. The thought is grotesque. He feels a buzzing in his head. He anticipates more pain.

Soon he is convinced that the body does not belong to his snow-white lover at all, but to Carmen Costello. The other maid. It is not the first time he has considered her. Carmen Costello has been on his mind since the haunting began. He was aware that she had gone to America after their short partnership to marry Earl P. Johnson VI. De Vere had even bumped into Six a couple of times at parties on the New York art circuit. Six had not recognised him and on those occasions he had not been with his wife.

But as the paintings continued to appear, Carmen began to gnaw away at de Vere's already troubled sleep. He decided to discover what had become of her and thanks to his computer, he has read every article he can find about Carmen Costello. He learned that she had divorced Earl P. Johnson VI in 1995 and was now living rather a glamorous life in California. Articles from celebrity websites showed photos of her posing with a red-faced man, a Santa Barbara television personality called Larry Pfister. But more recent articles have led de Vere to suppose that her life is not as happy as some might think.

He turns now to his computer and peruses some of his newer finds. He rereads the headlines that warn of imminent tragedy.

'IS SHE ANOREXIC? SERIOUS CONCERN FOR LARRY'S GAL' and, 'SOCIALITE CARMEN COSTELLO DENIES SHE HAS AN EATING DISORDER'. He recalls the appearances Carmen has made in his dreams of late. Not as the voluptuous minx of twenty-five years ago but as a bony witch, her skin as thin as paper.

There can be no more doubt. It is she who is the pitiful figure under the tree, and as de Vere heaves the painting up from his desk to return it to the white cupboard, he struggles with all his might not to look at it again, as if it were alive, as if it might suck him up inside if he so much as catches a glimpse of its deadly blue. He reaches the alcove and bundles the picture inside, slamming the door shut and fumbling with the key like a nervous prison warden struggling to secure a drooling maniac.

When the door is locked, de Vere returns to his desk, smoothing down his hair with only slightly shaking hands. The Le Mesurier Technique. There must be no delay with the lift. He closes his eyes, breathes in the fumes of his glass then drinks. *A long delivery down the throat*, he mutters. *The length is slowly descending. It's a very attractive descent.*

He passes through all the floors: one floor, two floors, three, four, five . . . all the way down to the bottom. When he arrives at the basement, the lift doors open and de Vere gets out. He walks along the corridor until he arrives at the fifth door on the right. He stops, opens the door, goes into the room and sits on the high-backed chair behind the teacher's desk. He closes his eyes, takes a few deep breaths then opens them, turns to one of the empty wooden chairs in front of him and starts to speak.

I bumped into your mother, Lady Merriwether Frost, towards the end of my time in New York. It must have been in 1989. She told me that you'd just turned twenty-one and were in the habit of locking yourself in the attic at Summer Crest Hall to paint. As she talked on about her plans to send you to finishing school, I remember feeling shock at hearing your name mentioned again. I'd succeeded in scarcely thinking of you since I'd left England at the beginning of the eighties. But I wanted to help you. It took me less than a morning to convince your mother that you had rare qualities which would only benefit from several years at art college in Rome.

You had only just graduated when you called me that day at my East End gallery. It was the end of March, 1997, a month after my marriage to Bárbara. I assumed you were ringing because you felt you owed me a debt – saving you from a fate of Cordon Bleu classes and months of walking round a room with a book balanced on your head. Yet the sound of your voice produced a strange sensation in me; I felt as though I were falling down a very deep well in slow motion.

I suggested meeting up that afternoon – it was a beautiful spring day – and yet when I put the phone down my secretary asked me if I was feeling quite myself. I realised that I'd let my Charles Frederick de Vere mask slip and what remained was the timorous face of the boy who messed alone. But I pulled myself together. I snapped that I had to go to an appointment. I called my driver and told him to take me to the National Gallery.

I recognised you immediately.

'Hello, you!'

'Freddie!' you said. 'You look wonderful.'

I chuckled. 'Not as wonderful as you, my dear Cosima.'

I was petrified. It had been nearly sixteen years. We hadn't seen each other since the midnight feast. You were twenty-eight years old now and I was fifty-nine.

I hadn't even written you a letter when I heard the news about Ellsworth. The evening I came to the house to view his so-called masterpiece, I left shortly after you went upstairs to fetch the picture you'd painted at school. It was only the next day that I heard the news and not until later that I read the reports in the papers about the police swarming through the house and I realised what you must have seen.

I ran off to New York like a coward. My first marriage was

breaking up and I wanted to forget what had happened that night at Summer Crest Hall. I thought that the years away from England might give me strength. But they only brought me money. Even when I came back to London, my run of success seemed unstoppable. And when I married the Spike a few years later, nobody realised what a cynical arrangement it was.

We walked through the various rooms of the National Gallery saying how uninspiring the pictures were. Do you remember? At twenty-eight, you'd become more formidable than when you were twelve, although not so much had changed otherwise. You talked a little about your life. I had the impression that men your age bored you. They wanted you to be their girlfriend and that was the last thing you wanted. We talked about fashionable British artists – the pickled sharks, the embroidered tents – we discussed places we liked in Rome, food we had eaten. You stopped in front of some painted skulls. 'It's funny, isn't it,' you said. 'How heads look like they're smiling when all the flesh has been scraped off.' You turned to me. 'Funny to know that even in the depths of despair you're actually grinning like an idiot.'

Do you remember?

I thought then that you might say something. Make some mention of it. But you didn't. And the longer you didn't mention it, the bigger Ellsworth became, the more monstrous, the more ravishing in my mind.

The staid, under-lit paintings we walked past reminded me of the stately homes Ellsworth and I used to raid in the seventies. I'd never intended going into business with him, but six months after the wedding, his child bride came to see me at Sévigné. She informed me that Ellsworth had hit the doldrums again. He'd taken to his studio in the tack room and wouldn't come out.

She wasn't just upset, she was angry.

Cosima, you won't like what I am about to tell you, but I beg you to allow me some honesty. I admit that I did feel some compassion for Bárbara. I had been the one, after all, to introduce her to

Ellsworth and living with him had been no easy feat. It wasn't long before she saw his sophistry for what it was. As a child, her grandfather had given her an excellent grounding in art and philosophy and she began to resent her husband's pompous harangues. When Ellsworth realised that she had seen through him, he started drinking again. The jibes followed. Having previously claimed a fascination with Bárbara's language, her culture, her opinions, he took to ridiculing them. Port was a disgusting drink, her family name was so ugly-sounding, the Portuguese Man O'War the only effective thing ever to have come out of her country . . .

And so she came to feel contempt for Ellsworth. She told me that she felt abandoned, betrayed, left to rot in a big, cold house in the middle of Gloucestershire and the English were so dirty, so slapdash. I tried to calm her. She was six months pregnant with Franck and I felt it my duty to do something. I told her I'd come up to see Ellsworth that weekend. I admit, part of me was excited at the prospect of visiting the 'haunted house' at long last.

When I arrived, I found him slumped in an arm chair in the tack room. He was holding a Sèvres porcelain cup in one hand and a bottle of whisky in the other. He was staring at an array of canvases he'd finally had shipped back from Tangier. I'd been drunk when I visited his studio in Paris, but looking at his work now, I was flabbergasted.

'What do you think, Freddie?' he said. 'Some people say they're abstract but I think they're more human than that.'

He explained that each painting was an emotional recollection of an event in his life – a meal, an excursion, a party – hence some of the titles that I read: *Drinks in the Petit Socco, Call To Prayer, Majoun Sunset*.

By now, I was more familiar with the paintings of modern artists – people such as Howard Hodgkin and Bridget Riley. I didn't particularly like their work, but there was definitely something convincing about it. Looking now at the swooshes and slashes in front of me, the hesitant splodges and the muddy blottings-out – I didn't just feel an emotional blank, I felt physically sick. It struck me that my friend had no talent whatsoever. If Ellsworth had meant his paintings to be playful, vivid, dynamic, they were only ever cautious, drab, lacking in rhythm. They were certainly not capable of 'stirring the world from its torpor', as he had once promised to do.

'Know what *majoun* is?' he asked, hauling himself up from the chair. The slur in his voice was becoming more evident.

I told him I believed it to be a variety of hashish.

'"A variety of hashish,"' he said, mimicking my voice. Then he roared, 'It's a cake! The most inspirational cake in the whole bloody world!'

He hiccupped and collapsed back into the chair. He stank of whisky. And there was something new in his eyes; something I didn't quite trust any more.

'You infuse the hash into some butter,' he drawled. 'You mix it with almonds and honey and spices. I became famous for it with Eddie's crowd.'

He sighed as he studied the label on the whisky bottle.

'I sort of became Eddie's cook,' he confessed. 'He was knocking off his house boy. Couldn't get any work out of him.' He unscrewed the top of the bottle. 'I was a damn good cook. I didn't just make *majoun*. I did couscous. And pigeon tagine – you'd have liked that.'

He filled his cup with whisky.

'Didn't get me anywhere though. Eddie kept saying he'd come round to my studio but he never did . . .'

He was about to drink but stopped suddenly. He looked up, beaming.

'Tangier was amazing to start with, Freddie. I thought I was Sinbad the Sailor! Got myself a *djellaba*, some little Turkish slippers. I went to the market and bought some ornamental birds. Peacocks. They used to wander through the house making this comical hoot.'

He became more animated as he talked about Eddie and his sparkling crowd: actors and musicians and poets, a couple of fashionable London hairdressers, the playwright who came to the unfortunate end. Sometimes, after dinner, Eddie would persuade Ellsworth to wander over to a carpet shop in the Kasbah – the Bazaar Delilah. Radio Cairo would be blaring out from an old transistor radio and Momo, whose shop it was, would let them smoke large quantities of hash before persuading them to buy some more at a highly inflated price.

'I'd try and get Eddie to visit my studio afterwards. It was so near . . .'

Ellsworth's face fell and he downed the cup of whisky in one gulp.

'But there was always some famous rock and roll star to greet back at his house. Or, more likely, another piece of "chicken" he had to hunt down.'

He started to swig from the bottle.

'He visited in the end. Boxing Day. It was about three in the morning. I was painting, but of course he hadn't come to see my art. One of his bits of "chicken" had let him down. He was acting strangely. I don't know what he was on but he came up behind me, brushed my hair back and started kissing my neck. I froze. He knew immediately he'd done the wrong thing. He backed off. We both pretended it hadn't happened.'

As Ellsworth threw his Sèvres cup furiously to the floor, my eyes were pulled back to his awful pictures which filled the room like bad breath.

He read my mind.

'You have more in common with Eddie than you realise,' he announced.

He flicked a limp hand at the landscape of half-hearted spontaneity in front of us.

'Eddie thinks they're crap too. "Monumentally untalented." That's what he told me that night. I pretended I hadn't heard. I went to get him some *majoun*. He said he didn't want any. Said we'd have to stop being friends because it would be, "Too hard to look at you without remembering your ghastly paintings and thinking, 'Yuk'."'

Ellsworth gazed down at the broken china.

'I tried to sound jokey. I said, "That's rather a horrible thing to say." But Eddie just looked bored. "Oh no, not horrible," he answered. "I'm only horrible to people I love."'

I didn't know what to say.

I started to walk round the tack room. In one of the horse stalls, I noticed a pile of rubbish – books, broken furniture, ancient kitchen utensils. On closer inspection, I saw that a couple of old paintings had been shoved down between some chair legs and a warped card table: a shepherdess reposing, a winsome huntress drowsing in a grotto.

The frames were tarnished and the varnish was covered in hair-line cracks.

'I say, Ellsworth,' I said. 'You really ought to do something with these.'

'I *am* going to do something,' he mumbled. 'I'm going to throw them out.'

'But . . .'

'Father's junk!' he exploded. 'I can't be bothered with it any more.'

I didn't say anything else, but when we went inside the house, what struck me most were the paintings in the Long Room. Strange fanciful stuff for such a gothic place: a frisky girl on a swing; a rather racy-looking sea nymph. The frills and the rouge and the swelling bosoms dazzled the eye and lightened the heart. I began to feel more cheerful. Ellsworth too seemed in better spirits.

'Filthy bugger, my dead pa,' he said, casting an eye over the walls. 'I blame those tarts in Shepherd's Market.'

He smiled. An Ellsworth grin. It made me see that everything was going to be all right. He wasn't depressed at all. He was just being rather more petulant then usual. I watched him sit down and throw his feet up on the shining surface of the dining room table.

'Actually, he's got a huge collection of eighteenth century fluff.' He paused. 'And I hear that *you're* rather a good salesman.'

I should have given Ellsworth up, but I realised I could make money with him. He made a solemn promise to control his drinking and what with his family's paintings and those we took off the hands of some of his friends, we started doing rather well.

There was still a lot of aristocratic treasure to be pillaged around the country in the seventies. If Dorothy Sykes had been my *entrée* at school, that role had now passed to Ellsworth. Every exceptional dealer aspires to know the whereabouts of all the best paintings and since many of them were in the homes of the British aristocracy, it was useful for me to have a spy whose background meant that he knew most of the great houses inside out.

To start with, I relished the masquerade of those visits. I played the serious art aficionado while Ellsworth was the good-natured, libertine son of well-born parents who was visiting to catch up on old times. We sold the paintings for high prices to Americans looking for some instant ancestors. By cutting out the middle-man we started to make some money. By 1974, I had enough to leave Sévigné and set up on my own at Claridges.

The year 1974 also coincided with the ending of one of Bárbara's love affairs. (I'd been aware for a while that she had found a new way of coping with her husband's deficiencies.) With extra time on her hands, she took to visiting me at Claridges. She was rather amusing in the early seventies. I remember Reception calling up one summer afternoon to inform me that there was someone waiting in the lobby. When I came downstairs, I was struck by the sight of a petite young woman tapping a tiny foot impatiently on the marble floor. Her hand was slung on the hip of a pair of fitted cream slacks and her slinky silk blouse was rippling in the breeze from the revolving door. When she saw me, she peered coquettishly over the top of her Jackie O sunglasses, purred, 'Ciao, gajo,' and announced that she had booked us a table for tea.

I followed the music of her dangly gold jewellery and when we were seated, I said I hoped that the strikes currently crippling the country hadn't inconvenienced her train journey from Gloucestershire.

'Puh!' She shrugged dismissively. 'Your little strikes. You should experience a revolution such as the one happening in my country!'

I was about to ask if she was looking forward to the democracy that seemed likely to follow April's coup d'état in Portugal, when the cake stand arrived. Bárbara ostentatiously removed all the scones and replaced them with a dozen pastéis de nata she had secreted in her Gucci shoulder bag. She whispered from behind a dainty hand that after flagging down a taxi near Paddington, she had stopped off at a Portuguese bakery in the Golborne Road.

'Let us hope,' she added, 'that the so-called revolutionaries will not be eating cake today.'

There was a loud jangle as she suddenly threw her hands into the air.

'Fifty years of brutal fascist oppression! That is what these mischief-makers are saying about my country's leaders!'

She composed herself before leaning forward and dabbing icing sugar from the corner of my lips.

'Let me tell you something, *gajo*,' she confided. 'The staff in my father's hotels always found Salazar to be a perfect gentleman.'

When she was happy that I had eaten enough of her custard tarts, she insisted on going upstairs to view my latest favourite painting. At first, she gazed quietly at the array of antique pinks and blues that I showed her. She nodded politely as I extolled their charms and virtues. It was only when I balked at taking her into my inner sanctum that her mood changed.

She snatched a mirror from her bag and began to touch up her lipstick. As she did so, she saw fit to inform me that the Sèvres tea cups were still being put to improper use in Gloucestershire and that her husband would often stagger off into the fields with his gun and his wolfhounds, forgetting to padlock the studio door behind him.

She snapped the compact closed and kicked a tiny suede heel in the direction of the paintings.

'Frankly,' she drawled, 'I have already seen most of this froth in half-finished states in the bloody tack room . . .'

A gust of wind shook the room.

When I opened my eyes, I was sitting on the crimson couch and Bárbara was telling me that this could be kept as, 'Our little secret.'

But I was only vaguely aware of her because an insane vision was erupting in front of me: Ellsworth being swept away in a torrent of water, his arms reaching out to me, screaming at me to help him, begging me to save his life and me doing nothing; kicking him away from the bank, letting the waters drag him off, drown him, suck him down dead into a drain.

He had lied to me, deceived me and so now the alluring woodland creature was dead to me.

When my anger subsided, I wasn't sure who I was any more. I'd always believed it was my passion for individual paintings that had propelled me into the art world. But maybe the truth was that I was more drawn to the showmanship and the pleasure of making a sale. What, after all, was this new emotion seeping into my chest?

It took me a while to register that it was elation.

It suddenly struck me as funny that while Ellsworth's own hideous work was genuine, the graceful works of art I had been selling for the past four years were fakes painted by the very same hand!

I said that your uncle had no talent for painting, Cosima. But what I should have said is that he had no talent for originality. What he had an incredible gift for was pastiche. In fact, he could only really be himself when he was copying someone else. His fakes were characterised by strong, confident lines and he had a startling ability to reproduce the world around him in oil paint: fabrics, jewellery, skin tones, foliage – you felt as if you could reach into one of his rococo scenes and ruffle the lace on a wispy *jabot*, stroke the squirrel trim on a blue silk pelisse.

There was a kind of genius to it.

Or so I told myself.

He'd done much of his homework in Paris. He'd worked for several months at an old masters' gallery in the Latin Quarter, handling thousands of prints and drawings of all periods, acquainting himself with the feel of hand-made paper. He learned ancient canvas-stretching techniques and made sure he procured all the right tools: an antique *camera obscura*, a porphyry stone for grinding colours. He'd gathered a coterie of charlatans around him – the Hungarian rococo expert, for instance, who could be relied upon to verify many an afternoon's work as, 'school of', 'attributed to' or 'preliminary study for', if not stamp it as work of the artist himself.

210

But if the idea of forgery had first come to him in Paris, it was in New York that he found his first customers. Silver Tony, his film maker friend from the Factory, used to ridicule contemporary art. He preferred the nineteenth-century landscapes that he'd find in junk shops or at the bottom of rubbish bins.

'Modern abstract art is nothing but atrocious graphics,' Silver Tony would rage from a table at Max's Kansas City as Ellsworth made figurative doodles in his 'trip diary' to try and calm him down: ladies with parasols, dandies with pedigree hunting dogs.

One afternoon, he took Silver Tony to the Frick Collection on Fifth Avenue. He led him immediately to the Fragonard room which he knew contained the painter's rococo masterpiece: a series of capricious panels known as *The Progress of Love*.

'Fragonard painted them for Madame du Barry,' Ellsworth told Silver Tony. 'And when he'd finished, she decided she didn't want them any more.'

'Bitch.'

'Whore, actually,' Ellsworth corrected him. 'The King's whore. That was the problem.'

He pointed to one of the panels.

'There's the culprit. *Storming The Citadel*, it's called.'

Silver Tony went to look closer at the rosy-cheeked man clambering over a wall as his lover thrust her hand melodramatically against him.

'People say that Fragonard became unfashionable in France because revolution was brewing,' Ellsworth said. 'But actually, Madame du Barry sent *Storming the Citadel* back for very apolitical reasons.'

'Which were?'

'She thought it suggested she was an easy lay.'

He slung his hands deep in his pockets.

'So she told Fragonard it didn't suit the décor of the chateau that Louis XV had given her. Poor chap died in poverty. *Plus ça change*, Silver.'

'But how did all this stuff end up in the States?

211

'A virtuoso salesman,' Ellsworth explained. 'Lord Duveen of Millbank.'

'Who?'

'An art dealer. A good one can raise you from the dead.'

Silver stepped back and looked again at the panels all around the room.

'Amazing. I mean, who can paint like that today?'

'I can,' Ellsworth said simply.

And that was how it began. If Ellsworth was impressed by Andy Warhol's silk-screen techniques, Silver said he knew plenty of society types who would be impressed with Ellsworth's ability to paint like an eighteenth-century artist.

Silver was an excellent businessman until his amphetamine habit got the better of him. Understanding that reliability was of the utmost importance in this new enterprise, Ellsworth decided to quit while he was ahead. On his return to London in the summer of 1966, he produced a few old master sketches for the owner of a chain of Soho strip joints, but on the whole, the money he'd made in New York was sufficient to tide him over while he tried to develop a style of his own.

When his world collapsed in Tangier, he decided that I would be a perfect business partner. The ultimate rock.

I should have stopped when I found out what he was doing, but I didn't. For a few weeks after Bárbara's revelation, I resolved to take the ethical stand of only selling to dealers or through salesrooms. I reasoned that such people earn their living from being able to tell the difference between the genuine and the spurious. I told myself that it was perfectly fair to pit my wits against theirs. But then, one of my 'ladies' called expressing interest in another lavish scene of *al fresco* gallivanting and I gave in, convincing myself that it was impossible to have a moral code in the jungle of art dealing.

Besides, my life wasn't entirely fraudulent. My work didn't only revolve around the bulky packages wrapped in brown paper that arrived in a white van from Gloucestershire once a month. When Ellsworth and I visited stately homes together, I had seen with my own eyes that the treasures we came away with had most definitely been marked by the passage of time and a few of the paintings at Summer Crest Hall actually were from the eighteenth century. Ellsworth's great grandfather, a notable London physician, had purchased them in the early nineteenth century when the likes of Boucher and Fragonard were still tainted by their association with the *ancien régime* and their work could be had for a song.

Still, I had long since recognised that finding outstanding eighteenth-century paintings was no easy task. I came across many fine pictures with regrettable subject matter: boys with podgy faces, gentlemen with bald heads, ladies who had reached a certain age all too quickly.

Many artists from the eighteenth century are virtually indistinguishable from one another.

I never confronted Ellsworth. We simply never talked about it. I did send some of the brown paper packages back, claiming that I couldn't sell them. But that was only part of the reason we began to grow apart. I felt some unease at having been forced, you might say, into an affair with his wife. Bárbara was happy enough with the afternoon entertainment I showed her on the chaise longue behind the Diana screen and the liaison served to avert any blackmail threats. Luckily, her modelling career was taking off and work trips abroad were expanding her horizons. After a few months, her twenty-two-year-old heart tired of me and she embarked on a new affair with a photographer in Rio de Janeiro.

Soon, I didn't need Ellsworth any more. There was still a small rococo market, especially a seam we'd tapped into for smutty mythological allegory, but thanks to Carmen Costello, I'd found a much more satisfying niche in the post-Impressionist market. By the end of the seventies the white van rarely ventured up to Claridges. Neither did Ellsworth, who preferred to stay in the country shooting birds and drinking himself silly, so I imagined.

*   *   *

All of this flashed in and out of my mind as you and I made our tour of the National Gallery, Cosima. I was so excited by your presence and yet so troubled by memories of Ellsworth. I was hoping that one of the paintings we walked past might rescue me from the alternating waves of nausea and euphoria. And yet, as we wandered from gallery to gallery, I found no picture capable of wrenching me back to the present. *So much blood on the walls*, I thought. *So much human emotion: greed, ambition, jealousy, passion. All captured and tamed in fine gilt frames. Domesticated savagery on a grand scale.*

And then I saw it. A painting that had somehow escaped my attention on the afternoon I spent here with Earl P. Johnson VI all those years ago. It showed Ganymede flying. The claw of an enormous bird was about to rip into the flesh of the boy's inner thigh. We stopped in front of it. Do you remember? I turned to look at you but you were already staring at me.

The moon white of your skin and a tender patch of flesh about to be damaged.

I stopped fighting the delicious sickness I could feel in my stomach. And the more I embraced it, the more famished I became. I hadn't felt hungry in years but my appetite returned that afternoon, and by the time we left the National Gallery, I was a starving man.

'Come to my suite at Claridges one afternoon next week,' I said. Do you remember?

Even now I'm not sure if it was you who was exciting me or if it was the corpse you were carrying on your shoulders. I thought you would save me from my memories, my nightmares. I wanted you to smother me, to suffocate the demons, but I also wanted you to show me a glimpse, to help me understand.

You had always fascinated me but now it struck me that I needed you. You had found a dead man in a bath of blood at the age of twelve. You were my ship in a bottle and part of the pleasure was that I knew I would never be able to extract the ship.

CHAPTER TWENTY-THREE

De Vere's bedroom at Claridges makes Cosima think she has been led into a forest in the middle of the night. Cornices and curlicues and arabesques sprout as far as the eye can see and everything shines in black and gold. De Vere has taken her to the inner sanctum, the forbidden chamber.

It is cold and rainy in the street outside but it is warm inside the bedroom. Too warm. Cosima notes the canopied four-poster bed, the black brocade on the walls, the paintings – Sickert, Picasso, van Dongen, Francis Bacon – a collection worth millions. The black velvet drapes on the window keep out most of the light and the stale waft of lilies hangs in the air along with a smell of fat, of roasting flesh.

'Sit down,' he says, surprising Cosima. Generally, if anyone orders her to do anything, she refuses on principle.

A small flame ignites inside her, and yet since last week at the National Gallery she knows that her old life has ended. She is impatient for the new one to begin as she sits down and contemplates the plate of caviar on the table in front of her. She wonders if he remembers about the eggs.

'Here you are,' he says, handing her a flute of champagne. 'To happy days!'

She can see he is nervous, in spite of the bluster. She looks at a framed woman on the wall. Black and green and dirty white. Fat flanks on soiled sheets. No face just a muddy hole.

Do you like my paintings?' he asks.

'They're better than the stuffed bird in the other room.'

'I'm going to get rid of that owl,' he tells her. 'I'm thinking of getting a cage of monkeys instead!'

He waits for the laugh but nothing comes. He hesitates. 'People tell me they'll smell bad. But I intend to spray them daily in the Empress Eugenie's favourite perfume!'

When their eyes lock, the smile drops from de Vere's face. He is a wizard or a druid you find in the woods, the stag who finds you bathing, the one you have to kill although you have to fuck it first.

He makes a clumsy lunge towards her and when she pushes him away she sees a black egg lodged between his teeth. 'I have no interest in kissing you,' she says. 'I possibly have an interest in using your dick.'

He gasps. He looks as if he has seen a vision. As if he might kneel down in front of her, worship her.

She gets up from the table, moves closer to him. Through his shirt she pinches hard on a nipple and he bends to the pain, twists with it. The public-spirited, unselfish gentleman drains from his face. His blue eyes turn weak. The flesh under his shirt is soft as the veal skin jacket he is wearing. Rib bones under soft flesh. Repulsive. She doesn't kiss him. She opens her mouth and lets him smell her breath.

But he is a magician.

'I wish I were able to suspend time,' he says, gently pinning her arms to her sides. 'Keep things exactly at this point. Because this moment is filled with endless possibilities.'

He feels her heart beating as he holds her.

'The sand trickles through the hour glass so quickly,' he whispers in her ear. 'Once it starts there's no stopping it. Much better to suspend time, prolong pleasure.'

He releases her.

'Don't you think?'

Now she is confused. He walks away from her, disappears through a door at the back of the room. She hears the sound of pans, the rattle of plates. She smells the roasting flesh again.

The huge voice travels from the other room.

'Have you read any Colette?'

She feels a tingling in her belly.

'No.'

He returns holding two plates covered with silver domes.

'Tante Alicia tells Gigi that learning how to eat boiled eggs and asparagus will prepare her for entry to polite society.'

He sets the plates on the table.

'The delicacy which prepares Gigi for the life of a courtesan is much more . . . complex.'

Cosima looks at the silver mounds as de Vere opens a bottle of red wine with a large letter 'V' and a golden laurel on the label.

'Some claim the greatest claret of the twentieth century to be the 1951 Pétrus,' he says. 'But a friend once told me that the night before he died he would drink a Mouton Rothschild 1945 – *L'Année de la Victoire*.'

De Vere has not tasted the *grand vin* since the mid-1950s when he tried it in Ellsworth's tiny school bedroom. He lets Cosima drink first. She takes the glass without saying anything. It tastes of hare's entrails and dungeons and dandruffy old men with nanny's treacle tart stuck between their teeth. She looks him in the eyes until she sees the deep blue drain to pale and she is confident again of her powers.

He stands up and removes one of the domes from its plate. Through a haze of steam, she sees a small roast bird scarcely bigger then a thumb. She can't help laughing.

'The songbirds!' she says.

He remembered, she thinks.

'My first time too,' he tells her with a smile. As he brings his chair closer to hers, he tells her that he obtained the illegal consignment of Ortolans from one of his French 'spies'.

She feels the warmth of his hands. In the murky inner sanctum, she is just aware of the brush of his fingers on her neck as he covers her head with a dark hood that pricks her face. Then his voice, a deep rumble that fills the room.

'Locked in a box and gorged on figs. Drowned in brandy,

then plucked and baked. Laid out to rest on a tongue. A heavy cloth to concentrate the fumes, to hide you from the eyes of God.'

There is a rich chuckle and then a flash of light as his hand reaches under the hood, crawls over her face, touches her cheeks, her lips, her jaw, eases open her mouth. 'Taste the guilt,' he whispers, sliding a weight of warm flesh on her tongue, closing her mouth, tightening the cloth over her face, his hands touching her bare shoulders, her throat, brushing her breasts, making her moan.

'Breathe deep,' he says, his face close on the other side of the hood. 'Taste the bird's whole life.'

His hand abandons her breasts, slides down her belly. The skin between her thighs is so soft, like feathers on the throat of a songbird. It makes him gasp. The exhilaration of another beginning. But he must restrain himself. He must only add to his pleasure, proliferate the possibilities. Why obey the striking of the clock? He must defy death, hold everything back at the start – the supreme indulgence. If the wings of a butterfly are to keep their sheen, they must remain untouched.

He takes his hand away from the warm, wet nest between Cosima's thighs, savouring her small cry of regret. He leaves her to make her way through the bird's life and lifts the second silver mound to begin his own journey. He puts a hood over his own head, closes his eyes and places the tiny creature on his tongue.

His teeth glide slowly through the tender flesh, his tongue savouring the succulence of tiny muscles. As he chews away in the darkness, he tastes the salt of Mediterranean air, the richness of Moroccan wood smoke, the sweet fumes of Armagnac, the tang of puddles and thistles. He feels the span of tiny wings gliding through sunny skies, he breathes in the euphoria of flight. He is momentarily conscious of his bliss when the cloth of the hood scratches his cheeks as he grins. And then he falls into a dream where he exists only as taste itself.

The pungent fumes take him away from the suite in Claridges, on and on he flies, over fields and seas, through time, far away to a bubbling pan of cream and vintage port. Two pigeon breasts, two bent forks and a glistening head of black curls. He chews harder on the Ortolan flesh but slower too, anything to prolong this flash of heaven.

Messing time. The kitchen. The other boys all gone. Ellsworth in the doorway, a dead bird in his hand. He goes to the sink, cuts off the limp neck with a pen knife, sticks his arm inside and pulls out a sausage of innards.

'Found some vintage Warre in the old man's cellar,' he tells de Vere. He hacks into the breasts. 'I'm going to fry them in butter, then add cream and the port.'

He turns to de Vere, wiping a bloody hand over his forehead.

'Should be all right, don't you think, Freddie?'

De Vere is shocked to feel a lump in his throat. Why is Ellsworth talking to him? Calling him by his proper name? Doesn't he realise that de Vere is now worse than a dog? A dog in disgrace. Since his interview with the headmaster this afternoon, his expulsion is certain. He has packed his belongings. His train leaves for Scotland at nine o'clock tomorrow morning.

Ellsworth doesn't wait for a reply. The butter is already sizzling in the pan, the pink breasts follow, then the cream and the port until the bubbling sauce, the warmth of the stove, the proffered fork and blue-rimmed enamel plate make de Vere feel as though he is being lifted out of a cold sea just in the nick of time.

But the cloud is passing. The smells of cream and port vanish, the pale forehead smeared with pigeon's blood disappears under a thick mist. All that remains is a pair of glassy black eyes pleading with de Vere in the gloom of a French jazz club. De Vere is sneaking off early, back to the Hotel Bristol. Only, as he glances round to check that Ellsworth hasn't noticed him, their eyes meet. For a split second, he has the impression that Ellsworth wants de Vere to pull him out of the well of monster's blood that is starting to drown him. Under the hood, de Vere now sees that this is the instant an artist might have captured in a portrait, a moment of weakness that makes every human being moving. It was a second when everything could have changed. But it passed. Ellsworth turned away, back into the jazz club, the lustre of his curls disappearing into the smoke and the gloom.

De Vere crushes the Ortolan's pea-sized lungs in his teeth and the last dregs of fragrant air dry up on his tongue. A sadness seeps on to his palate that soon engulfs his whole body. The sweetness of the songbird has passed and all that remains is the bitterness of bones. The sickening crunch, a drunkard's laughter, a rictus of sneer on cherubic lips.

Ellsworth at the bottom of everything.

De Vere starts to choke. He rips the hood from his head, gasping for breath. Cosima has returned from her journey and sits staring at him. He turns away, snatches for his glass of wine. *L'Année de la Victoire.* And yet, as it rushes down his throat, it brings him no relief. He groans as he feels the taste of victory bleeding into his body. *The horrifying taste of victory!* Ellsworth hisses in his ear.

He panics. He imagines the hourglass. His only hope. He sets it on its head but immediately, a weight of panic falls into his guts, a tidal wave of fear that threatens to sink all his lily pads and damn him to mortality. He takes hold of Cosima but as he carries her to the bed, all he is aware of is sand slipping inexorably through his fingers.

Soon he slobbers and squelches over her arsehole like a warlock doing black magic. Now that the outpouring has begun, he has determined to profit from every grain. She turns to see murder on his face, black tar dripping from his mouth as he writhes on a polluted sea and then he dives in, he goes under, shouting like a gaga old man from an old people's home rolling around in a filthy bath.

She marvels at his ability to cast off, to give himself up to the deluge that pours faster and faster down on him, rushing through this body, reviving every piece of skin. She sees the monogrammed suitcase by the bed as he turns himself onto his front, his pale, desperate arse in the air.

'Do it,' he rasps. 'Do it now!'

He pushes his cock down into the mattress, he spreads his legs, spreads his butt cheeks.

'Say please,' she tells him.

'Do it!'

'Say please.'

His grey head twitches with irritation but she slaps him into submission with a lash of her belt. He gasps. He soaks up the pain, drinks it in. She teases the leather tail over the angry red marks.

'Say please.'

'Please give me some more.'

She removes an implement from the case.

'You want some more?'

He whimpers at the creak of leather, the jangle of buckles.

'Oh . . . God.'

He's ready to give it up now. Give up the grouse and the fine wines and the household staff and the trustee meetings and the, 'Can you imagine his despair, Mrs Thoroughgood!' The unselfish, public-spirited gentleman wants to not exist for as long as he possibly can. He gasps as the black rubber slides back and forth, deeper and deeper. And now he strains, he wails like a man who's seen a ghost, a wail of fear – silly and melodramatic and electrically honest.

'Yes!' he calls, desperately. 'Do it now!'

When they finally come to, there's broken glass in the sea and fizzing surf all around.

She comes to see him more and more. Sometimes he orders in seafood and champagne and they go crazy. She can hardly believe it the next day. The things they've done. Sometimes they have grouse and claret and then his arms and shoulders are cliffs, his hair is a forest, his hands are slabs of granite and when he passes

221

her a glass like a priest at mass passing a chalice, she takes it, inhales the dangerous fumes and already, before the wine is halfway down her throat, she knows it has turned to blood.

It thrills her. She is giddy. The flayed skin, the twisted nipples, a lump of head between her legs, a mouth that's gagged with hair and muscle. A union of vipers convulsing on the bed, his head in her mouth, begging for the slaughter. And when he finally falls over the edge of the precipice, crashing with a howl into the raging sea below she jumps too, without thought of a parachute. Because she never falls, she only rises. She takes off into the skies, higher and higher, turns into vapour and covers him in dew, in wet.

And afterwards, when the naked Atlas sprawls in the tangled sea of pungent sheets, surrounded by a debris of greasy bones and cheap sex toys and tipped-up bottles of *grands vins*, she wonders at the power that she wields, the rock that he is. She watches him balance the telephone on his broad chest, his face flushed and petulant against the battered pillows as he chides the director of the Rijksmuseum in Amsterdam about import fees and, 'Entry via Rotterdam as I have told Henrich to proceed with a hundred times!'

They see each other every day when de Vere is not travelling. They give each other watches as presents, to remind each other that time is still ticking away. Soon, de Vere is with her even when he is away. His voice begins to eat inside her head. The mould grows like the map of a country that swells to the size of a continent. Like clumps of spores growing on the wall of a cold cellar, you can't stop them once they've begun. The black eggs that took up residence when she was twelve years old now begin to spread throughout her body. Dirty voice, damp thoughts, spunking on her clean skin. Like roaches in a building: once they're in they'll never leave, you have to burn it to the ground.

And then one day it is too late. She sees that the ground is hurtling towards her and she doesn't know how to stop.

One afternoon, as they collapse into the bed after their respective explosions, her hand lands on his arm. The pale, slender fingers clasp the old skin for several seconds, before they spring away in a shock of awareness. It is an event that does not pass unnoticed by Charles Frederick de Vere. It has been a source of irritation to him that Cosima will not let him kiss her. And naturally, she has kept up her promise of the first day that *she* has no intention of kissing *him*. Indeed, he marvels how so seasoned a whore could be coiled up so deeply inside such a gentle little cat.

De Vere determines to make her drop her guard. He knows from his business ventures that everyone has their price and he imagines he knows what Cosima's is.

They lie together in the four poster bed and he begins to talk of escape.

'We'll drive across America,' he says.

'Yes, Dog!' she says. 'Yes!'

She is the only one he allows to call him 'Dog'. He tells her that nobody else knows about the name, although he omits to tell her who christened him.

'In the middle of nowhere,' he says, lighting a cigar. 'Just you and me.'

'Nobody to bother us, Dog!'

'Nobody at all,' he chuckles. 'We'll catch a fish from a stream and roast it.'

'A trout!' The delicate fingers close tighter on the old arm.

'A trout,' he says, watching his smoke rings float up to the ceiling. 'And we'll serve it with a *soupçon* of butter . . .'

She sits up.

'But . . . where would we get the butter from?'

Her hands have left him now. Her arms are clasped around her naked breasts. He tries to calm her. He strokes her with his warm hands.

'Baby,' comes the purr. 'I'd just happen to have some with me.'

She frowns, she leaves the bed.

'You wouldn't have any butter,' she says. 'Because where would we get butter in the middle of nowhere?'

He's not sure if this is a joke. He wonders if he should laugh.

'Well,' he stumbles, 'I'd . . .'

'That proves you wouldn't really go on the journey. You wouldn't dare to run away with me.'

His eyes cloud over as he watches her rage.

'I'd go on the journey!' she says, desperately. 'I'd dare to do it!'

'Yes,' he sighs, all the Charles Frederick de Vere puffed out of him. 'I think you would.'

Then he begs. 'Baby,' he says, softly. He holds his arms open to her. She knows she only has a small amount of time before he goes back to the Spike. 'I have duties,' he says, wearily.

'You didn't have to marry her!' she accuses.

De Vere looks at her as if she has struck him. 'After he . . . died, I thought I owed it to her.' He looks away. 'I thought I owed it to Ellsworth.'

This is the first time he has mentioned his name. They never talk about him. Once, by accident, when she mentioned the words 'Uncle Ellsworth', she witnessed him sag. He began talking pompously about an, 'incredible new painting' he had just acquired. He made a patronising dig at the apparent 'gaps' in her art-history knowledge. He hinted that she should dress more elegantly.

She was shocked by his cruelty. She felt herself shrink inside her paint-speckled man's shirt. Suddenly her arrows were all gone. She didn't even have her quiver. *I've let him grow too confident*, she thought. *I've let him have too much.*

Then she regrets how she let him tickle her palm as they walked hand in hand in Brook Street in the early morning when he knew it would be deserted. She regrets how she let him slip inside her, how he thrust inside her and she saw a tiger being slaughtered, a colonial master spearing an animal and she was so excited she wouldn't allow herself to come. She hates this memory now although the colour and shape of it will be forever burned into her mind: ivory and orange, brutish, the blood-soaked sabre teeth. And afterwards, how he stayed inside, trolling around like a tank roaming through the rubble, searching for spoilings in the depths of the ruins, the very last pieces.

She regrets all of this now. She feels hopeless. And yet she rises up, stands up to the naked Atlas: 'Just because Uncle Ellsworth died you didn't have to marry his wife!'

'Baby . . .'

'That doesn't make it any better! It was too late to make things better!'

He drinks up her lost, frightened eyes and soon there is a new light in his. Excitement, maybe. An unnameable lust.

'Please . . .' he humbles himself before her, trembling with anticipation. 'I felt it was my duty . . . you know what happened . . .'

He looks up, a mad hope shining in his eyes. 'You of all people saw what happened.'

But she won't give it to him. What he wants.

'Her of all women – the Spike.'

He pleads. 'My baby, I have responsibilities. I . . .'

She stands above him, watching him wanting her. He wants to be a rich man but loved as if he were poor. She looks at his scratchy schoolboy trousers laid over a chair, she thinks of his old man arsehole all green with barnacles.

When she finally kisses him, his lips are cold and musty. She thinks of torn plastic sheet from a shanty house flapping in the breeze and inside, an empty cupboard, a bare pantry with shelves all scrubbed and never any food.

For a while, this gives her strength.

*   *   *

Charles Frederick de Vere turns to the chair in front of the teacher's desk. He asks the question he always asks before he leaves his underground room:

Cosima, are you there?

And then:

Are you all right, Cosima?

225

As always, the chair remains empty. Yet something is different today. When he turns and goes to open the door of his room, he decides not to leave the basement just yet. He opens the door and steps into the hallway but instead of turning left and walking back to the lift, he makes a few steps to the right and lingers a while in the damp blackness, listening to the echoes coming from the other end of the corridor.

Soon, he thinks, Carmen will know the truth about Charles Frederick de Vere, master thief, stealer of youth, polluter of dreams. The man who let Cosima drink from his poisoned cup until she lost the will to live.

As he carries on looking into the shadows, fragments of sound start to work their way into his ear. Subtle hints and disconnected words come floating down the icy hallway until some of them string themselves together and he believes he hears a voice.

'I wanted to kill myself,' it says. 'But I didn't want to be dead.'

He trembles. His whole body starts to shake.

Cosima.

Yes. That is who he can hear. He is certain of it. A smile radiates over his face.

He starts to see it all now.

He goes back quickly into his room. He remains inside for much of the day before finally leaving, going back to the lift and climbing – *ten, nine, eight, seven, six* – all the floors up to his East End gallery.

CHAPTER TWENTY-FOUR

Carmen is surprised to note that Cosima's grip is reassuringly tight as she grabs her arm and drags her away from the monkey painting, out of the attic room, down the granite stairs and along the drafty corridor until they are standing outside room number 1981.

'We need to go into your bedroom,' Cosima says, catching her breath. 'Is that all right?'

Carmen nods. She's still wondering what Cosima must be like in the sack to have snared de Vere. She follows her into the bedroom – a tangle of lips and black hair and hot white skin flashing through her mind – and goes to sit next to her on the edge of the bed.

There is an awkward silence before Carmen decides to speak.

'You said your paintings were good for releasing stuff,' she says, tentatively. 'But I guess you still have a lot to release with de Vere . . .'

Cosima snaps on her drawing room mask.

'Don't start talking like a shrink,' she warns. Then she catches Carmen's eye. 'I'm sorry,' she says, touching the mythology tiles on the headboard of the bed. 'Do you remember that first day in my studio?'

'Sure,' Carmen replies, thinking of the piece of sheepskin and her naked butt.

'You told me that Picasso warned his lover to take things slowly because there was only a limited amount of sand in the hour-glass.'

'Well, I . . .'

'The thing is,' Cosima says, 'De Vere and I . . . our hourglass was stopped rather abruptly.'

'Bummer.'

'Yes. I wondered what to do with all the sand.'

She takes her hand away from the tiles.

'This is Ellsworth's old room, you know.'

'Yeah? You probably know who all those mythology people are then.'

'What?'

'Orpheus and Eurydice,' Carmen says, pointing to the lettering under each picture. 'I know that's an opera. And Theseus and the Minotaur, that's the bull story. But the guy with the winged shoes. Perseus. What did he do?'

'He slayed Medusa.'

'The snake chick who turned men into stone?'

Cosima looks annoyed. 'Zeus turned himself into a swan to rape Leda. But he doesn't get typecast as a repulsive monster.'

'I guess not,' Carmen says, thinking back to the Fragonard swan porn de Vere showed her that first day in his suite.

'It was the Greeks who turned Medusa into a monster,' Cosima tells her. 'She was revered before that. In ancient Libya, she was worshipped as the Mistress of the Beasts.'

Cosima sighs. 'De Vere once told me that when Perseus hacked off Medusa's head, the blood that fell from the stump of her neck created a fountain. It was where the muses would drink when they needed inspiration.'

'Gross . . .'

'He said that art's blood is dirty because it springs from the blood of the monster. The Gorgon's neck. But what is dirt, Carmen?'

Carmen thinks she'd better keep quiet.

'It's female mystery and wisdom. The untamable forces of nature and all that. That's what Medusa originally was.'

A smile appears on the corner of Cosima's lips. 'Still, I can't deny that I found de Vere's concept of dirty art quite exciting.' She gets up and walks over to the casement window. 'When I met him again as an adult. I hoped he'd make my blood dirty. And he did. We built a house of cards, made it higher and higher. We set a glass on the very edge of the shelf.'

She watches a cobweb blowing in a draft through the closed window. 'I was the glass. But I didn't realise that until I was broken.'

She turns round and comes back to the bed. 'It was quick. We met at the National Gallery and then he invited me back to his suite at Claridges.' She makes a smile of mock horror. 'The forbidden bedroom. It was very funny. Monogrammed silver hair-brushes and things.'

Carmen smiles but she doesn't get the impression that Cosima found it funny at the time. She can't resist asking what the sex was like.

'The best sex I had in my life,' Cosima replies.

As she gives Carmen time to digest this piece of information, she recalls how speedily she'd bedded de Vere. Memories of the art dealer had certainly crossed her mind over the years, and yet it was only the marriage notice she'd spotted in a newspaper one day that made her decide to see him again. When the newsprint turned blurry on the page and she became aware of a pounding in her throat, Cosima construed it as a sign that she was about to embark on another voyage of discovery.

She had long ago decided that in order to avoid being haunted by gruesome memories from that hot August night of 1981, she would have to keep on moving, keep pushing herself to the limit. A life of thrill and adventure and risk. After all, her uncle Ellsworth used to insist that experience was sacred to every artist.

She became rather enchanted by the idea of an affair with one of her mother's friends. Aunt Spike's new husband. And the fact that de Vere was fifty-nine – nearly an old man – meant that he would be grateful to her. Even if he wasn't, she was no longer a blushing ingénue; she was twenty-eight and equal, she told herself, to take on a man of the world such as Charles Frederick de Vere. A young corporate lawyer had recently caused her some heartache and she reasoned that de Vere would be good for her confidence.

Except there was little reason in the air on the afternoon they met at the National Gallery. When Cosima finally let herself gaze into the sparkling eyes, she felt a bolt of lightning in her chest. Her childhood awe of de Vere had blossomed into desire and as she stood in front of *The Abduction of Ganymede*, she knew that her life was about to be turned on its head once again. She relished the prospect and knew that unless she acted fast, she might not act at all.

'Unfortunately, the blissful part didn't last very long,' she tells Carmen. 'I remember leaving Claridges one day and starting to cry in the street. Despair, I suppose you'd call it. My imagination started to relish horror. Something like a horror film entered my head. It would slow down and I'd have to stop and have a really good look. It struck me that I was having a nervous breakdown. I didn't want to kill myself but I feared that I'd be drawn to it. I couldn't breathe for thoughts of gruesome porn and botched suicides: women flailing at necks with broken glass, mangling their limbs in shiny blades, bodies falling from bridges and blood oozing down windscreens like lumpy sauce . . .'

'So . . . you killed yourself.'

'Kill myself!'

A breeze of a laughter fills the room.

Carmen looks puzzled.

'But I thought the people who run this place all killed themselves.'

'They did,' Cosima says. 'Apparently.'

'So . . .'

'Oh, I'm not one of the nurses. I just like to paint. I have to paint.'

She makes a lop-sided smile.

'Although I always have an appalling confrontation with myself whenever I finish a picture. I always think, "Is that it? Is that all there is?"'

She touches the Perseus tile again.

'Poor Freddie. Do you think I've been too harsh on him?'

'I guess you never know what people will see in a painting,' Carmen says, sheepishly. In spite of the shock of seeing herself, she has secretly admitted that the monkey picture is a powerful work of art. It makes her think of Francis Bacon *but without the queeny drama*. And yet, she has become accustomed to keeping her feelings buried, so all she says now is, 'People bring their own story to everything. I suppose artists just have to paint what they see . . .'

'Yes,' Cosima says, glumly. 'There's no hiding with painting. You look at the picture you've just finished and you see that *that's* what you are. Whether you like it or not.'

She takes her hand from the tile and turns back to Carmen with a smile.

'I can't deny that I thought about suicide a lot.'

'But you didn't take the final step?'

'I wanted to kill myself but I didn't want to be dead.' She folds her arms as if she's suddenly very cold. 'I think people assumed I did commit suicide. The thing is, since my very early childhood I've suffered from melancholia. The headmistress of one of my schools sent me to a shrink when I was ten. He told me I was psychotic. But he was wrong. It's only my imagination that's psychotic.'

She looks up.

'You've seen my pictures.' She makes a wry smile. 'When I grew up I found a good shrink of my own. Dr Michaels. He explained it all quite simply. Said I had a tendency to suffer from manic depression. He said that most creative people suffer from some kind of mood disorder.'

She stands up.

'My uncle Ellsworth suffered from the same thing. But much worse than me.' She pulls the sleeves of her painting shirt over her hands. 'The thing is, when the Freddie horror film came, I knew what to do. I went back to Dr Michaels and things started to clear after a few months. As a matter of fact, I was feeling much better the spring afternoon that I died in the tack room. Almost a year since the affair had begun. I was twenty-nine.'

She folds her arms again. 'I suppose I still am.'

'How did you die?' Carmen asks.

'I fell. From a rotten beam.' Cosima looks around the bedroom. 'Funny to wake up and find myself still at Summer Crest Hall. The old dump hasn't changed much. Just a bit colder. More dilapidated. At least we have the pre-meds now.

'Why were you at Summer Crest Hall in the first place?'

'De Vere was living here at the time. With his new wife. Bárbara her name was. The Spike. He married her a few years after Ellsworth died.'

Carmen narrows her eyes.

'Ellsworth died?'

'Oh yes.' Cosima sighs. 'Ellsworth died.'

She gets up from the bed and walks over to the closed bathroom door.

'Though he left his masterpiece.'

She hesitates in front of the door. She hasn't been inside the bathroom since she was twelve years old. And what a surprise lay in store for her that night – not ideal for a stomach still gurgling with scrambled eggs and caviar, not to mention the sardines and the condensed milk.

When she'd turned the light on, the flies were everywhere. She remembers how she didn't see them at first; it was just the smell. The stench of putrefaction. And then she saw the shimmering, the glowing – hundreds, millions of them, like black eggs everywhere, writhing and churning in the crevasses. What a feast they were having.

Ellsworth had told them what happens when you die. One night at dinner, he'd told Cosima and Franck about the Avar chieftain, Haji Morad. When the Cossacks slayed him, blood flowed from his head and crimson spurted from the arteries of his neck, soaking the grass.

Franck didn't see the body in the bath but he imagines it. The noble Roman way. Slitting your veins lengthways and letting the blood flow into the warm water, a flush of red diffusing like

232

steam. The polish of death more perfect than the sheen on a perfectly painted taffeta dress.

Franck imagines a bath full of calm, the only visible thing, a head above crimson water, the only light, the moon shining in through the bathroom window on to a head whose lips, in spite of everything, still bear a kindly, child-like expression. A valiant head, a hero's death.

But it wasn't like that at all. Under the electric light bulb, the body looked bloated and she was drawn to the face in a way she'd never been drawn to any painting. It was still alive, still moving, although not human any more. It was retching with flies, a butcher's shop closed down. Not quite a master-piece, yet better then the fakes. The arms were flung back like a ghoulish hug, the jaw was a rictus of smile, the tongue was black and lolling. A steak knife lay crusted on the ledge of the bath pointing towards the dirtiest bath water she had ever seen.

The thing about death, twelve-year-old Cosima had decided as she looked at the melting Dracula, is that you can't ignore it. And yet somehow it was not as scary as the sticky holes and the stretched skin in the *Deep Crack High* she'd flicked through earlier at the midnight feast. The colour was lamentable. A hope-less red spurted all over the walls. Dull and thick and yellowing at the edges, cracking in the heat. Mainly it was the smell that impressed her. She was surprised to note that the smell of death was not entirely unfamiliar to her. High game. And something else too. Something horribly sweet.

That was when she felt the black grains brushing against her lips, her eyelashes, her ears. It was when she started to feel the buzzing, the terrible noise through the oppressive heat of the night that she hadn't heard until now. She'd drunk a lot of wine with de Vere. The world had seemed apocalyptic just now, down in the kitchen with the scrambled eggs and the caviar, but looking at the bloated shape in the bath, she thought only of practical things. She had found the body so it must be her fault. Like spilling a glass of wine on a tablecloth, she suspected she'd get into trouble. She knew where the cloths were, the detergent, the scrubbing brush. Elbow grease, she thought. She would clean. She would mop things up.

CHAPTER TWENTY-FIVE

Now it is Carmen's turn to look pale.

'Oh my God! You poor thing!'

She throws her hands over her face.

'And in that August heatwave . . .'

'Yes,' Cosima says. 'The police said he'd been there for three days. He'd meant for Freddie to find him sooner. Maybe he imagined that fresh blood would have made a prettier picture . . .'

She turns away from the bathroom door and comes back to sit on the bed.

'Everyone thought that seeing Ellsworth like that should have screwed me up. But it didn't. I think Freddie was waiting for some grand revelation from me too. But I didn't have one for him. I just remember looking at my uncle in the bath and thinking, "Thank goodness that isn't me."'

Thinking about it now, Cosima recalls no one asking her how she felt, although she does remember it as the only time her mother ever hugged her. 'We have to look after Franck now.' she'd said. So she and Lady Merriwether Frost left their own house and came to live at Summer Crest Hall. Ellsworth's bedroom was locked up and nobody seemed to remember who had the key. The Spike came and went when she felt like it, turning Franck into a kind of surrogate husband until he lost his Oedipal charm and she decided it was Freddie that she really wanted.

Carmen shakes her head.

'Poor Ellsworth. Was his art that bad?'

'I think he was a forger.'

'A forger?' Carmen narrows her eyes. 'Did de Vere know?'

'Yes,' Cosima says. 'Although I didn't.'

She frowns.

'I should have worked it out that day at the National Gallery. I could tell that Freddie was worried by something. When we got near to the French eighteenth-century room, I suggested we had a look inside – I thought all that ridiculous hedonism might distract him. Besides, I hadn't been back to Summer Crest Hall since my time in Rome and I was feeling strangely nostalgic for all the peachy skin and the plump fingers and . . .'

'The marshmallow flesh?'

'Yes, all that.' Cosima smiles. She turns away. 'Freddie didn't seem very keen, but we went to have a look anyway and he was soon pointing out things of interest: the royal mistress, the dove-borne *billet doux*, the sumptuous beadwork of a dress.

'But the commentary stopped when we came to the final picture in the room. It was a Boucher. Not a particularly good one – a couple of fleshy nudes taken unawares by some Arcadian sprite. Soft porn, really. Rather bland. More Studio of François Boucher than François Boucher himself. Freddie hurried past it, saying we should go on to the Impressionists. I flirted with him. I made some joke about the naked ladies not being to his taste and demanded to know what he thought of the painting. So he glanced back at it . . .'

Cosima sighs.

'There was so much going on that day. I didn't pick up on it at the time. The expression in his eyes.'

'What did you see?'

'A few seconds of blind panic.'

She gets up from the bed.

'I put it to the back of my mind because shortly afterwards we came across this bizarre painting – a gigantic eagle abducting a beautiful boy. It was rather erotic. I saw something else in his eyes then. Something murky at the bottom of the periwinkle blue. It made me feel excited. I felt something like cruelty stir inside me and I could hardly wait for our affair to begin . . .'

She shrugs.

'I suppose I didn't want to know that the Boucher picture was quite possibly Studio of Ellsworth Stokes. I'd always claimed to be indifferent to my uncle, but the truth was that I'd held him on a pedestal. He'd been a painter, after all – an apparently successful one. Even when I got into his abandoned studio that Easter, I made sure I didn't dwell on the significance of the pieces of ripped canvas I found – the shards of velvet slipper, the strips of draped taffeta . . .'

She turns to face Carmen. 'I don't really care that Ellsworth was a forger. He was a very good one, after all.' She looks down suddenly. 'It's just a shame that I had to kill him.'

'What?' Carmen jumps to her feet. She's pretty sure that Cosima is joking, although it crosses her mind once more that maybe Cosima is a murderer. She wonders if you can be murdered if you're already dead.

'Don't worry,' Cosima says with a smile. 'I'm over it now. Although red wine on a white tablecloth can still make me rather nervous.'

Carmen recalls the glass of pre-meds she spilled on the cloth that first night at dinner.

'Listen Cosima,' she says. 'You are *so* not responsible for your alcoholic uncle committing suicide.'

'Oh, I know that Uncle Ellsworth was a sick man,' Cosima tells her. 'But you have to chose a reason to die, and the air is always full of good reasons.'

'I guess . . .'

'Ellsworth wanted his death to be a masterpiece and I think he was right. I think that suicide is an act you prepare quietly inside yourself. Like a great work of art. You never know when the inspiration will strike.'

'What do you mean?'

'By the time your own personal horror film hits you, you're already an exquisitely sensitive soul.'

Carmen reflects how she never really understood about the

237

soul. When she thinks of a soul she thinks of a stomach. A big sack filled with salad. That's the good people.

'Deep despair strains your inner resources to the limit,' Cosima explains. 'It leaves your life hanging by threads.' She shrugs. 'It can be a small thing that finally breaks the threads.'

'Such as?'

'A random piece of indifference. Or an act. Forgetting to say good morning. Letting the dogs make too much noise or . . .'

'Spilling wine on a tablecloth, Cosima?'

Cosima gets up and walks over to the window. She looks out on to the orange gloom.

She was never clumsy. She prided herself on it. And surprisingly, neither was Ellsworth in spite of the amount he drank. That last night at dinner, the floor boards under the blue carpet had shaken with the incredible bulk of her forty-three-year-old uncle as he'd jigged around the Long Room brandishing the ram's horn cheese toasting fork. And yet he'd never stumbled, never banged into anything.

'Remember that last book I told you to read, Franck?' he warned, coming over to joust the glinting utensil at his son. 'What's the point of art? Come on now . . .'

'We have art in order . . . not to die of the truth, Pa?'

'What did you say?'

Franck's spoon began to rattle against his bowl of custard as he watched the silver prongs hover dangerously close to his eyes.

'Not to die of the truth, father.'

'Louder! And with conviction, damn it!'

'WE HAVE ART IN ORDER NOT TO DIE OF THE TRUTH!'

'Good man!' Ellsworth erupted, hurling the cheese fork into the air and catching it skillfully as his son blushed with pleasure.

'Remember, Franck,' he panted. 'Anyone and everyone can *say* things. But *asserting* them is the business of manliness!'

Ellsworth had always fed Franck weighty books on military history, made sure he read tomes by muscular philosophers such as Nietzsche and Schopenhauer. He now claimed to feel contempt for 'fey French philosophers', such as Albert Camus. Indeed, the older he got, the more he dreaded the merest hint of anything that smacked of weakness. In the past few years, having nearly successfully forgotten his own colourful past, Ellsworth had been obsessed with a confused notion of 'manliness'.

'And what happens if we don't have art, son?' he said, suddenly. 'Do we die?'

Franck blinked. He hadn't anticipated a trick. He glanced at Cosima and then over at his father who had started to cackle uncontrollably. Franck took the cue and started to laugh as well – a high-pitched whinny as his father launched into another drunken prance around the room, working himself up into an even greater sweat and becoming increasingly manic at the thought of presenting his final offering to de Vere.

'Let's see what the Dog has to say this time! Just wait until he comes!'

It was at this moment that Cosima knocked a plate she was removing from the table against a bottle of red wine. As if in slow motion, it toppled over and rolled to and fro, gurgling its guts out all over the white cloth. The shock delayed her reaction. When she finally managed to snatch the bottle up, it was empty. Ellsworth looked from the dark, creeping spot on the tablecloth to Cosima who dared meet him in the eye. At first, she was hopeful. She thought she might be all right. That she could fix him with her stare. Her talent hadn't let her down yet. And to start with, it seemed to work. He froze in her gaze. It seemed as if he didn't recognise her any more. She noted the sweat pouring down the ruddy face, the drool at the corners of the mouth, the trembling of the chapped purple lips. But then something went wrong. He wasn't turned to stone at all. There was a sickening clang as he hurled the fork into the fireplace.

'Sorry, Uncle Ellsworth,' she muttered. 'I didn't mean to . . .'

Fido and Phèdre rushed to her side but it was too late to stop the raging, the tears, the recriminations . . .

'Like I said,' Cosima turns to face Carmen, 'it can be a very small thing that finally severs the cord. And then you are guilty of their death.'

Carmen sighs.

'Jesus, if you put it like that then I'm a mass murderer. I must have not said, "Good morning" to hundreds of people in my life.'

She suddenly feels exhausted. She flings herself down on the bed. *Talk about taking your sex drive away,* she thinks. *But I guess that's purgatory for you.*

She asks Cosima why she came back to Summer Crest Hall that day anyway.

'Were you planning to bust in on de Vere and the Spike in their bedroom?'

Cosima walks back towards the bed.

'Oh no. I wanted to re-live the night I found Uncle Ellsworth in the bath. I wanted to see if the memory of it would shake Freddie off my back.'

She snorts.

'Of course, I never reached the bathroom.' She smoothes her hands over the bathroom door. 'In fact, I haven't been inside since I was twelve.'

Carmen feels nervous. 'Do you think . . . it's a good idea?'

But it's too late. Cosima has opened the door. She pulls on the frayed tassel and finds herself in a room with moist walls, a gurgling wooden commode and a smell of damp carpet.

She turns to the lion-footed bath tub and for a few seconds, it rears up in front of her as if it is bigger than the whole of the bathroom. But it is clean. Just scratched and rusty around the taps. She sits on the edge. She hears de Vere's voice in the hallway:

Did you find your painting, Cosima?

She'd promised to show him the acid trip painting. The one she did at school after the night in the woods with the dyke.

Cosima, are you there?

Like the purr of a cat.

She'd wanted to show him the painting. But she couldn't. The clogged-up water. The mopping up. No time for cats.

Are you all right, Cosima?

Such a lovely voice.

'Cosima, are you all right?'

It is Carmen, coming into the bathroom. She sees Cosima looking almost serene.

'Franck's convinced that Ellsworth's death was your fault, right? That's why he keeps insinuating you're a murderer...'

'Franck can't let go,' Cosima says, running her hands along the side of the bath. 'He idolised his father and you can't mourn for someone when you still see them as a god.'

She stands up. 'His past is his whole future. So I suppose he doesn't belong to this world or the other one.'

'Is that why he keeps appearing and disappearing?'

But Cosima's face is impassive. When Carmen follows her back into the bedroom, she finds herself voicing a thought that has been brewing in her head since she first saw the monkey woods.

'Cosima, did you paint me into that picture as ... some kind of weird sex game between you and de Vere?'

When Cosima swings round and glares at her, Carmen has a momentary image of tiny snakes writhing around in the pale girl's pupils. She knows she's sounding clumsy but she makes herself go on.

'What I mean is ... did you use me just to frighten de Vere? Or did you ...'

'... Did I have other feelings for you?' The furniture eyes surface briefly as she looks at Carmen. And then she turns away.

'My uncle used to believe that being an artist was only half a life,' she says. 'And he was probably right.'

She walks towards the bedroom door. 'The only way I can possess people is through drawing them. And once I've possessed them I have to let them go.'

It is then that a warmth of emotion puffs up in Carmen's chest. A pang of regret. Of something too late.

Cosima is about to leave the room when she stops.

'Did you believe Franck?' she asks, her back still turned. 'About me being a murderer?'

Carmen hesitates.

'Some days I wasn't sure . . .'

Cosima opens the door.

'No blood on my hands, Carmen,' she says. 'Just a trace of paint on my fingers.'

CHAPTER TWENTY-SIX

The Cage is black tonight.

Charles Frederick de Vere finds himself in Paris. Another contemporary art dinner. The room is awash with the usual loutish behaviour. But de Vere is only half-aware of the tirade on wood oven cabbage steak coming from the man sitting next to him. Cabbage that's supposed to taste like steak.

'It's rubbish,' the man is saying. 'You're not telling me that's steak. I'm from Ireland and I'm telling you that's bloody cabbage!'

The man is one of his new artists. De Vere has no idea if he has any talent or not. He has a hunch that the man will make him some money. He is half-distracted by the arrival at the table of a procession of black Marilyn Monroes wearing aprons printed with the name of a mobile telephone company. The party is billed as *La Fête Noire* but it is not like the days of Mr Cheeks. There is no gyrating the night away to Sidney Bechet. No evening black tail coats or Klimt *femme fatales*. De Vere watches the black hands clear away plates of black food – cuttlefish ink risotto, seaweed *chiffonade*, wood oven cabbage steak with black truffles – and replace them with plates of black dessert: cherry purée, liquorice ice cream.

'Steak, my bloody arse!'

De Vere drinks his champagne. The sharp, spiteful bubbles prick the back of his throat.

'Hey Freddie, do you want a top-up?'

De Vere's hand is gripped, claw-like, around his glass. He watches the bubbles fizz up from the bottom like a diver's air pipe severed with a dagger. It is said that the golden foil on the neck of the bottle saves one from the vulgarity of knowing that the champagne has ended. But there is never any end to the champagne. Cosima used to make him put a teaspoon in the neck of the bottle to stop the bubbles from escaping but now there are too many bubbles. The bubbles never stop.

'Come on, Freddie! Pass your glass over. It's all free!'

So what if she hadn't committed suicide after all? She was still dead, wasn't she? She'd still gone too soon.

So much left unsaid. So much sand stuck inside.

De Vere foresees the terror of going deep down under the earth for a final time. The lift. Or maybe oblivion. He feels the foam from the overflowing glass run down his hand, caress his wrist like wet blood, as if his veins have already been slit open and he is saved the bother of doing it himself.

He picks the glass up and wrinkles his nose as the rich aroma hits his nostrils. More and more, de Vere finds, his champagne smells of vomit.

The lights go out. The Marseillaise begins to play and the room fills with a chorus of cheers and jeers as a fleet of trolleys bearing jeroboams of champagne is wheeled out. The trolleys are shaped like mini chariots and are decorated with a line of fizzling Catherine wheels.

'Jeroboams, Freddie!' His artist nudges him. 'Is that four bottles' worth or six?'

De Vere pulls the wire top from a stray champagne cork rolling on the table. As he stares at the Catherine wheels, he twists the sharp metal in his fingers, thinking only of Ellsworth. How his friend's life got faster and faster until finally it burned itself out. He throws the top down on the tablecloth and clasps his hands together, inter-lacing his fingers as if in prayer. He is surprised to note the feeling of hope this gesture brings him, a motion he has not performed since he was a child.

He notices a bead of red on his finger.

'Bad idea to cut yourself in public,' his artist slurs, pointing to the crushed wire cage. 'In this day and age, if you know what I mean, Freddie.'

Another waft of sick hits de Vere's nostrils and he pulls his hands apart. He excuses himself from the table and walks quickly from the noisy room, searching desperately for quiet. He comes to a kitchen where only a handful of people remain. He makes sure that none of them see him as he slips in, walks behind a line of tall refrigerators and eventually finds himself in a large store cupboard which gleams with kitchen implements and metal surfaces.

He closes the door and sits on a stool, finding a kind of relief in the clean, inanimate objects surrounding him. He shivers as he feels the cigar-cutter in his pocket – a single-bladed guillo-tine. He lets out a deep sigh, props his back up against the wall and closes his eyes. Going down: One floor, two floors, three, four, five . . . all the way, lower and lower he goes. Just a trace now of the party, *la Fête Noire*: the black Marilyns, the black crow in the diamond necklace, the dark, gooey chocolate, the black shit in the toilet the next day. All that is fading now as he reaches the basement.

CHAPTER TWENTY-SEVEN

It would be foolish to suggest that Ellsworth killed himself because of a double 'G'. But I have no doubt that this was a contributing factor. His suicide note was as pretentious as I might have imagined. A quote from Seneca: 'He who reaps the profits has committed the crime.' A more suitable epitaph might have read, 'It is in the ability to deceive oneself that the greatest talent is shown.'

Still, the gist was not lost on me. And I should have been more vigilant. To put a picture on the market, to sell it to Sotheby's of all places, a fake Fragonard signed, if you please, with two 'G's. It was asking for trouble. It was a mistake unworthy, one would have thought, of Charles Frederick de Vere, master of illusion, conveyer of immortality, blessed with the luck of the devil.

It even seemed remiss for Ellsworth. When he was sober, he was exact, fastidious. Nobody guessed that my holy relics were mere pig bones and rags and we made a fortune in the seventies – the good old days when art scholarship was rather patchy. His Bouchers and Fragonards appeared in galleries, museums and richly illustrated catalogues around the world. *Artemis gathers her nymphs about her. 65 by 50 in. Painted c. 1766. The dimensions of the work, the tenderness of brush stroke, the frivolity of subject matter, make of this previously unrecorded work an authentic masterpiece by François Boucher.*

Ellsworth needn't have killed himself. The whole affair was dealt with in a very civilised fashion. The chairman of Sotheby's Amsterdam had been at school with both of us. He didn't want trouble. He'd had wind of Ellsworth's recent problems. I fudged and said I'd never have thought him capable, said how shocked I was that Ellsworth could have tried to pull this off, the scheme of a clearly demented mind. I breathed a sigh of relief and considered myself lucky that he hadn't seen all the other filth Ellsworth had painted over the years. Boudoir pornography for the very rich. Naughty circus scenes, saucy mythological vignettes, giggling maids fiddling with each other. Harmless stuff.

To start with I assumed it was all genuine.

To start with I believed in Ellsworth.

In the beginning, admirers flocked to your uncle because he was only playing at being a monster in those days. The trouble came when his vanity started to eat into him and he began worrying what people thought. As he himself had foreseen, it is one's own smells that corrupt, not other people's.

De Vere gets up from the school desk and walks slowly around the room, his hands slung deep in his pockets. Occasionally, he turns to address the empty wooden chair.

And yet you never come to see me, Cosima. In spite of all I have told you. Is it because of Bárbara that you never come? Are you still piqued by the farcical marriage I made with her? That I still, for my sins, must maintain with her?

He stops walking. He closes his eyes and lets out an audible breath of weariness.

I'd assumed our short fling in the seventies had served to obliterate any thoughts of blackmail she might have harboured. But in 1997, Bárbara's memory was jogged by a series of unfortunate events. She was about to turn forty-five, her long-standing affair with a top plastic surgeon had come to an end and her father had just died leaving her almost nothing in his will.

It transpired that democracy in Portugal had done no favours for Senhor Vasconcelos de Souza's bank balance. When revolution erupted in Lisbon in 1974, it wasn't long before its former colonies of Mozambique and Angola began to demand independence as well.

Unfortunately for Bárbara's father, many of his hotel properties had been located in these 'overseas provinces', as he termed them, and the consequences to his business were catastrophic. Bárbara had hoped that her inheritence would make up for the fact that her lucrative modelling contract for an anti-ageing cream had not been renewed. She still received a small income from tenants in a couple of cottages on the Summer Crest Hall estate, but her dead husband had left no other provision.

She came to visit me at my East End gallery. She reminded me of the fortune I had made from her late husband and began to talk of marriage. She made it clear that I would be unable to resist her charms. And I did not resist.

De Vere laughs bitterly.

You mustn't think for a moment that I have found happiness with the Spike. Or that she has found happiness with me. She believed I was a safe bet but she couldn't have been more wrong. She was away in Uruguay the night Ellsworth decided to sully his bathwater in such a dramatic fashion. She didn't realise that my mind has been slowly unravelling since that day. And if I was undone then, I feel as if I am undoing now at an ever-alarming pace.

De Vere scans the room hopefully.

Cosima, are you there?
   Are you all right, Cosima?

He frowns as he returns to his high-backed seat at the teacher's desk.

Are you angry because I deserted you that night when you were a child?
Drove back to London and left you to mop up your uncle's mess?
It was unforgivable. And yet when you went to look for your painting, I became nervous. I opened a second bottle of wine and downed it

248

rather quickly. I became paranoid. I was so tipsy I feared I'd charge into Ellsworth's room at any minute and challenge him to . . .

To what? I didn't know. I tried to find you upstairs but you seemed to have vanished. I decided the best thing would be to leave. I told myself I'd call Ellsworth in a couple of days when my head was clearer.

He flinches as he looks at the empty wooden chair in front of him.

The thing is, Cosima, I had a premonition that night. I think that deep down I knew what Ellsworth's 'masterpiece' was going to be. If the abandoned tack room at Easter hadn't been a warning, then the awful exchange I'd had with him two weeks earlier certainly was.

He came to my suite at Claridges. It was the opening of the grouse season: 12 August 1981, The Glorious Twelfth. I'd just come back from a late lunch with the Duke of Beaufort. Carmen was still with me. Ellsworth was giving her a hard time so I took him into my office. I tried to calm him down but it was no use. He was pissed. Abusive.

'Don't forget who you're speaking to, you bastard! Remember when I was . . .'

He frowned, as if bewildered by the memory.

'When you were someone, Ellsworth?' I suggested. 'I thought you were the most glamorous person I'd ever met. But look at you now.'

Even as I said it, I was afraid of him.

He fixed me briefly in the blackness of his eyes. 'Don't fuck with me, Dog,' he said. 'I hear the wine's very bad in prison.'

I went to the safe and took out an envelope. He snatched it from me. He was about to leave the office when the sight of *The Dead Stuff* stopped him in his tracks. He'd sent me the painting nearly two years previously but for some reason I hadn't returned it. I knew there was no possibility of selling it, and yet something about its startling physicality mesmerised me.

You saw something in it too, Cosima. Do you remember? When I brought it back to Summer Crest Hall two weeks later and bumped into you in the kitchen in the middle of the night?

I see that painting now as a cry for help. If I'd stopped to think, I'd have realised that Ellsworth's work had been getting increasingly angry. His fakes now were occasionally tinged with the horrific, a fact which was all the more shocking given that his work was still executed with his trademark precision.

I watched him bend forward and brush his fingers over the glistening entrails of the mangled peacock.

'You didn't sell my *Still Life With Game*, then?' he said, airily. 'I think it's rather good. Very "School of Desportes."'

He straightened up and strolled back to my desk.

'I painted it that time in Tangier,' he said, settling himself into my chair. He stretched his legs out, clasped his hands leisurely behind his head.

'You think you're the most spectacular art dealer of all time, don't you?' he sneered. 'But you're not. The best salesman I ever met was Momo from the Bazaar Delilah. "Just look at this rug," Momo would go. "The *quality*! I wouldn't show this to just anybody. I'd only sell it to you!" Even Eddie gave up haggling in the end.'

A manic cackle filled the room and then suddenly stopped.

'Momo could have sold it,' he said, nodding viciously at the painting. He hesitated. He began biting his nails.

'It's an ostentation of peacocks,' he said. 'Did you know that, Dog? A nye of pheasants, a covey of partridges . . .'

A trace of a smile appeared.

'A murder of art dealers.'

He swivelled the chair round and gazed down on to Brook Street.

'I painted that peacock from a still life,' he murmured. 'Funny, it was only after Way Out Eddie told me how shit my art was that I realised how its squark wasn't comical at all. When Eddie stomped off into the early hours, the house suddenly seemed very quiet. The

250

only noise was the damn peacocks. It struck me what a horrible sound it was. A mournful hoot of disillusionment. A desolate cry for help.'

Ellsworth was trembling when he turned back into the room.

'So I thought I *would* help them. It took me quite a while. Feathers everywhere, Freddie. Very messy. But I knew that my house boy had cleared it all up, because when I came back from my walk there were smears of blood all over his *djellaba*.'

He seemed dazed.

'Peacocks,' he whispered. 'So beautiful. So useless.'

It was the last time I saw him alive.

Ellsworth, who once saved my life.

De Vere drags himself up from his chair. So much shame in his life. Hanging over his head like a musty hood. And the person he wants to see is not here. She is never here. Why does she never come? He stands up, breathing faster, scanning the room with his eyes.

Cosima! Dear God, where are you!

He walks round to the front of the desk, puts his hands tenderly on the back of the wooden chair.

Sometimes, you'd act as if you knew there wasn't much time left. A look in your eye. I can't deny that I relished that look at times. I thought that if I could sink you, you who had seen everything, then I could sink Ellsworth too, get rid of both of you, be free at last.

But of course, I didn't want to get rid of you. Although sometimes what we did in bed seemed to verge on murder. You went inside me, you made me vulnerable. A dirty bitch, my snow-white succubus.

In the end you didn't give me what I wanted at all. I didn't want to know about Ellsworth any more. I didn't want to see. I had you now. I thought I had you. You were the one who filled my waking hours. You had almost completely blotted him out.

He scans the room once more.

So why do you never come?

He strains his ears, but fails to hear her this time. He lurches to the couch in the middle of the room, falls into it, appears on the verge of passing out. And then suddenly, he sits bolt upright. His body stiffens, his eyes open wide as if a revelation has come to him.

Listen!

He scrambles to his feet, glances around the room. He starts to pace up and down, breathing heavily.

Murderess!

A deranged new light shines in de Vere's eyes. He licks his lips.

You know what your uncle Ellsworth was drinking the night you upset him so much? Did you see the label on the wine bottle as it rolled back and forth on the stained cloth? Did you see it, Cosima? No! Of course you didn't see it. But I did. It was the Mouton '45! He was drinking the wine he said he'd always drink for his last supper. Do you understand what that means . . .

His head flails round the room.

It didn't matter that you spilled the wine, Cosima! The Mouton '45. Don't you see — he'd already planned everything! It was nobody's fault. I saw it, Cosima! I saw the bottle rolling on the tablecloth that night, even though I was miles away in London. I've seen everything, Cosima, do you understand? I've imagined everything! Seen it all in my head! I've made it all all right so that now you can come, now we can be together.

Cosima!

He crumples back on to the couch and buries his head deep into his hands. It is only when he begins to look out through the bars of his fingers that he sees it. Lying on the desk.

A shirt.

A paint-splattered man's shirt. The rolled-up sleeves. The stains of Prussian blue.

He grabs it and soon he is collapsed on the floor, hugging the shirt, smelling the shirt, clasping the shirt to his face as if it is a woman in a beautiful backless dress at a dance, burying his face in her neck, kissing her, breathing her in – the bitter almonds, the ladies' furs – until she enters his body like a vapour, glides through his veins, glitters in his pores. She is the genie who dissolves into his flesh, she takes him to the very edge of the cliff. He groans.

Charles Frederick de Vere is no longer a mountain. He is just a pile of wet washing. He kneels in the pose of an altar boy or perhaps of a nymph, head lowered, feet pointed together, sobbing into the reeds, a man dissolving before our very eyes.

I saw you as my ship in a bottle, but I didn't anticipate the shipwreck to come. My baby, like a sinking ocean liner that sucks down everything with it, you're still pulling at me. And the fumes start to seem attractive. The monkey woods are not so frightening after all. There was always something trapped about your art. Something under glass. But death has let it out. The fumes emerged and they were blue. Not the cold blue bruise of death. An ethereal blue, beyond this world.

A call to the infinite.

Shall I follow you?

He looks up and sees a painting on the wall. Leda and the Swan. The blandness, the soulless perfection. He thought he was safe in his room. Nothing had come to disturb him before. His eyes harden, his jaw clenches. He feels something solid wrapped up inside the paint-splattered shirt. Clean, gleaming. Surprisingly sharp.

He lunges like a madman at the painting but another comes. Then another – an array of perfectly executed lace ruffles and velvet skirts, the Boucher nymphs, the girl on a swing, Ellsworth's Cunt. The paintings spring up endlessly.

De Vere staggers backwards. His head thrashes from side to side, his eyes screw tight shut until a huge glass tower suddenly appears behind them. Then hot steel passes through cold butter and the room shudders abruptly in an explosion of sand and vivid red. Amidst the shattering of glass and the clattering of metal, a stream of blood as shiny as oil glugs like wine from a bottle, thick and fresh and changing colour with the light so rapidly as it unblocks and undams that it seems to de Vere a marvel, a shiny silk scarf, a snake you can never capture, a liquid serpent filled with all the colours of the world. Soon, his feet are soaked in blood, it pours into his eyes like rain, it floods out of every pore of his skin. And at every gust of laughter, more of the thick juice belches out and he gurgles in blood, until spirals of energy twist on top of his head, dancing their dance until all the life is gone.

When he finally opens his eyes, he gasps to see that someone has come at last.

It is not Cosima.

Sitting on the wooden chair is the boy who took him into his bed that night. The night he thought his life was over. The business with the maid. Seventeen and sacked. A tall, dark forest towering over his head. Drumming his fingers on the teacher's desk is the friend who'd called him 'Freddie' at messing time, fed him pigeon breasts and vintage port, held him close for the whole of the night, absorbed the shadow of his dark secret so it seemed not so dark the next day.

De Vere stands transfixed. As if someone went inside his mouth with a rusty coat hanger and yanked out his soul. His sex drive. There is no body left to him. Just a stuffed velvet suit where a body should be.

I stumbled to your room. The night I was sacked. An intoxication of despair. I got into your bed and I wept. I cried for a long time. It was the shame, you see. I whispered in your ear, 'Ellsworth, Ellsworth,' and you held me tight, you kept me safe. We didn't do anything. The warmth of your arms. The faint smell of port still on your breath.

Always Ellsworth at the bottom of everything.
The figure rises from the wooden chair.

No! Please don't go, Ellsworth!
Let me come with you this time!

But he walks out of the room into the cold hallway. De Vere follows him, turning right down the corridor away from the lift. He pursues him down the long passage which now echoes with the sound of two pairs of footsteps on damp concrete. He walks past cobweb-draped alcoves, past walls studded with black fungus and doors on either side of different shapes and sizes. Finally, at the very end of the corridor he sees something that looks like a huge dungeon door.

It is ajar. De Vere sees a crack of faded blue carpet, a slice of window ledge with a rusty toasting fork on top.

He hears voices inside.

Vernissage

When Carmen pushes open the attic door the next day, she can hardly believe her eyes.

The eggs have hatched.

The ship is free.

There is no blood, only sea, a blue vapour.

It pours in through the windows of the attic room, deluging Carmen with light, a huge beam of delphinium all over her body. She spreads herself wide and laps up the rays: warm, celestial, electric.

I should have left then, only I didn't. It was 10.25 in the morning, the exact time of my birth. Knowing the logic of Summer Crest Hall, I should have suspected that something was about to happen. And it did. I had another of the cream and fruit flashbacks. Only this time, I could see a little clearer. I could make out the private room of a Mayfair strip club with Larry and a couple of naked girls. There was a menu at one side of the room that said:

Private dance: £100

Private dance with fruit, cream and chocolate sauce: £100

That's when I remembered. My last thought before the blackout. It still bugs me if you want to know the truth – the free fruit and the free cream? What's up with that? And then I noticed something horrible. It wasn't the spectacle of Larry writhing around like a fish on a slab as the girls shot an aerosol gun of modified milk compounds up his ass and lubricated his tits with chocolate sauce while he screamed, 'Get another woman up . . . hire a hooker . . . let's get crazy!' (Typical Larry, he never did learn to appreciate life in the present.) No, that wasn't the thing that grabbed my attention. It was the woman sitting at the side of the room that made me afraid. Skinny as hell. Like a skeleton. She was perched there, watching the scene in front of her like it was daytime TV and the coke she was shovelling up her nose was a packet of stale potato chips.

There was a ton of coke. A whole pile of it heaped up on a table. I could have blown it all away. Saved my life right there and then. But you know what? It seemed like too much work. Too much work to do on *myself,* as the shrinks like to say. Besides, bathing in the groovy blue sun was more relaxing than any flotation tank I'd ever gotten into. Even when I got a second chance – suddenly, I'm in an ambulance and a British guy is shouting at me in that London accent I never could understand. 'Miss Costello!' he's going. 'Can you hear me, Miss Costello?'

Even then, I just turned away to toast the other side of my face in the funky blue haze. I guess I missed the boat. And it's too late to go back now. The varnish has almost dried, you might say, and here I am, stuck like a fly in gradually setting amber. It's not a completely unpleasant sensation.

See, the thing about purgatory is that it's not that bad. There's the food, of course. That sucks. Pigeon every fucking day. Charred and tarry. But sometimes it's squidgy and sometimes it comes with potato smiles, and sometimes you feel a piece of lead shot in your teeth and you say, 'Bullets in your food. The veggies miss out on that, huh!' And without fail Marie-Thérèse will shriek '*les pigeons*!' and burst out crying. I mean, obviously, it gets boring after a while but this is purgatory after all.

I figure that my time here is like the champagne process. The longer you allow a wine to 'sleep', the more complex it becomes and when you finally open it up, it pours out in a cascade of bubbles – just like Cosima did that morning in the attic, leaving this trail of heavenly azure in her wake.

Like I say, purgatory's not that bad. You soon adjust to the way things are. Take Franck. Turns out I was right about the 'living dead' because Franck's not actually dead at all. Only kind of. Like Cosima said, he can't let go of his past so he appears and disappears at whim. Some kind of extra privileges, I guess. Typical aristocrats, right? But hey, if life's not fair, why should death be?

I'm happy just taking things easy. Nothing too deep. Sometimes I talk about stuff with Sykes and Kenneth Sketch. I tell them that the idea of eternity is actually perfect for a bulimic.

'It's like an all-you-can-eat buffet,' I say.

Sykes looks blank, so I explain.

'It's like a never-ending feast!' I exclaim. 'It goes on and on. For ever and ever.'

And she snaps on that puritanical 1950s face of hers and yells, 'Starters, main and sweet would be enough for me! Do you know how long I've been stuck in this bloody place?'

Then she marches out of the room.

She can be such a killjoy.

Luckily, I can always rely on Kenneth Sketch. Talking to him is like biting into a big old American hamburger – warm and soft and bland.

'You know,' he says, cutting another picture out of a magazine. 'There's the theory about deanimation. Timothy Leary was big on it.'

'The LSD guy?'

'Yeah,' he drawls. 'He thought you could die and live on in computers. Or something.'

Kenneth Sketch doesn't seem to care that he might be dead.

'It's not that different from being alive, as far as I can remember,' he muses.

It turns out that I did meet Kenneth Sketch in Claridges back in the day. Kenneth Sketch met de Vere too. He was tottering back to his room in New Romantic drag early one morning when he bumped into a 'distinguished-looking guy' in the elevator.

'He was very open-minded,' Kenneth Sketch tells me, picking up the glue stick. 'In fact, there was something very honest about him.'

'De Vere!' I go, in my scoffing kind of way. 'Honest!'

And that was when something broke in Kenneth Sketch. When he turned to look at me, there was a new sharpness in his green eyes.

'You know, Carmen,' he says. 'The day comes when you can't hide in the woods any more.'

*   *   *

The next morning, when Carmen Costello comes into the Long Room, Kenneth Sketch has disappeared. All that remains is his collage. The heads have opened up and three necks are spewing iceberg lettuce, olives and asparagus tips up into the sky.

Carmen notes that the incredible blue light is slightly dimmer today, although if she were honest, she would admit that the colour has been fading and the warmth diminishing for a while. She looks out of the window, pulling her cashmere wrap closer as she sees that the light is returning to the sticky orange of old.

And yet when she turns back into the room filled with soufflé satins and pink shepherdess gowns, she can't help smiling. She forgets her goosebumps as she looks up at the tender colours on the walls and breathes in the beguiling world of stolen kisses and amorous dalliance. The paintings take her back to her glory days at Claridges, to Charles Frederick de Vere who introduced her to more than just the *volupté* of rococo decadence.

Marie Antoinette might have had her little shepherdess game, Carmen thinks. *But I had a pretty good act myself.*

She remembers how de Vere had shown her a glimpse of the best toy farm in the world, a gilded menagerie filled with the most colourful of creatures. The Cage had certainly had its ups and downs, *but it doesn't seem to have done me any harm.*

She thinks longingly to her next bout of delicious Summer Crest Hall sleep, smiling as she reflects how wrong Southie's Father Lock had been about, 'The arduous slopes of purgatory, Carmen!'

She feels a prickle on the back of her neck.

She hears de Vere's voice as if he were here in the room.

'Remember, Carmen,' comes the purr. 'Eighteenth-century France began with the toilet of Venus, but it ended with Marat dead in the bath.'

When she looks back at the walls, she is convinced for a few seconds that they are dripping with the somber palette of French Neoclassicism: Roman soldiers pledging oaths, Greek philosophers dying for their beliefs. No more pastels, no more puppy fat. Just edifying hymns to self-sacrifice and moral rectitude. Allusions to hard times ahead. The Terror.

Carmen's legs buckle under her and she has to hold on to the dining-room table. She glares down at the white tablecloth, refusing to look back at the walls to see if the *bunch of fucking party poopers* really is there.

The icy steam she sees coming from her nostrils pulls her to her senses. She stamps her feet on the carpet to get her circulation going. *Fucking art history*, she mutters. *Goddamn art doesn't mean a thing*.

It is only when she removes her hands from the tablecloth that she notices the two extra places which have been laid for dinner.

She does what she always does when she needs reassurance. She heads for the kitchen, for the cupboard under the sink where the wine bottles are kept, each one containing the same vital elixir.

She hears the familiar squeak of the hinge as the cupboard door opens, but she reels back in shock as a set of empty shelves looms up before her. There is a violent thud and when she swings round, she sees a man slapping a brace of dead birds down on the table. He has matted black curly hair and his coat is covered in mud.